INSIDE DARKNESS

hudson lin

Riptide Publishing
PO Box 1537
Burnsville, NC 28714
www.riptidepublishing.com

Cover art: Natasha Snow, natashasnowdesigns.com
Editors: Sarah Lyons, May Peterson, maypetersonbooks.com
Layout: L.C. Chase, lcchase.com/design.htm

ISBN: 978-1-62649-788-7

First edition
June, 2018

Also available in ebook:
ISBN: 978-1-62649-787-0

INSIDE
DARKNESS

hudson lin

For those who go into the field,
and those who live with darkness.

TABLE OF CONTENTS

CHAPTER ONE

Excited shouts rang out across the open yard. Cameron Donnelly turned to see a plume of red dust rising in the far distance, shimmering in the heat of the scorching Kenyan sun. Several minutes later, a rumble echoed through the air, announcing the impending arrival of a convoy of trucks, and Cam's team of UN staff broke off their conversation.

Word of the supply delivery had spread like wildfire through the refugee camp over the past few days, and a crowd of people were gathering in front of the warehouse, eager for whatever goods came laden on the trucks. If they were lucky, this would be one of their more generous supply runs. After all, the convoy had special guests this time, an audience that UNHCR headquarters in Geneva wanted to impress.

Patsy, Cam's second-in-command, had been in charge of leading the convoy, and the status updates she'd sent during the three-day round-trip between the Dadaab refugee camp and Nairobi had been promising. The paramilitary groups manning checkpoints along the route had been generally cooperative, and they'd only lost a minimum amount of supplies along the way.

The convoy rolled to a stop in front of the warehouse, and a crowd quickly congregated around the vehicles. Cam's staff corralled them back to create space for the trucks to be unloaded. Patsy elbowed her way through the throng, backpack thrown over her shoulder, platinum-blonde ponytail standing out in the sea of dark black hair. She strode over to Cam with a wide smile.

"Hey, boss." The Australian accent rolled off her tongue, slow and easy, more suited for a beach lined with surfboards than the middle of a refugee camp.

"Hey, Patsy. Good trip?"

"As good as can be expected. Although, probably more exciting since we've got precious cargo."

Cam grunted at the mention of *precious cargo*, code words they'd been using for the two journalists Cable Broadcasting Network had sent from the States. Most of his staff had been excited about the prospect of getting on TV, but in Cam's opinion, they were little more than necessary evils. He had said as much to Teresa, Cam's boss at UNHCR headquarters, when she called to give him the news.

"Play nice," she'd said over the staticky Skype connection. *"When was the last time Dadaab was in the news? We need the publicity."*

He might not have liked the prospect of having to babysit some journalists, but Teresa was right. So he bit his tongue, and now they were here.

Next to him, Patsy sighed dramatically and made googly eyes back in the direction of the convoy. Cam followed her gaze. From the chaos emerged a tall Asian man, looking impossibly immaculate for someone who had traveled all the way from the States.

The trip from New York to Nairobi usually took a good twenty-four hours, and most people looked like the walking dead by the time they made it all the way to Dadaab in eastern Kenya. But not this man. His shiny black hair had that artfully tousled look, like it was meant to be falling over his forehead at just that angle. The snug-fitting baby-blue polo shirt had no visible wrinkles and sat tucked neatly into khaki slacks that somehow maintained a crisp crease right down the front. Aviator sunglasses shielded the man's eyes, but there was no hiding the easy grin that graced his lips.

Something stirred in the depths of Cam's consciousness, an old and familiar feeling that had his eyes lingering over the shape of the man's jaw, the stretch of blue fabric around a biceps. Cam snapped his head away and adjusted his Oakley sunglasses as he quickly scanned the people around him—had they noticed his little slipup? He couldn't be sure.

"Cameron Donnelly?" The man's voice reverberated from somewhere in the middle of his chest, low and resonant, designed for seducing listeners over the airways. And the way it caressed his name—settling on the accents and lilting over the consonants—made

Cam acutely aware of the attraction awakening inside of him. He clenched his jaw and tamped down the desires he had learned to hide so many years ago.

"Tyler Ang, CBN." He held out a hand. Long tapered fingers topped with cleanly manicured nails.

Cam hesitated. It was irrational—it was only a handshake—but his palm already tingled with his body's natural excitement of touching someone he was attracted to. He sucked in a breath as he stretched out his hand, as if that would dull the impression of Tyler Ang's soft skin and strong grip. It didn't. Cam pulled his hand away a fraction of a second too early, but if the other man noticed, he didn't show it.

"This is my cameraman, Douglas Mann." Tyler Ang nodded at the man standing next to him. "I'm told you're going to show us around this week?" His tone was friendly and unassuming, like his presence there was par for the course. But it wasn't normal, at least not to Cam—the TV-ready journalist looked out of place in the rough, arid landscape and ignited reactions in Cam that he couldn't afford to indulge.

"Yeah, look. You're welcome to shadow any of us, but don't get in our way. We're not here to babysit you." He glanced back to the truck that held their bags and equipment. "And grab your gear before someone makes off with it." The words came out much harsher than they needed to be, but better to push the guy away than risk too much interaction.

Besides, it was true—they were busy, he didn't have time to roll out the red carpet. He turned away to search for his logistics supervisor, but didn't miss the eyebrow that popped up over the top of the aviators, or the shrug that Patsy gave in response to Tyler Ang's unspoken question. Let Patsy deal with them—she was better with people, anyway.

"Robinson!" Cam shouted as he spotted the tall, dark-skinned Kenyan man. Robinson was directing the flow of boxes and crates from the trucks into the warehouse.

"Boss!" Robinson greeted Cam as he approached.

"How's the shipment looking?"

"Eh—it's good. With this, we'll have enough inventory for two months, maybe. Oxfam should have a shipment next week, so that will help."

"Good. When's our next scheduled delivery?"

"Eh . . ." Robinson chuckled. "Soon."

"Great." Cam was anything but excited at that news. Two months' worth of supplies, maybe three—he did some quick calculations in his head—wasn't a lot of buffer, but he'd worked with less before.

"What does 'soon' mean?"

Cam snapped his head around, arm half raised in defense. It took him a moment to recognize the perfectly tanned Tyler Ang, standing over his shoulder, much too close for comfort.

"Whoa, sorry. Didn't mean to startle you." Ang held up both hands, palms facing out.

Cam clenched his jaw against the sudden spike of adrenaline in his system. He sucked in a slow, steady breath through his nose, barely catching Tyler Ang's next words.

"I wanted to know how frequently you guys do supply runs. I overheard your guy say that this shipment brings you to two months' worth of supplies? Is that the typical inventory level you maintain?" He had pulled out a small notebook from somewhere and was already scribbling away.

When Cam didn't respond, Tyler Ang raised his head, eyebrows lifted above his sunglasses. *"Play nice."* Teresa's words rang in his ear.

"'Soon' could mean any number of things—next week, next month, or never. 'Soon' means we have no fucking clue."

Tyler Ang paused, pencil poised. "So there's no schedule?"

He sounded so surprised that Cam almost laughed out loud. "Supply runs happen when the donor gods deign for them to happen. No one really knows when that's going to be."

"Then how do you know whether you've got enough to last you until the next run?"

"We don't." The two short words were pointed, with enough force to stop the next question from coming out of Tyler Ang's mouth. He snapped it shut as Patsy ran up to them.

"Hey, Tyler," Patsy said, eyes shifting quickly between them. "Doug's pulled all your gear. Why don't I drive you guys back to

Admin Block and get you settled in your tent? You've got a couple of hours before the sun sets to familiarize yourself with the place, and then you can head out into the camp tomorrow."

"Yeah. Sounds great." Even through the opaque lens of the sunglasses, the look Tyler Ang gave him felt like a dissection.

Cam gritted his teeth again. There were things inside of him better kept hidden from the light of day.

Tyler Ang backed down first. "Guess I'll see you later, then." He nodded once before following Patsy to the idling Land Cruiser, already loaded with their gear.

He walked with a sure, confident stride. The way those khakis pulled taut over Tyler Ang's ass, the taper of his back to a narrow waist, registered in Cam's brain before he could stop himself. He spun around with a jerk.

Don't look; don't be gay. Indulging in those desires only led to people getting hurt out here. He'd learned that lesson in the worst way possible, and he wasn't about to make the same mistake again.

He felt a call to retreat back to that dark corner of his mind where nothing penetrated, where he was safe from the outside world. The call had been stronger lately, the dark corner growing larger, and his resolve to resist was eroding by the day. Soon, Cam told himself; his days in the field were numbered, and then he'd be able to shake this darkness and go back to normal. Whatever the hell normal was.

"Hey, boss!"

Cam blinked back the darkness—that was for later. Right now, there was a crisis to ward off. Soon couldn't come soon enough.

CHAPTER TWO

Cameron Donnelly did not like Ty. That had been clear from the moment they'd met with the sun beating down on them and nowhere to hide but under that threadbare tree.

Donnelly hadn't been fazed by the sun, though. He probably wasn't fazed by much, if that firm jaw and stern brow were anything to go by. Ty had read somewhere that there were three types of aid workers: the wide-eyed newbie who wanted to save the world, the weary veteran who had accepted that they were not going to save the world, and finally the gives-no-fucks lifer who had no interest in saving the world. Donnelly was a lifer.

Which really made no difference to Ty; he was here to get his story. Except he'd been here three days already and wasn't anywhere near getting his story, not while following Donnelly around from meeting to useless meeting. At this rate, he'd end up with some stock footage and would never get promoted off the Chinatown beat. Interviewing Chinese grandpas about the latest mugging, or thug teenagers about the most recent car accident had been great for his first few years at CBN, but now he wanted to cover real stories that affected the course of world history.

Dani, Ty's editor, wanted stories that would shock and awe: poor starving children, mothers holding dying babies, ramshackle shelters, and overrun health clinics. Meetings and spreadsheets were not going to get Ty his promotion.

Doug was still snoring into his pillow when Ty slipped out of their tent. The early morning air was cool against his skin as the sky began to brighten along the eastern horizon. He strolled down the row of tents reserved for short-term visitors, heading away from the mess hall and offices toward the edge of Admin Block, the fresh smell of dew tickling his nose. A quiet stillness reigned over the land, broken only by a few chickens clucking away in the distance.

He'd always liked the morning. A memory surfaced of himself as a child, wrapped in blankets as his mom drove to a park near their house. It was still dark when she pulled him from the car and they snuggled together on a bench overlooking a little drop-off, waiting for the sun to appear. He'd been too small to think to ask what they were doing, but he'd forever associate mornings with that sleepy happy feeling and the smell of roses that had always lingered on his mother's skin.

The memory dissipated as quickly as it had materialized. That little boy felt like a stranger to him sometimes, someone who might have looked like him, but who would have walked a much different path than the man now walking between the quiet rows of tents.

He reached the end and stopped. Apparently, he wasn't the only person awake. In the barely lit dawn stood Donnelly, one leg propped up on a fence as he stretched. His T-shirt hung from his frame as if it was several sizes too large, and his jogging shorts drooped so low on his hips that Ty was certain they'd slip off. The fanny pack he wore around his lower back wasn't much of a belt.

Remembering how easily Donnelly had startled the other day, Ty made a noisy approach. Donnelly straightened from his stretch and turned. Maybe it was the early hour, or maybe he'd been caught off guard, but the Donnelly that faced Ty did not look like the same man he'd seen around the camp the past several days.

The Oakley sunglasses that normally obscured Donnelly's eyes were sitting on top of his head, revealing dark bags and weather-worn wrinkles. His lips, often pressed tightly together and obscured by a scruffy auburn beard, were parted, full and plump. His shoulders were slack, and he had yet to pull his long wavy hair back into his man bun.

Donnelly looked him over with an appraising glance, as if wondering what the hell Ty was doing there. Then something sparked in Donnelly's eyes—a flash of recognition, perhaps something more—before he blinked, and it was gone.

The transformation was incredible. One minute Donnelly was tired and world-weary, and in the next, his shoulders tensed, his posture straightened, and that . . . something in his eyes was replaced by the Donnelly he'd seen around camp. The give-no-fucks lifer.

"Good morning," Ty called out.

"Morning."

"You're going for a run or something?"

"Yeah."

"Mind if I join you?"

It was impossible to miss the way Donnelly stiffened at the suggestion, or the second, much more deliberate head-to-toe survey of Ty's body. "Dressed like that?"

Ty quickly assessed his linen slacks and light polo shirt. Okay, it wasn't what he typically wore to go running, but he could make it work. "Sure, why not?"

Donnelly shrugged, slipped the sunglasses over his eyes, and pulled his hair back like he was putting his armor on. "Suit yourself."

He took off at a light jog, leaving Ty to catch up. They set a steady pace, and Donnelly led them through the streets of the camp. *Street* was a generous word for the lanes between the uniform tents, white with the UNHCR logo emblazoned in baby blue across the sides. Some had morphed into Frankenstein-esque shelters as residents had built onto the tents with scraps of plastic, metal, or wood.

Here and there, Ty spotted evidence of residents taking pride in their homes. Wreaths made of questionable materials hung atop makeshift doorways. Colorful fabric covered the side of a tent. A series of ribbons were tied to a nearby tree.

In front of every tent were women mixing packets of powder with water, young children sweeping dirt yards with brooms made of branches. As they passed, people looked up and nodded at them, as if it were customary to see Donnelly running through the camp. They were all quiet, though, a sharp contrast to the raucous crowds that gathered later in the day.

A million questions ran through Ty's mind, but the rhythmic beat of their feet hitting the dirt ground and the meditative cadence of their breathing kept him from asking—the morning was too perfect to be disturbed. They continued for a while before Ty noticed a group of kids following them, most in bare feet, all keeping pace with no difficulty.

Ty glanced over at Donnelly and what he saw surprised him. Donnelly was smiling—an honest-to-god smile with lips curling and cheeks full. This was the first time Ty had seen something warmer than sternness on Donnelly's face. A couple of the kids shouted something that Ty didn't understand. Donnelly reached out, gave each of them a fist bump, and they all kept going.

The farther they went, the bigger the group of kids became, and the nods of greeting from mothers morphed into shaking heads at the two foreigners leading a bunch of kids through the streets. By the time they stopped in an open square, the sky had brightened and their posse of followers had grown to about twenty.

They were a mix of boys and girls, all with shortly shorn hair, covered in a fine layer of red dust from the run. Excited, they smiled and jostled each other. When Donnelly kneeled, they swarmed him, the bigger kids elbowing the smaller ones out of the way.

"Polepole," Donnelly said, waving them back with the palms of his hands. He reached into his fanny pack and came out with a handful of colorfully wrapped candy. But rather than distribute them, he asked each kid a question and each one listened with intent concentration. Only after they'd answered his question to his satisfaction would they get their treat.

"Kumbuka kuweka hii siri, sawa?" he asked them, placing one finger vertically across his lips. They nodded, eyes wide, mouths full of sweets. He held out his hand again and collected the candy wrappers before stuffing them into his fanny pack. "Can't leave any evidence around." He tossed the comment over his shoulder so casually that Ty almost didn't catch it.

"Mjomba." One of the kids leaned in close and murmured to Donnelly, as the rest shifted their stares up at Ty, towering above them. "Nani huyo? Chi-na?"

"Chi-na! Chi-na!" The kids all started shouting as Donnelly peered at Ty, eyes obscured by the reflective colors of his sunglasses. His smirk was obvious, though, as if he thought this was the most amusing thing in the world.

Donnelly translated. "They want to know who you are. Specifically, if you're from China."

The unexpected question hit Ty like a blast of cold air, leaving him feeling like an imposter in his own skin. He forced himself to smile. They were kids. They didn't know any better.

"No, I'm American." Even he could hear the touch of resentment in the declaration. He suppressed a cringe.

Donnelly didn't respond right away, but the smirk wasn't as smug as it had been a minute before. Then he turned back to the kids with a shake of his head. "Si Chi-na. Marekani."

"Marekani! Marekani!" they all started shouting.

He shouldn't be so goddamn sensitive. They didn't care if he was Chinese or American or an alien. All they wanted was something to shout at him and then giggle about afterward.

When Donnelly stood, Ty was surprised to find himself on the receiving end of a smile—the same one the kids had gotten. It only lasted a second before Donnelly blinked, and it was gone, leaving Ty wondering if he had imagined it.

Donnelly turned toward the kids again. "Kwenda shule sasa." He waved them off, and they all ran back in the direction they'd come from. "Kwaheri!"

He and Donnelly stood in the square until the last kid disappeared.

"You do this often?" Ty asked as they walked back toward Admin Block, the streets now full of people shouting out greetings to each other.

Donnelly's stare weighed on him through the lenses of his sunglasses, and Ty wished he had his own aviators to deflect. Donnelly stared for so long that Ty didn't think he'd respond. Then he turned away and muttered, "A few times a week."

"And what were you talking to them about?"

Donnelly chewed on his bottom lip before answering. "A bunch of things: how school is going, how their health is, their family. I like to check in and make sure any concerns are being taken care of."

"Is it always the same group of kids?"

"Do you ever stop asking questions?"

Ty let a grin spread across his lips. "I'm a journalist. Asking questions is what I do."

Donnelly grunted and fell silent for a moment before answering. "I take different routes through the camp, so it's more like I rotate through the kids."

A crackle interrupted before Ty could ask his next question. "Alpha-Romeo-1, this is Alpha-Romeo-12, message, over."

Donnelly dug a handheld radio out of his pack. "Alpha-Romeo-12, this is Alpha-Romeo-1. Send, over."

"This is Alpha-Romeo-12. There's been a break-in at the health clinic in C Block. Can you be on-site? Over." The radio distorted the voice, but Ty managed to pick out Patsy's Australian accent.

"Fuck," Donnelly muttered before raising the radio to his mouth and pressing the Talk button. "This is Alpha-Romeo-1, affirmative. ETA ten minutes. Out."

Donnelly took off at a jog, not bothering to put the radio back into his pack. Ty followed him, wishing he had Doug with him to film whatever it was they were heading into. "Does this happen often?" he asked as they ran.

"Only every other fucking week." Donnelly took a sharp right.

How the hell Donnelly knew where they were or where they were going was a mystery to Ty. Every street was variations of the same patched-together shelters, opening suddenly onto little community courtyards filled with loitering people.

"What about security?"

"What *about* security?"

"Don't you have security on these places?"

From the way Donnelly tilted his head at him, Ty was sure that Donnelly was throwing him some serious side-eye, and he was spared the sharp edge only by the sunglasses. Ty wasn't surprised when Donnelly didn't answer the question.

When they made it to the health clinic, a massive crowd of people already filled the small courtyard, most of them women with children of varying ages. They approached Patsy, who was talking with a couple of uniformed men, and a woman wearing a Médecins Sans Frontières vest.

"What happened here?" Donnelly approached, and everyone stepped aside—it was clear who was in charge. Ty hung back to observe and pulled out the notebook he'd had the foresight to grab when he left his tent this morning.

"The same fucking thing that happens every time, Cam." The women in the Médecins Sans Frontières vest spoke with a heavy French accent.

"Angelique, I'm sorry." Donnelly was calm and sincere but also resigned. "You know we don't have the extra staff to man every station every night."

"Right, and the fucking thieves aren't idiots, you know. They can figure out the rotation schedule. You have to, I don't know, randomize!" Angelique spoke with one hand on her hip, the other waving around to emphasize her point.

His jaw clenched, Donnelly turned to one of the uniformed men wearing a burgundy beret. "Sergeant?"

The officer nodded once but didn't speak.

"How much did we lose this time?" Donnelly asked.

Angelique shook her head and headed for the concrete building. "These thieves are smart, I tell you! They only take what they know they can use, and . . ."

Ty didn't follow them inside, instead debating whether he should borrow one of those radios to get Doug to come out here. Dozens of people stood or sat in a line that wound around the clearing. Some stared at him with curiosity. Others were hunched over, rocking back and forth, clutching a body part.

The weirdest thing was how eerily silent the place was. No people shouting, no animals braying. Nothing more than an occasional sniffle or a shuffle of feet against the dirt.

"You went on a run with Cam this morning, eh?"

Ty turned at Patsy's question. "Yeah, it was . . . interesting."

"Did he hand out sweets to the kids?"

"Yeah, that was unexpected. Didn't fit the image I'd been building of him."

Patsy chuckled, loud in the stillness of the yard. "He wasn't always so . . . rough around the edges, you know."

Ty cocked his head, his interest piqued. "You've worked with him for a long time?"

She eyed him, as if deciding how much she should share. Ty kept his expression innocent and waited out the awkward pause.

"Several years now. But Cam's been around for ages. A bit of a legend, he is."

"What made him so 'rough around the edges'?"

She barked a laugh before casting her gaze around them. Then in a lowered voice, she said, "Have you seen this place? We're all bound to end up rough around the edges. Cam's fared better than most if you want my opinion. He's lasted a hell of a lot longer than the vast majority of people who come out here."

"And how long do most people spend in the field?" Ty asked.

Patsy seemed to ponder the question. "Let me put it this way: A lot of young folks come looking for glory. Only a handful become lifers." She patted him on the shoulder before turning to join the others inside.

"Only a handful become lifers." It sounded like a rarified goal. But at what cost?

CHAPTER THREE

Cam clicked on the starred email again for what must have been the one hundred and eighteenth time since he'd received it a month ago. It was from Teresa, written formally in the vein of an official email from the UN, approving his request to be transferred to UNHCR's New York Liaison Office.

He remembered his conversation with Teresa months ago when he first brought up the idea of leaving the field. The Skype connection had been patchy, and she'd made him repeat himself to make sure she'd heard correctly. As if he hadn't almost choked on the words the first time.

"But that job is in New York," had been Teresa's response.

"I know." Cam had hesitated with his next words. *"That's why I want it."*

"But you're a field guy."

That was the same reaction he'd gotten from most of his staff. The only person who had been excited about his decision to leave the field had been Patsy. She'd pulled him into a long, uncomfortable hug and said, *"Good for you."* She hadn't let go until he'd finally relented and hugged her back.

Two weeks until his contract at Dadaab ended, and he was already scheduled on a UN-personnel-only flight out to Nairobi for an in-country debrief. That should take a couple of days, then to New York via London. Then he'd be home.

Cam didn't remember feeling this terrified when he was twenty-three and waiting for his first overseas posting. Now, the thought of going home made his stomach churn, but the thought of staying out here wasn't much better. He was fucked either way.

"Hey, boss." Patsy poked her head into Cam's office, and he quickly closed the email.

"Hey, what's up?"

"Those CBN guys are leaving tomorrow; thought you might like to say goodbye."

Cam didn't like Patsy's mischievous expression as she kicked the door shut and dropped into a chair. "Why would you think that?"

"Oh, I don't know," she teased him. "Perhaps a smoking-hot journalist had caught your eye."

Cam's gaze shot to his closed door, and he listened for the sound of footsteps in the hallway.

"Oh, come on. There's no one out there," Patsy said dismissively.

Cam lowered his voice to a stage whisper. "You don't know that."

"What I do know is that man is hot as hell, and I've seen the way you look at him."

Cam cringed and buried his face in his hands. Shit, if Patsy had noticed, who else had also noticed?

"Cam, it's fine!" Patsy leaned across the desk and pulled his hand away from his face. "You're allowed to be yourself."

He leveled his sternest gaze at her. "Not that part of myself. Not here. If I'm outted, I'm not the only one who bears the consequences. Other people could get hurt too."

Patsy's sigh was more of a huff. "Well, I'm not saying you should have sex in the middle of camp. What's the harm in chatting with the guy?"

Cam knew she would never fully understand, but he also knew she was only looking out for him.

"Besides," Patsy continued. "You should at least come hang out with us. You don't have too many of these nights left, you know."

A fresh layer of guilt piled onto his already heavy burden. His staff was capable; they knew what they were doing. So why did he feel like he was hanging them all out to dry?

Cam swallowed the mix of fear and shame, and nodded. "Yeah, sure. I'll be there in a minute."

"Sure thing, boss." She let herself out.

Cam started packing up his laptop. His staff were more than simply his staff; they were family, and they'd been through a lot of shit together. Patsy was right: he should go and spend what little time he had left with them.

Loud voices and laughter drifted down the hall as he approached. More guilt hit him as he stood in the doorway and watched his people unwind from a long day of work.

Cam's eyes drifted to a certain tall Asian with the perfect hair and easy grin. One of his female staff leaned in a little too close and giggled at his oozing charm, and something sour and sharp spiked in Cam's belly. He tried to ignore his reaction, but he couldn't tear his eyes away from the way Tyler Ang laughed readily at a joke, or stared intently into the eyes of someone speaking to him, as if that person were the only person alive on the planet.

Cam almost backed out of the room, suddenly in no mood to share his people with this outsider.

Robinson caught sight of Cam. "Boss! You made it!"

Too late.

He went inside, dropped his backpack on a couch that was probably older than he was, and accepted the lukewarm beer that was handed to him.

"Eh, boss, how much longer you with us?" Robinson asked.

"Two weeks and counting."

"Ay, you're going to miss it here, aren't you?" Robinson gave him a friendly punch on the shoulder, but coming from someone who was six feet four inches of muscle, it didn't feel friendly when it landed.

Cam rubbed his bruised shoulder. "I don't know, man. I don't know." And that was the truth; he'd miss the people, that was for certain, but would he miss the long, dirty grind? Probably not.

The hairs on the back of Cam's neck stood up, as if someone was staring at him. A glance over his shoulder confirmed that Tyler Ang was the culprit.

Yes, after a full week of the posh journalist running around his camp, he still thought of the man on a first-and-last-name basis. It kept him at a distance and staved off the hope that Cam could ever have a chance with him. Aside from that early-morning run they had shared, Cam had managed to avoid the other man altogether. Now, he only had to get through one more night, and then he'd be free.

"Hey, Donnelly." Tyler Ang's voice always came as an unwanted yet pleasant shock, resonating so much lower than he could brace himself for. "I wanted to thank you and your team for hosting us this week. I think we got some really interesting stories. The health clinic break-in will definitely get decent airtime."

Cam nodded. "No problem." He hid the slight crack in his voice with a quick gulp of his beer. Where the hell had Robinson disappeared off to?

"You've got a great team here."

Cam nodded again and took another gulp of his beer. The beer at camp was little more than flavored water, barely strong enough to give the slightest hint of a buzz, never mind getting drunk off it.

"I heard you're leaving soon."

"Yeah, in two weeks." Cam was almost done with his beer and debated whether he should grab another or go back to his cabin for something stronger.

"You're going to be missed, you know. They can't stop talking about what a loss your leaving is going to be."

Cam's throat closed with yet more guilt. They would be fine, he reminded himself; he wasn't irreplaceable by any means.

Cam stared at the bottle in his hand, but he could feel Tyler Ang's gaze heavy on him, demanding his attention. When he finally succumbed and raised his head, their eyes locked in terrifying clarity. Light-brown eyes, almost bordering on hazel with a slightly golden hue. Those eyes were observant, intelligent, probing. If Cam wasn't careful, those eyes would see right through his mask, meticulously crafted by many years of fending off the most inquisitive of people. And yet, not having to wear that mask anymore was exactly the reason why Cam was leaving the field.

"You're allowed to be yourself," Patsy had said. And he only had two weeks left.

"Do you want something stronger than beer?" The words were out of Cam's mouth before he had the forethought to stop them.

Dark, thick eyebrows rose, and the full mouth curved into the same easy grin that the girls had been giggling over. Apparently, that grin didn't only work on horny young female aid workers; it also worked on horny old gay aid workers.

"What do you have in mind?" His voice rumbled low, awakening parts of Cam that had been repressed for a long time.

He didn't trust himself to speak. Shit, he shouldn't trust any part of himself at this point. But that didn't stop him from nodding toward the door, grabbing his backpack, and leading the way outside.

Though the sun had set several hours ago, residual heat still lingered in the air as Cam headed toward his cabin with Tyler Ang in tow. Bringing someone back to his cabin—a man, no less—ran counter to the central principle that had protected him in the field for the past ten years.

Just drinks, Cam told himself. Nothing had to happen. Like Patsy had said, it couldn't hurt to chat with the guy.

As Cam held the door open, his heart raced at the knowing look he received from golden-brown eyes under strong eyebrows. Cam's mouth went dry, and he ground his teeth together against the heat that tickled his skin.

"Nice place."

Cam lit the kerosene lamps, slowly turning up the flames until they threw flickering light against the walls of his cabin. His bed was little more than a cot, and the only other pieces of furniture were a small table and two chairs, one of which served as his nightstand. He removed the books and the bottle of water from the chair by his bed and brought it over to its partner, then went to his closet to dig out the bottle of whiskey he kept stashed there.

"I hope neat is okay with you." Cam poured the amber liquid into two plastic cups stolen from the staff kitchen.

"Sure. I imagine ice cubes are in short supply around here."

Cam grunted as they settled at the table. Tyler Ang's tall frame sat slightly slouched in his chair, and his long legs crossed at the knee. With one arm thrown lazily across his lap and the other holding his cup on the table, he exuded an easy confidence that was both enticing and irritating.

He studied Cam. Cam studied the liquor he swirled in his cup.

"Thanks for the whiskey," Tyler Ang said, and Cam nodded his acknowledgment. "We should toast." He uncrossed his legs and leaned forward, holding up his cup.

Again those eyes, watching him, seeing him. Cam swallowed around the lump in his throat. "To what?"

Tyler Ang's eyes narrowed as if in thought. "To your many years of service and the sacrifices you made. And to a new future."

Cam's heart thudded so loudly, he was sure it could be heard from across the table. A new future. There was no way this self-assured man could know how much the idea of a new future scared the living fuck out of Cam. This had been his life for the past ten years, and there was still so much work left to do. How was he supposed to leave it all behind?

Cam raised his cup and bumped it against Tyler Ang's in a dull clunk. Downing its contents, he stood abruptly. "I need a smoke." His hands shook as he stepped outside.

He lit a cigarette and let the acrid smoke fill his lungs as the nicotine worked its way into his blood stream. The red-orange tip of the cigarette glowed in the inky black of night.

"Seems like everyone smokes around here." Tyler Ang followed him outside and leaned against the doorjamb a few feet away.

"It's mostly the expats. It's how we up our field cred." Cam stared at the burning end of his cigarette.

"By smoking?"

"The more someone smokes, the crazier the shit they've been through. The chain smokers have the most field cred."

"So, are you a chain smoker?"

Cam eyed him through a cloud of gray wisps. "I can be."

Tyler Ang pushed away from the doorjamb and came to stand so close that Cam shuffled backward half a step. When he took the cigarette from Cam, Cam tried not to focus on the brush of their fingers.

Without breaking eye contact, Tyler Ang took a nice long drag. The cigarette glowed bright, and the crackling burn punctuated the silence. He exhaled slowly, and the space between them filled with gray tendrils of smoke. Gazing at the cigarette with a lazy grin and half-lidded eyes, he said, "God, it's been a long time since I've had one of these."

"What? You trying to build your field cred?" Cam surprised himself with the hint of flirtiness in his voice.

Tyler took another short drag, with the long white cigarette pinched between his thumb and forefinger, and his lips pursed lightly around the filter. "Maybe. Is it working?"

Cam's lips parted as his lungs searched for more air. Tyler's proximity and the thickness of his voice did more to suck the oxygen out of the atmosphere than the smoke that surrounded them. He wanted to kiss those lips and find out if they felt as soft as they looked. He wanted to taste the stinging, bitter mix of whiskey and smoke.

He caught himself right before he swayed into Tyler and those undeniably kissable lips. What the fuck was he doing? About to kiss a man in the open where anyone could catch them? Fear prickled his skin as he cast his gaze in a wide arc around them, pausing in the darkest shadows to search for impressions of figures lurking close by. He didn't see anyone, but that didn't mean no one was there.

Turning sharply, he went inside and braced himself, arms straight, against the back of one of the chairs. He only had to keep his shit together for two more weeks. He had done it for ten years, so why did two weeks feel so impossible?

He needed to remember: his actions had consequences, not only for himself, but for the people he was here to serve. Eyes were always watching, always judging—the smallest slipup could mean life or death in societies where being gay was not allowed.

Cam jumped at Tyler's hand on his shoulder.

"Hey, are you okay?"

No, he was not fucking okay.

He grabbed the whiskey and poured himself a generous shot. He tossed it back and poured another; it would probably be easier to drink from the bottle.

"Whoa." Tyler took the bottle from him, and Cam resisted the urge to snatch it back. "What's going on?"

Tyler's one hand rested on Cam's shoulder, its heat seeping through Cam's thin T-shirt and warming his skin. He was right there with his golden-brown eyes, high cheekbones, and full lips. All Cam had to do was lean over a few inches, and he could learn the feeling of those lips on his own, those shoulders under his hands. And yet, they felt like miles away.

For ten long years Cam had watched every word he uttered and the way he said them, looked over his shoulder, and questioned every suspicious glance in his direction. He was so goddamn tired of constantly protecting himself. He wanted to be himself, consequences be damned.

And Tyler was a temptation that Cam didn't have the strength to resist.

The tip of Tyler's tongue slipped out from between full lips and wetted them as if inviting Cam in for a taste. Tyler's eyes were heavy lidded, and the hand on his shoulder squeezed. Cam drifted closer, compelled by a desire he no longer wanted to deny.

The first brush of lips against lips was a tantalizing taste that his body yearned to indulge. And yet he hesitated, held in check by years of conditioning. Tyler must have interpreted his pause differently, because he leaned in to kiss Cam again, ruining Cam's self-control. He kissed Tyler back like a man carried by the crest of a wave, propelled forward by a force not his own. Cam's fingers found their way into his thick hair, and he leaned into the hardness of Tyler's body. They stumbled in Cam's eagerness until Tyler was backed up against the wall.

God, he tasted good: like whiskey and smoke, and the spices from that night's biryani dinner. Cam slipped his tongue inside Tyler's mouth, and he groaned when Tyler's tongue fought back. He'd forgotten how deliciously good it felt to kiss another man, how his body lit up at the nips and licks they exchanged.

Tyler grasped Cam's ass, squeezing hard and grinding them against each other. The realization of how much he'd missed this—needed this—sent deep shudders tearing through him. He couldn't stop shaking.

Cam tore himself away from Tyler's delectable mouth, struggling for some semblance of control, only to have Tyler kiss and lick at his neck, nibble at his earlobe. Cam let his head fall back, his fight for control no match for the wave of passion carrying him forward.

Tyler pulled Cam back into a tonsil-deep kiss, and the hand that had been clutching his ass drifted around to the front. When the heel of Tyler's hand pressed against his throbbing dick, Cam let out a cry and jerked. He clung to Tyler, fingers digging into the sloping muscles of his arms.

Then, with a deftness that escaped Cam's befuddled mind, Tyler unbuttoned and unzipped Cam's pants and pulled his boxers low enough for his hard, leaking cock to spring out. Cam almost died when Tyler wrapped long, hot fingers around his dick. The foreignness of another man's touch was so much more stimulating than his own.

He moaned and shook, surrendering to Tyler and to the part of himself that he had repressed to work in the field. It didn't take long, one tug and then two. A twist of Tyler's hand across the head of Cam's cock, and a swipe of his thumb against the leaking slit. And then Cam was coming, his body tensing as he unloaded all over Tyler's hand.

Shame and embarrassment followed close on the heels of the euphoria of his orgasm, chasing him as he retreated into his familiar dark corner. He pushed himself away from Tyler, and pulled up his pants as he stumbled against a chair. He couldn't look Tyler in the eye. He didn't want to know what the other man thought of being jumped by a scrawny, unkempt aid worker, or what he thought about Cam's sudden ejaculation.

He wanted it all to go away—the impossible demands of aid work, the years of self-denial, Tyler and his all-seeing eyes. He wanted to hide in the distant safety of the darkness.

"You should go." Cam's throat was raw.

"Wait, what?" Tyler's sounded raw too.

"You should go." Cam repeated a little more forcefully, backing as far away from Tyler as the small cabin would allow.

"You're kidding, right? You can't tell me to leave after something like that." Tyler held up his hand. "I've still got your jizz all over me."

Cam grabbed a stray T-shirt from where it lay on his bed and tossed it at Tyler. He leaned against the wall, eyes shut tight as a complex mix of hormones and emotions coursed through his veins.

Tyler wiped up his hand and dropped the soiled T-shirt on the table. "What's going on here? You—"

Cam held up a hand, palm out, ignoring the way it trembled. "Please, just leave."

"Seriously?"

"Just. Leave."

Tyler scoffed. "Fine. Good luck with your future." He spat the words out like a curse.

When the door slammed shut, Cam collapsed into a heap on the chair, elbows braced on the table, head held in his hands. He sank into his darkness, a blanket of safety protecting him against the world. He reached blindly for the whiskey, and instead his hand landed on the soft fabric of the soiled T-shirt. Cam couldn't snatch his hand back fast enough, his eyes flying open at the abrupt reminder of what he had done. His brain suddenly registered the smell of his semen and the lingering scent of arousal, pungent in the enclosed space of his cabin. Pushing away from the table, he barely made it outside in time for his stomach to force his dinner up his throat and onto the dusty Kenyan earth.

CHAPTER FOUR

Two weeks later, Ty set his carry-on bag on the floor of the lounge and dropped into an empty seat facing the tarmac at Heathrow Airport.

He was late in returning to New York, but the change of plans had worked in his favor. The colleague who was supposed to cover the start of trade talks between the US and the UK had a wife who'd gone into early labor, and Ty had happened to be there to step in. Two foreign reporting assignments in a row—things were looking up.

Ty was exhausted, but it was the good kind of exhaustion which came from work he enjoyed and that contributed to something worthwhile. He would welcome the exhaustion any day of the week over the monotony of muggings and car accidents in Chinatown.

He'd gotten some good stories the past couple of weeks. His favorite was the one with the school children singing and dancing, a spot of joy in a roster of depressing stories. There was a foreign correspondent position opening soon; if he could polish this raw material to a shine, there should be no reason why they wouldn't give him the job.

Something flashed in the window overlooking the tarmac, and Ty caught the reflection of a figure walking behind him. He snapped his head around but couldn't find that auburn man bun, or the tensed shoulders that swam in oversized clothes. He must have imagined it—what would be the chances?

But, now reminded, his brain wouldn't let go of the thought of Donnelly and that strange night in the cabin. Ty wasn't an idiot—he knew why Donnelly had invited him back to that cabin. He'd had all the reasons in the world not to go. Top of the list was not mixing work and play, lower down was that Donnelly wasn't really Ty's type. But he'd still gone, because he'd seen something in those bright-green eyes that belied the gruff exterior Donnelly showed the world.

He leaned forward in his seat and pulled out his phone. By force of habit, his fingers took him to Twitter, and he scrolled through updates without really reading them. Instead he replayed that night in his head: the hazy expression of surrender on Donnelly's face as he came, dissolving into outrage and disgust—not directed at him, Ty was certain of that, though he couldn't explain why. But then, directed at who?

He tapped away from Twitter and called up the results of his search efforts the past week. There wasn't much out there on a Cameron Donnelly who worked for the UN. Ty had tried every search combination he could think of, and had only managed to find a bare-bones LinkedIn page and a protected Facebook profile with a picture of Donnelly that must have been taken when he was in college.

Clean-shaven, ruddy cheeks, wide smile, auburn hair cut short and smart, and green eyes that shone even on the small screen of Ty's phone. The man in that picture was Ty's type, but that man was a far cry from the Donnelly he'd met in the refugee camp.

The PA system crackled to life.

"Good afternoon, ladies and gentlemen. This is a preboarding announcement for British Airways flight 175 with service to New York JFK. Please have your boarding pass ready for inspection and your passport open to the photo page. We will begin boarding by zone numbers."

Ty locked the screen on the picture of young Donnelly and stuck his phone in his pocket. As he joined the line of people inching toward the counter, he brainstormed additional search terms. He was acting like a bona fide stalker. At this rate, he'd end up staking out UN buildings and tailing Donnelly back to his apartment.

"Welcome aboard, sir."

Ty nodded at the flight attendant with an automatic grin, then checked his boarding pass for his seat number: 15C. Shuffling down the aisle, Ty stopped short before he reached his row.

"You've got to be kidding me, right?" He laughed out loud.

Sitting in 15A, by the window, was Cameron Donnelly, with his curly man bun and scraggly beard. He turned from the window at Ty's exclamation and blinked once. Recognition morphed into surprise, which melted into a frown and lips pressed into a line. Ty bit back a snarky comment and stashed his carry-on in the overhead compartment.

"That's really your seat?"

Ty sat down. "Yeah. Don't worry. I'm not trying to stalk you." An ironic thing to slip out, considering the search results still on his phone.

Donnelly's jaw clenched as he turned back to the window.

"Didn't realize the UN splurged for business-class seats."

"Only for those with enough field cred."

Ty snorted. Field cred, right, which Donnelly apparently had a fuck-ton of because he chain-smoked.

He waved down the friendly flight attendant—the tag on her uniform said her name was Ann. "Miss, can I get a glass of red wine, please?"

"Of course." She turned to Donnelly. "And for you, sir?"

"Uh, a whiskey, please."

"Certainly, I've got Johnnie Walker Red and Jack Daniel's."

Donnelly hesitated long enough for Ty to notice. "Uh, Johnnie Walker?"

"Excellent. I'll be right back." She smiled and headed down the aisle, scooting past other boarding passengers to the galley.

Ty snuck a glance to Donnelly, who was staring resolutely out the window, his expression closed. His nose looked like it used to be straight but had been broken at one point; pale freckles decorated the tops of his cheeks, so subtle they could only be seen by someone sitting close and staring hard. Ty turned away, annoyed at himself for noticing, and yet his eyes kept drifting back.

Donnelly should get rid of that beard, or at least trim it up so he could show off his jaw properly. Or some beard oil, to make it more pleasant to nuzzle against.

Ty jerked his head away and held his chin with his hand as if that would stop his eyes from seeking out Donnelly of their own accord. Where was that flight attendant?

"Weren't you supposed to have gone home weeks ago?" Donnelly asked, gaze still fixed firmly out the window, his flat tone not giving away any clues as to what he was thinking.

"A colleague of mine was supposed to be in London to cover the US-UK trade talks, but he had a personal emergency. So I stayed an extra week and a half to cover it for him."

All he got in return was a short, curt nod.

Ann came back with their drinks. "Would you like a newspaper? We've got *New York Times*, *Wall Street Journal*, *Guardian*, *Daily Times*, *Financial Times*."

"*New York Times*, please," Ty requested, having difficulty returning Ann's smile.

"And for you, sir?"

Donnelly turned away from the window but didn't respond. A frown of concentration marred his forehead, and when Ty raised a questioning eyebrow, the response was a nervous flick of the eyes.

"I'm good, thanks," Donnelly finally offered after the silence stretched into awkwardness. Ann was professional enough to smile and leave. Donnelly drained his whiskey in one swallow. Ty wondered if he should do the same with his wine.

Left on their own, the tension in their little two-seat row thickened in the dim hum of a boarding airplane. Ty had never been so grateful as when Ann came back with his newspaper. He shook it out and refolded the pages to fit in his lap. Holding the crinkly gray newsprint in his hands always felt comforting; it was the smell, the texture of the paper, the way the ink smeared across his fingers. These days, most of his news came through newswires, word of mouth from colleagues, or Twitter. It had been a while since he'd sat down to read a newspaper front to back, and what with Donnelly glowering in the corner, this newspaper was going to be a welcome distraction.

The distraction took Ty through final boarding, pushback from the gate, and takeoff. It wasn't until the seat belt sign turned off that he noticed Donnelly had fallen asleep next to him. And then, only because Donnelly was twitching in his sleep, face all scrunched up, mumbling incoherently under his breath.

Ty hesitated, loath to disturb him if he was going to settle into a deeper slumber. But the longer he waited, the more agitated

Donnelly became—the mumbling grew louder and the twitching more violent—until it became clear that he wasn't going to settle on his own.

"Hey." He shook Donnelly's shoulder, gentle but firm.

"Wha—" Donnelly jumped. His eyes flew open and his arms jerked up in defense.

"Whoa." Ty snatched his hand back and held it up, palm out, to deflect any flailing limbs coming his direction. "I think you were having a nightmare. You kept twitching and mumbling."

Donnelly blinked the wildness out of his eyes, rubbed his hands over his face, and slumped forward in a whole-body sigh. His shoulders still trembled with what was no doubt the adrenaline of being woken up mid-nightmare.

"You okay?" Ty asked, though he already suspected what the answer would be.

Donnelly didn't respond. It was several minutes before he let his hands fall into his lap and leaned back into his seat. "How long was I out for?"

"I'm not sure." Ty checked his watch. "Max thirty minutes?"

Donnelly sighed again, and Ty got the distinct feeling that short, uneasy sleeps were common for him.

"Are you okay?" Ty asked again.

The weariness etched in the lines on Donnelly's face had to do with more than lack of sleep. "I'm fine." He leaned his head back and stared off into the distance.

He didn't look fine. Patsy's words resurfaced in Ty's memory: something about Donnelly being rough around the edges because of all the things he'd experienced in the field. But maybe those experiences hadn't just affected the edges.

Aid workers with PTSD couldn't be that uncommon; after all, they worked in conditions not dissimilar to the military. If Donnelly had really been through all the shit people claimed he had, it wouldn't be difficult to imagine him with some sort of trauma-induced mental illness.

Ty went back to his paper, more staring at the page than reading. Donnelly had closed his eyes, but his posture was too stiff for sleep, his every breath a gasp and then a sigh.

The next time Ann walked past, Ty waved her down. "Can we get refills, please?" He pointed to their empty glasses.

"Certainly. I'll be right back."

Ty flipped to the next page of his paper and refolded it.

"Thank you," Donnelly whispered. "And I'm sorry."

It was more the tired and resigned tone of his voice than his words that gave Ty pause. "For what?"

Donnelly stared at the empty glass sitting on his tray table, brows furrowed low over his eyes. "For waking me up. And . . . for how I reacted . . . that night."

The apology was so sad, so defeated, that without making any conscious effort, Ty found himself forgiving Donnelly for the outburst and putting it behind them. Holding a grudge at this point felt like kicking a man when he was down. Ty was intimately familiar with what it felt like to be on the other end of that foot. "Don't worry about it."

Donnelly pressed his lips together in what Ty assumed was supposed to be a smile, but it looked more like a grimace.

He ventured forward. "I take it the nightmares are a regular occurrence?"

Now that was definitely a grimace. "It comes and goes."

"Is there something that triggers it?"

Donnelly shifted in his seat. "I don't know. Maybe?"

He pushed a little more. "Have you seen anyone about it? Like a therapist or someone?"

Donnelly chuckled humorlessly. "No." He shook his head.

"No because you don't want to? Or you've never had the chance to go?"

Donnelly finally turned toward him and stopped the questions with a single pleading look. Whatever burdens Donnelly carried covered him like a heavy shroud, making every breath and blink labored. The raw vulnerability on Donnelly's face was enough to shut Tyler up and leave him aching to comfort the man.

Ann came back with their drinks. He thanked her and took a sip of his wine. Donnelly did the same with his whiskey, and by the time they set their glasses down, the weight of the air between them had eased.

Ty went with a safe topic. "So, are you excited about heading back to the States?"

The hesitation before Donnelly spoke was answer enough. "Sure, I guess. I mean, it's home."

"You don't sound convinced."

"I haven't lived there for over ten years."

Ty nodded his understanding. "Do you have any family in New York?"

The corners of Donnelly's lips curled in a small grin and then grew into a genuine heartfelt smile, like the one he'd given the kids at camp. It softened the world-weary lines on Donnelly's face and was so infectious that Ty couldn't help but smile along. He'd known Donnelly for all of a week, but he could tell that that smile was rare.

"My sister lives in New York. My parents are up in Westchester County."

The smile lingered with unspoken memories. What must it feel like to look forward to being with family? "You're close to them."

"Yeah." The smile grew wider, the crinkles around Donnelly's eyes deepening.

Lucky. "They must be happy to have you back." Some wisp of his own envy must have slipped into his words, because Donnelly regarded him with a touch of curiosity. Ty retreated behind his journalist mask, polite and charming, but markedly removed. "Well, aren't they?"

Donnelly's expression softened again. "Yeah, they probably are. They're generally an enthusiastic bunch."

For the life of him, Ty could not imagine Donnelly coming from a family described as *enthusiastic*. But then, what the hell did he know about families?

"How about you? Do you have family in New York?" Donnelly's words were hesitant, and he worried his bottom lip with his teeth.

The mannerism reminded Ty of that night when he'd been nibbling on that lip with his own teeth. It took a second for him to refocus on the question. "No. I don't have family."

"None?"

Ty shrugged. Everyone always seemed surprised to hear that, but there was nothing surprising about it to him; it wasn't like he knew any different.

"I'm sorry."

Ty paused at the unexpected response. "For what? It's not your fault I don't have family."

"I know, but it's . . . it's nice to have family."

He'd bet it was. "I wouldn't know."

Ty waited for Donnelly to ask the inevitable question of what happened to his family. But even though Donnelly glanced over at him several times, the question never came. He should have been grateful—he hated explaining his nonexistent family. Instead he started talking.

"I don't know who my dad is. He was gone before I was born, and my mom never talked about him. My mom died from breast cancer when I was eight. We didn't have any other family or any close friends, so I grew up in the foster system in Jersey." Ty couldn't remember the last time he'd willingly spoken those words to another human being. Maybe he had finally grown out of his discomfort, or maybe it was Donnelly, but talking about his childhood wasn't as painful as Ty had remembered it to be.

"Oh."

Ty braced himself before checking Donnelly's expression. He hated the pity he'd gotten from teachers and the disgust from other children, as if being an orphan and a foster kid defined who he was, and made him weak, difficult to handle, or even dangerous.

But Donnelly didn't express any of that. Ty only saw acceptance, like his sob story was the most normal thing in the world. It was the reaction Ty had always wished for, but now that he'd gotten it, he wasn't sure what to do with it.

So he kept talking. "My mom was an only child, at least as far as I know. Her parents were in Asia—Singapore, I think—but they were estranged, or maybe they were dead. I never knew what happened there." Why the hell was he sharing all this?

Donnelly cocked his head, but no shock yet. "Have you ever tried to find them?"

"No." The thought had never occurred to Ty. "My mom never really spoke about them, and she didn't leave me any information that I could use to find them. I've never really thought of myself as someone with grandparents."

He wished Donnelly would say something, anything, so he could react to it, or at least change the damn topic. But the silence stretched and, despite knowing better, he succumbed to the urge to fill it.

"When I was a kid, I figured if I had grandparents who wanted to know me, they would have tried to find me. But I never heard from them. And Child Welfare hadn't been able to track them down." He shrugged. "It never bothered me that much."

Donnelly nodded and didn't press the matter, but instead of feeling pleased, Ty found himself fighting back irritation. It was like he'd been saving this story his whole life, and when he finally shared it, the reaction was disappointingly anticlimactic.

"What made you want to become a journalist?"

The change of subject only brought up more memories of his mother.

"My mom was a journalist. Or, at least, she worked at the local newspaper. So, who knows. She might have been a secretary." He fingered the paper that sat folded in his lap. "But there used to be stacks of newspaper at home. They lined an entire wall, taller than I was." The image of the hallway that housed the towers of newspaper was clear in his memory.

"After she died, I used to steal old newspapers out of trash bins. I liked running my finger over each line until my skin turned black. I would stare at the pictures, studying every detail. They were like portals into a new and exotic world, an escape from whatever I was living through at the time."

Now they were even—an odd exchange of secrets that had no purpose and no end. It wasn't how Ty did life, and he wasn't sure how he'd feel about it when they landed and went their separate ways. But in the closeness of their two-seat row, somewhere over the North Atlantic, it felt like the most natural thing to do.

"So where are you headed from here?" Tyler asked him as they stood next to the luggage carousel, waiting for their bags to come out.

Oh, the number of ways Cam could answer that question—most of them some variation of *Who the fuck knows?* But that wasn't what

Tyler was referring to. "I'm crashing with my sister for tonight, and then we're driving up to my parents' house for the weekend."

Tyler nodded. "Where does your sister live?"

"SoHo somewhere."

"Ah right, you mentioned she was a fashion photographer," Tyler said.

Being stuck in close quarters for eight hours and unable to sleep had unlocked Cam's sharing side, or maybe it was Tyler and his constant barrage of questions, pulling personal information out of Cam that he would never have thought to divulge.

"Yeah, she's a bit of a diva."

"Is she coming to pick you up?" Tyler asked.

"No, she's got a shoot scheduled or something. Besides, she doesn't have a car, so we'd be cabbing it anyway."

Cam jumped when the light on top of the carousel flashed and the loud horn blared, the metal conveyor belt groaning to life. Fuck. He clenched his jaw and balled up his fists as he waited for his heart rate to normalize. From the way Tyler eyed him, he was pretty sure his reaction had not gone unnoticed.

"I'm not far from SoHo. Over in Tribeca. You want to share a cab?" Tyler carried on, and Cam gave small thanks that he hadn't pressed the issue.

"Um." It was a simple question, but his brain was still preoccupied with that blaring horn, and it took him a moment to formulate the answer he wanted. "Yeah, sure."

Bags started sliding out from the mysterious belly of the airport, and passengers rushed forward to grab their belongings. Cam kept one eye on the conveyor belt and the other on Tyler, standing next to him with a sleek leather satchel slung over his shoulder and a navy sports coat tucked over an arm. He stood tall and straight-backed, almost regal with his coifed hair and crisp clothing.

He looked like he belonged in New York.

Cam's hair was falling out of its ponytail, and his raggedy clothes hung on his body. His rundown backpack lay at his feet, heavy with his banged-up laptop. Who was he kidding? He was a field guy—what made him think he could cut it at a desk job in New York?

A silver hard-backed luggage case slid out onto the conveyor belt, and Tyler moved forward to pull it out. As he bent over, Cam couldn't help but notice the way his jeans hugged his thighs, the curve of his buttocks. By habit, Cam flicked his eyes away, scanning the crowd for anyone who might have caught his indiscretion, but no one was paying any attention.

This was why he'd come home. So he could be himself without constantly looking over his shoulder or feeling like he was putting the safety of everyone around him at risk.

Tyler dragged his suitcase toward him with a grin, and for the first time, Cam let himself stare. The memory of Tyler's lips under his, the smoothness of his skin under Cam's hands—he might be allowed to look now, but Cam doubted he'd ever get to feel Tyler's body the way he'd felt it that night.

Pushing the idea out of his head, he caught sight of his bag as it dropped onto the metal conveyer belt. He jogged to grab it and drag it back to where Tyler waited, again with a sting of embarrassment when he placed his bag next to Tyler's. His wasn't even a suitcase; it was an oversized military-grade nylon duffel bag with handles barely attached and covered in duct tape.

"Ready?" Tyler asked.

"Yeah." He followed Tyler out of the baggage claim area. As the automatic doors slid open, they were greeted by a huge crowd of people, signs, flowers, and even a large bundle of balloons floating off to the right. The din of emotional reunions bounced off the sleek metal walls and reverberated through the airport terminal.

He fought to breathe through the overstimulation, seeking some of the cool calm of his dark place.

"Cam!" a female voice shouted, and he turned to find Isabelle marching toward him with a giant smile on her face.

Izzy dodged around passengers with carts full of luggage in her stiletto boots. Cam dropped his bag and caught her as she threw her arms around him.

"Hey, Izzy." Her hair flew into his face, but he didn't mind. She always had a massive mane of thick red curls, and underneath whatever expensive shampoo she used was the smell of home. It unlocked the part of himself that he held so tightly in control, and suddenly he was fighting to keep back the tears. "I thought you said you had to work."

Izzy pulled back, and her smile quickly morphed into a frown. "Skype has been good to you, brother. You look so much worse in person."

Cam winced. "Thanks."

"Cam!"

Beyond Izzy's big hair, he saw his parents approaching. Oh god, his parents had driven all the way from Scarsdale, north of the city, to pick him up from the airport. He blinked at the tears, but felt his eyelashes dampen.

Hugging first his mom and then his dad in turn, a few drops rolled down his cheeks, and he tried to wipe them away before anyone saw.

"How was your flight? Are you tired? Did they feed you?" Cam's mom fired off questions.

"Wendy," his dad said. "I'm sure they fed him on the plane."

The corners of his mouth curled up. His mom was about as good an interrogator as Tyler. Oh shit, he'd forgotten about Tyler. He stood a few steps behind them with a polite if somewhat formal smile on his face.

"Mom, Dad." Cam stepped to the side. "This is Tyler Ang from CBN. He was in Dadaab covering the refugee crisis, and we happened to be on the same flight home. Tyler, these are my parents, Wendy and Bill."

Tyler shook his dad's hand, and then his grin deepened as he turned to Cam's mom. "It's a pleasure to meet you. You have a most impressive son."

"Oh, thank you."

Cam almost rolled his eyes as his mom flushed at Tyler's praise.

"And I'm Isabelle, Cam's sister." She stuck her hand out and met Tyler's gaze with an elegantly raised eyebrow and a shrewd look. It had been a while, but Cam recognized it as the look she gave to all the boys he brought home, as if she was trying to size them up.

"Isabelle. A pleasure to meet you too." Tyler returned Izzy's look with nothing but charm.

Then Tyler turned to him with the same pleasant professionalism as the first time they'd met on the fields of Dadaab. Gone was the snarkiness from early in the flight, the gentle concern when Cam had awoken mid-nightmare, and the easy rapport they'd fallen into afterward—it bothered Cam more than he wanted to admit.

"I take it your transportation plans have changed," Tyler said casually. "It was great chatting with you. Take care."

They shook hands, and like that first time, the smoothness and warmth of Tyler's palm against his own was unmistakable. "Yeah, same to you."

Tyler gave him a nod and strode toward the exit in long confident strides, his shiny silver luggage case rolling alongside him.

"What's the deal with him?" Izzy asked, staring after Tyler, her arms crossed.

"What do you mean?"

She turned her scrutiny on him for a moment before shaking her head. "Nothing. Never mind. Come on. Let's get you home."

As they headed out to the parking lot, Cam couldn't help glancing over his shoulder one last time in the direction Tyler had walked off in. But he'd disappeared, and the space between them filled with people waiting for loved ones.

CHAPTER FIVE

Saying that Cam had deep reservations about this party was the understatement of the year. This was the last place in the world he wanted to be, and for the life of him, he couldn't remember why he had agreed to come.

He took a sip of his whiskey. The Macallan Rare Cask was the only redeeming factor of the evening, its fragrance a rich vanilla and raisin. Cam stood in the corner, half-hidden by a giant plant that was more suited to some jungle forest than a New York living room. Out beyond the plant milled a growing group of men, all impeccably dressed and incredibly handsome. He took another sip of his whiskey—if he had to be here, he would be here drunk.

Cam's best friend from high school and the unlikely host of the party, Cary Davis, found him in the corner. "Hey."

"Hey, Cary."

"You made it."

Cam eyed his friend. "I don't know why you have these parties if you hate them."

Cary shrugged with a touch of resignation. "I have a reputation to uphold."

"What reputation is that?" Cam scoffed.

Cary smirked but didn't respond. Cam should have left it at that, but his accelerated consumption of excellent whiskey had loosened his tongue.

"Does your reputation have anything to do with sex parties?"

"Is that what Izzy told you this was?" Cary asked, amusement lightening his voice.

"She said it was a full-on orgy. Full-on gay orgy, to be exact." Cam thought of Izzy's cringe when Cam told her where he was going.

Apparently, invitations were highly sought after and hard to come by. Cam had no idea his childhood friend had become so notorious while Cam had been overseas. "So, is it?"

"I will neither confirm nor deny."

"Orgy, it is." Cam nodded. Not that he was opposed to getting laid—which was probably why he had agreed to come in the first place, now that he thought about it. But all the back and forth that preceded the act of fucking was enough of a turn off that he'd rather go home with his own hand.

"You can't believe everything Izzy tells you." Cary shook his head. "She's prone to exaggeration."

"That's true. So, this *isn't* an orgy?"

"I didn't say that."

"So, what the hell kind of party is this?" He threw Cary some side-eye.

"It's not an orgy. But people do tend to disappear at the end of the night in groups of two, or three, or more." Cary shrugged again. "What they do after they leave is none of my business."

"You're unbelievable. The things you get up to when I'm not around to supervise."

"*Pish*, as if you were ever the one supervising. How many times have I had to bail your ass out?"

Cam pressed his lips together and didn't answer.

"Like I said, I have a reputation to uphold." Cary swirled his drink in his glass. "I should go make the rounds." But he didn't move.

They gazed out at the party that moments ago had seemed so far away. But as guests—all men—continued to trickle in the front door, the mingling crowd closed in on their hiding spot, and the room shrank down around them.

"I need a new drink." Even with the plant as a shield, Cam felt the press of bodies on his skin and heard the cacophony of voices ringing in his ears.

"Bar's that way." Cary nodded across the room.

Cam narrowed his eyes and debated how long he could hold out for. That was when the hum of the room faded, and the moving bodies slowed to a standstill. A newcomer stood by the door—Tyler Ang.

"What's he doing here?" Cam asked.

Cary shot him a questioning look, but Cam ignored it, his eyes trained on how well Tyler's suit showed off the width of his shoulders, the narrowness of his hips. The collar of his shirt was undone, and his tie hung loose, leaving that little hollow at the base of his neck exposed.

Tyler had been making regular appearances in Cam's thoughts during the past month since they'd flown home together. A month full of sleepless nights or bone-shaking nightmares, no appetite, and zero attention span at work. Then Cam would spot Tyler on TV—segments from Dadaab, or ones closer to home—and it would trigger Cam's memories of warm eyes and a sly grin, his trim body and soft, long fingers.

"Tyler Ang? He's been a couple of times. Usually quite popular. I've heard he gets around. There are probably some people who came tonight solely to try to catch him."

When Cam didn't respond, Cary continued. "Do you know him?"

Cary was watching him, but Cam didn't want to take his eyes off the man across the room.

"We met in Kenya."

"Yeah?" Apparently, Cary wanted more.

"We sat next to each other on the same flight back to New York."

His view of Tyler was suddenly blocked as Cary stepped in front of him, lips tilted in a smug grin. "And?"

"And what?"

"Exactly. And what?"

"And nothing." Cam stepped sideways, telling himself he wasn't trying to look around Cary.

"I don't believe you."

"Well, then you can fuck off."

Cary's grin slipped. "Look, Cam. I know I invited you to a sex party, and I was hoping that you'd get laid tonight. But Tyler Ang's not the person you want."

Cary had his full attention now. "Why not?"

"He's kind of a jerk, and kind of a slut."

"And how would you know?"

He didn't like how Cary hesitated before answering.

"There's a grapevine. And this is my party. Look, he's one of those guys who only looks out for himself, sights set on the top of the corporate ladder. I've heard he's good in bed, but I think you deserve someone who isn't a jerk."

That description of Tyler wasn't surprising, but then Cam remembered the way Tyler had reacted to his nightmare on the plane, the way he'd spoken about his mother and his lack of family. Cam knew all about how someone's appearance might not match what was going on inside.

"I've been away a long time, Cary." He felt every one of those years in that moment. "How do you know I'm not just as much of a jerk as he is?"

Cary flinched at the statement but didn't argue. "All I'm saying is I don't like him for you."

"Fine. Thanks for the warning." Cam moved in front of the damned plant, done with pretending he wasn't trying to stare at Tyler.

When Cam found the tall, dark-haired man again, he was leaning in close as someone spoke into his ear, his hand on the other man's arm. The casual grin on Tyler's lips deepened as he listened, and then he burst out in laughter.

Cam's stomach clenched—he needed that refill now. He did a quick scan of the room and mapped out the fastest route to the bar. Weaving through the crowd was risky, but at least safer than potentially running into Tyler by going around.

With a fortifying breath, Cam took off, squeezing into open spaces between bodies, side-stepping those who unexpectedly moved into his path. He was making good progress until a short, slim man dressed in tight purple leather pants and a long-haired fur vest materialized out of nowhere.

"Hey, gorgeous." Maybe it was the lilting voice and the way he stood with a hip thrust out to the side, or the obvious interest in his kohl-lined eyes, but Cam took a step back, his defenses on high alert. His mind ran through all the exit routes he'd cataloged when he first arrived.

"Whoa, easy there, tiger." The twink smiled at him, but rather than appear charming, it made Cam's skin crawl.

"Excuse me," Cam bit out from between clenched teeth, his heart pounding and his skin buzzing, every instinct in his body telling him to run.

"Oh, come on now. I'm Bobby. What's your name?"

The twink took one step forward, and Cam matched him with another step back, his arm rising of its own volition to fend off the unwanted attention. "Not interested." Sweat broke out across his forehead, and his collar felt too tight. "Sorry."

The sickly sweet smile dropped from the twink's mouth. "Well, good evening to you too." He glared at Cam and melted back into the crowd.

He made it to the bar and chugged his first refill before waving the bartender over for another.

"You should try to savor that. It's really good," the bartender said as he poured another glass. He was right, but Cam didn't care.

He took his glass, turned, and assessed the room for the best course to the French doors leading out to the rooftop terrace. His lungs itched for a hit of nicotine to complement the sting of alcohol in his gut. It required some fast ducking, but he made it outside without incident, shivering at the chilly September night.

He set his drink on the ledge that overlooked the twinkling lights of downtown New York, and pulled the pack of smokes out of his pocket. A quick spark of the lighter and a deep inhale. His nerves responded to the rush of nicotine and settled with a warm mouthful of whiskey.

The call of the darkness echoed, and Cam welcomed the sweet oblivion it offered, a protective buffer from the organized chaos of the party and of the world beyond. Cam exhaled, and tendrils of smoke curled around him. With slightly shaky fingers, he switched his cigarette to his left hand, afraid that the tense grip of his right would break the slim cylinder in half.

He'd left the field to escape the uneasiness he felt in his own skin, but he'd been home now for a month, and things were not getting better. Whatever this was—this sense that nothing was quite right, despite nothing really being wrong—had followed him back across the Atlantic Ocean and was sinking its claws deep. His only escape route was a constant flow of nicotine and increasingly regular jolts of alcohol.

"Hey."

Cam whipped around in defensive mode, armed with the heavy glass in hand.

"Whoa." Tyler took a step back with palms raised. "Sorry, I forgot you startle easily."

The rush of adrenaline counteracted the chemicals already running through Cam's veins, pulling him in and out of the darkness until he had to hold on to the ledge to steady himself.

"I wasn't sure if it was you. But I think that reaction confirmed it." Tyler's laughter faded into a touch of concern. "Hey, are you okay?"

Cam took deep drags on his cigarette and drained what was left of his whiskey in hopes of falling back into his dark place. "I'm . . . fine." His voice cracked in the middle of the sentence as he bent over the ledge, elbows on the cold stone.

Tyler didn't say anything, much to Cam's surprise. Instead, he leaned a hip against the ledge, crossed his arms, and studied Cam with such intensity that Cam's skin heated.

"I like the new look."

"Huh?" Cam frowned.

"Your new look. You got rid of the hipster."

It was only as Cam's hand floated to his face that he remembered he no longer had a beard or a ponytail. "Izzy dragged me to a barber before I started my new job." The good thing about his dark place was that he felt safe in it. The bad thing was that it loosened his tongue too much.

"She's got good taste."

Cam grunted, his gaze trained on his empty glass. Behind them hummed the din of the party, and in front of them hummed the City of New York. But on the terrace, silence fell, awkward and uncomfortable. Cam was in no condition to brave another trek back to the bar. And the cigarette he'd been working through had burned down to the filter—he debated whether he should light another.

"I didn't expect to see you here."

"I could say the same to you."

"Really?" Tyler's voice held a hint of amusement. "I've never seen you at one of these things before."

He had a point. Cam scowled at his glass. "I'm friends with the host."

"Cary Davis?" Tyler sounded surprised.

"We went to high school together."

"Wow, I did not see that coming," Tyler muttered, more to himself. "I would have thought he went to some fancy private school, considering his family is old money."

"We did," Cam deadpanned.

"Oh."

If he wasn't so preoccupied with the overstimulation of the party, Cam would have laughed at the awkward silence that followed.

"Anyway, so, you know what usually happens at these parties, right?"

Tyler leaned down so their elbows lined up next to each other, close enough that Cam could smell whatever intoxicating cologne Tyler was wearing—the scent was a match to the kindling of attraction deep in Cam's gut.

"I was duly informed that these are sex parties."

The laughter that burst from Tyler was a deep rolling thunder that reverberated across the stone ledge, up Cam's elbows, and into his body. "So, are you planning on having sex with one of these fine gentlemen tonight?"

The thought of having to *talk* to any of those gentlemen gave Cam anxiety; he wasn't sure how he would get to the sex. But there was one man he didn't mind talking to. He worried his bottom lip before answering. "I hadn't been planning on it earlier." The words came out in a croak, and his heart raced.

"And now?" The question was uttered low and quiet, adding fuel to Cam's growing desire. Clasping his hands around the tumbler did nothing to stop their shaking, so he gave in and lit another smoke.

As his lighter sparked a flame, Cam peered over his cigarette at Tyler. He had a look reminiscent of another inky-black night in the middle of the hot Kenyan savannah. Eyes half-lidded, mouth half-open, the tip of his tongue sneaking out to wet his lips.

When they parted ways at the airport, Cam had thought that would be the last he saw of Tyler, and he had satisfied himself with his brief memories of the man. But the truth was, he wanted another chance to feel the weight of Tyler's body pressed against him, and he hadn't realized how strong that desire was until now.

"Donnelly?" Tyler did that thing with his name again, his intonation dipping in all the right places as if he savored each syllable the same way Cam savored a sip of excellent whiskey.

Cam swayed toward him until their shoulders bumped. As the contact registered in his brain, alarm bells sounded—he was in public, touching another man, about to kiss him. All his instincts told him to clamp down on his desires and run.

But he wasn't in the field anymore.

Still, he couldn't help a quick look over the shoulder at the people inside. They probably would have cheered for the free show, but the potential audience was enough to keep Cam from closing the last inches to get at Tyler's mouth.

The darkness pushed him forward. The instinct for self-preservation held him back. The tug-of-war pulled Cam so taut he felt like he'd rip in half. With a trembling hand, he brought his cigarette to his lips, the red-orange tip dancing erratically in the night. The nicotine wasn't helping. "I need another drink."

"How about somewhere less crowded?"

Tyler's eyes were filled with desire, but apparently observant enough to understand Cam's behavior. It was unnerving, and if Cam were slightly less drunk, or slightly less eager to get into those slim-fitting pants, he might have tried to throw up his mask.

Instead, his darkness urged him toward that pretty face, trim body, and all that calm, cool collectedness. A sudden image flashed through Cam's mind: Tyler under him, hair tousled, lost in the heated haze of lust. He needed that more than he needed a drink.

Cam pulled himself to his full height, his body warm with the heat of desire. He took one last drag on his cigarette and then dropped the filter into his empty glass. "Let's go."

Tyler's apartment looked exactly as Tyler did: straight out of the pages of a magazine. Everything was decorated in shades of gray, anchored by a black hardwood floor and white walls, with crystal accents throughout the space.

"Nice place." Cam was afraid to touch anything.

"Huh?" Tyler looked around as if seeing it for the first time. "Oh, thanks. I hired a designer and let her have free rein."

That explained it.

"Here."

Cam took the glass tumbler from Tyler's outstretched hand, with a brief brush of fingers. The cab ride from Cary's had been uneventful, but rather than settle his nerves, it had only served to increase Cam's anticipation. The small touch was like a waft of oxygen across slow-burning embers.

"Cheers." Tyler held up his glass.

"Are we toasting again?" Cam asked, remembering the last time they'd shared a drink together.

Tyler's eyes narrowed. "I'm not sure that ended so well."

"Good point. Cheers." He clinked his glass against Tyler's and took a sip.

How that night ended was an elephant in the elegantly decorated room. Tyler must have thought he was unhinged; Cam supposed he would have been right. But things were supposed to be different now.

"Um." Cam swirled the amber liquid in his glass, not sure how to approach the subject. "About that night."

Tyler moved to the couch and sat down, his long legs extended in front of him, crossed at the ankles. "Yeah?"

Cam followed but left enough room for a third person to sit between them. He braced his elbows on his knees, glass cradled in his hands.

"I, uh . . ." The inside of the glass glistened from the thin coat of whiskey. "Um, it's . . ."

There was movement beside him, and Tyler's hand covered his own, bringing the swirling glass to a stop.

"What is it?" he asked quietly.

The scent of Tyler's cologne penetrated that strange dark place inside Cam, drawing him closer. There were little black specs in Tyler's golden-brown eyes, and although those eyes saw too much, Cam couldn't help but be captured by them. His breath quickened. "That night. That's not me anymore."

Tyler's thick brows furrowed. "What do you mean?"

"I mean, I'm not like that anymore. Or . . . I'm trying not to be like that."

"Like what, exactly?"

Like crazy, Cam wanted to say. Except there had been times since returning home that he had felt crazy—and they seemed to be increasing in frequency. "Freak out. I'm not going to freak out this time." At least he hoped he wasn't going to.

It took a moment before Tyler's lips curled into a heat-inducing grin. "Good. That's good."

Putting his glass on the coffee table, Cam leaned in and paused millimeters away from Tyler's lips, waiting for that instinct of self-preservation to kick in. All he sensed was the tingle of anticipation and the stunning sense of liberty, so striking that it paralyzed him. He dragged in a shaky breath, desperately wanting but unable to close the final distance.

Tyler did it for him with a small tilt of his head and a simple press of lips. That was all Cam needed to sigh and melt into the kiss.

Finally, his actions aligned with what he knew was true on the inside, and it was a drug more potent than the alcohol he'd drunk tonight. Cam reached for Tyler and pulled him closer in chase of more of that high.

They lay horizontal on the couch, arms and legs tangled together. Tyler's hands were all over him—in his hair, running down his back, squeezing his ass—each touch setting his body alight, proof that this was who Cam was meant to be.

Tyler nipped at his lip, and Cam gasped, only to be treated to the intoxicating scent of Tyler's cologne. His mind was frazzled by that scent, and his lips wandered across Tyler's jaw and down Tyler's neck in search for more.

"Fuck," Tyler whispered, arching into him, shaking.

Cam rubbed his face against the delicate skin at the base of Tyler's neck, letting the mix of cologne and man fill his senses, enough to tease, but not enough to satiate.

"Ah, Cameron." Tyler gasped, his fingers tightening painfully in Cam's hair. "We need . . . Fuck. Condoms, Cameron. In the bedroom."

His mind preoccupied with the delight of being intimate with a man again, it took some tugging and pushing to get Cam to stand up and follow Tyler down the hall. Even then, his hand in Tyler's gave him the same thrill as the first time he'd held hands with a boy, despite there being no one here to witness it.

At the end of the hallway was a bedroom decorated in the same grayscale as the rest of the apartment, with an overstuffed armchair in the corner and a bed piled high with pillows.

Tyler wasted no time in getting naked, stripping off his clothes in practiced, certain motions and tossing them across the armchair. His casual confidence was such a sharp contrast to Cam's nervousness and trepidation, leaving Cam to wonder why the hell Tyler would want to spend the night with him anyway.

"Like what you see?"

Who wouldn't like that? Cam thought as he traced the lines and curves of Tyler's body with his gaze. He hoped to hell that Tyler didn't expect Cam to have a body to match.

"Come here."

The words were spoken quietly and with enough huskiness that it made Cam's mouth go dry, and stirred the glowing embers of desire. Cam didn't consciously move, but suddenly Tyler was within arm's reach, pulling him closer, and Cam's hands settled on Tyler's narrow hips.

Cam's lips parted at the gentle coaxing of Tyler's tongue, and he drank greedily from Tyler's mouth. He pressed their bodies together and felt the unmistakable bulge of Tyler's dick, still trapped in a pair of tight black boxer shorts, plumping against Cam's hip. The evidence of Tyler's arousal for him broke through Cam's doubts, and he tore at his clothes with an urgency to feel skin on skin.

They tumbled onto the bed with less grace than Cam would have expected for a guy like Tyler, arms wrapped around each other, legs hooked around knees. Whatever Tyler's reasons were for wanting to be with him, Cam would take it. He slipped his hands under Tyler's underwear, filling them with the firm muscles of Tyler's ass, and ground their cocks together, separated by nothing but two thin pieces of fabric. The embers burst into a steady flame, burning through Cam's body and fueling his need to be inside another man and find completion.

"Ah, Cameron." Tyler gasped. "Condoms." He slapped the bed, pawing at the sheets.

Cam shifted to let Tyler sit up and grab what he needed. He pressed a foil packet and bottle of lube into Cam's hand, then tilted his hips up to push his underwear down. Tyler's dick lay across his stomach, hard with his foreskin retracted.

With a trembling hand, Cam traced the length of it with the tip of his finger, awe making him slow the movement to savor the heated, soft skin. He swiped the pad of his thumb across the contours of the head and thrilled when Tyler tensed and his dick jumped. The long-forgotten sense of wonder filled him as he took Tyler's cock in his hand, the weight and heft of it both new and familiar at the same time. Gently, he drew the foreskin up over the end of the length and back down again, reacquainting himself with the profound satisfaction that came with bringing another man pleasure.

Cam stopped when Tyler tightly grasped his wrist.

"Are you going to tease me all night, or are you going to fuck me?" Gone was the normally composed, smooth-as-hell Tyler Ang. In his place was a man whose eyes were glazed over with lust, lips parted with heavy breathing.

The fire burning in Cam's gut intensified, feeding off the look of want he read on Tyler's face. Shucking off his own underwear, he rolled the condom on with an unpracticed hand, the coated latex slipping out of his fingers before he got it into place. By then, Tyler had repositioned himself, pulling his knees up to his chest, exposing his entrance to Cam's view. The image etched itself into Cam's memory: Tyler's black hair messy against the white sheets, his skin shimmering from sweat, his hands under his knees, opening himself for Cam. Tyler was everything Cam was not, and yet he offered himself to Cam with no pretense or expectations.

Unwilling to look away from the sight before him, Cam patted the bed until he found the lube and squeezed a generous portion onto his hand. He shook as he bent over Tyler, touched to the core at having this man underneath him, surrendering to him.

Tyler's eyes drifted shut as Cam's fingers breached the tight ring of muscle. His breathing deepened, and Cam matched each inhale and exhale with the in and out of his fingers. Tyler was beautiful like this, skin flushed, chest heaving—Cam could stay like this all evening.

"Jesus, Cameron. Enough with the fingers. Fuck me already," Tyler demanded as he reached for a kiss. Cam groaned into Tyler's mouth and extracted his fingers to get himself into position.

Slowly, he fed his cock into Tyler's body, then held himself still until they both adjusted. It had been so long since he'd been inside another man, he trembled with the need to fuck and feel alive again. "I'm not going to last long," he warned.

"Then make it count," Tyler growled back, wrapping his long legs around Cam's waist.

The first pull out and hard thrust in left them both gasping for air. Cam dropped to an elbow and grasped Tyler's hip with his other hand. His forehead fell against Tyler's shoulder, the smell of Tyler's skin driving him forward as much as Tyler's cries of "harder, faster, harder."

The pleasure of fucking Tyler roared through him like a raging fire until it consumed him. He buried himself deep into Tyler as relief overcame him. When Tyler came and yelled his name, it reverberated into the dark corners of Cam's mind.

Cam collapsed on top of Tyler in a hot sticky mess of sweat and come. They caught their breaths while still entangled together, the air gradually cooling on their damp skin. As he drifted in and out of consciousness, Cam was vaguely aware of a dip in the bed as Tyler got up and then returned wearing his briefs.

By the time Cam recovered enough to open his eyes, Tyler had cleaned himself up, fixed his hair, and lay next to him, head propped up in his hand.

"Hey." The rawness of Tyler's voice warmed Cam's insides.

"Hey," he responded.

Postcoital bliss hovered around them, silent and still save for their breathing.

"So, um, if you want, I can call you a cab. Or you're more than welcome to stay the night."

Cam blinked as the circumstances of their joining came back to him—this was how sex parties ended, he supposed.

"No, it's fine." Cam cleared his throat as he pushed himself to sitting with shaky arms. "I'll call my own cab."

CHAPTER SIX

"But I thought you said they liked the segments?" Sitting in his editor's office, Ty clamped a hand over his knee to keep it from bouncing.

"They do. Those segments were great, no one is denying that." Dani sat behind her desk, elbows propped on the arms of her swivel chair, twirling her pen between the fingers of both hands.

"So, why am I still stuck on the Chinatown beat?" Ty's grip tightened as his irritation spiked.

Dani's eyes narrowed. "You're not on 'the Chinatown beat,' you know that. It's the City Desk."

"Except the only stories that I get to cover are in Chinatown. How is that the City Desk?" Ty bit out with too much force. He tried to walk himself back and channel that cool collectedness he'd spent decades fine-tuning.

Dani had the decency not to dispute him but pressed her lips into a flat line. "You're effective in Chinatown. You're getting good stories there. Management is noticing that."

"I'm effective there?" Ty shifted forward, leaning his elbows on his knees. "What you mean is that I blend in because I'm Asian, right? This is a racial-profiling thing?"

Dani raised both hands, palms out, a forced smile on her face. "It's not racial profiling. Please, Ty, we don't need a lawsuit. But you're doing good work there. The stories are engaging, they're impactful. Isn't that enough?"

"No, that isn't fucking enough. I've been with the goddamn network for six years now, and I can count on both hands the number of times I've worked outside of Chinatown. This is bullshit."

Ty jumped up, paced around the office until he stood behind the chair, and braced his arms against the backrest. "You know I don't speak Chinese. I don't even fucking like Chinese food. What other advantage would I have there other than the color of my fucking skin?"

Dropping her pen on her desk, Dani sighed heavily, rubbing her temples with her fingers.

"Ty, I'm going to say something you're not going to like." Dani spoke with her eyes still shut. "You're a really instinctual journalist. You know when to be aggressive and push for answers, and when to sit back and observe. You're friendly and don't come across as intimidating as some others." She nodded out toward the bull pen. "People feel more comfortable talking to you and that gets you the story. A lot of that is because of your natural talent and your training as a journalist, but some of that *is* because of your skin color . . . at least in Chinatown. So yeah, being Asian is an advantage in Chinatown, even if you don't speak the language and you hate the food. You might not like that fact, but it's true."

Ty pulled himself to his full height and slipped his hands into his pockets. His heart pounded in his chest as nervous energy flowed through his veins. He hoped that Dani wouldn't notice how much he was trembling. This wasn't the first time they'd had this argument, but it was the first time Dani had admitted to the less-than-subtle racism at the network.

"So, what? I'm supposed to go back to the Chinatown beat?"

Dani winced. "Ty, you know I love you, right? You're one of my best journalists, and I'm not just saying that. But . . ." She shook her head. "This network is a bureaucracy, and there's a deeply ingrained culture that is not about to change anytime soon. I get why you're upset, I really do. But I don't think there's anything you can do about it here."

The writing was on the wall, but he didn't like what it said.

He'd given CBN six years. Not that long in the grand scheme of things. But with the way Dani couched her words and the apology in her eyes, it was clear his days here were numbered.

"Listen, this world is all about who you know. You've got lots of contacts out there. It might be a good time to see what they're up to." She paused and glanced quickly out the glass walls of her office to the bull pen. "I've got a lot of contacts too. I'll let you know if they come up with anything."

He'd worked hard to be a part of the team at CBN and show he deserved to be here as much as anyone else in that bull pen. It was a slap in the face to be told that he'd never be good enough. The offer to help softened the blow, but it still hurt.

Not that he should be surprised, Ty reminded himself as he left Dani's office. He walked past his desk, grabbed his jacket off the back of his chair, and headed straight for the elevator. After a lifetime of being underestimated, his mistake had been letting down his guard, thinking that maybe he'd found a home at CBN. But life was a hustle, and CBN was no different.

Shouldering his way through the people loitering in the lobby, he escaped out into the cool autumn New York air. The streets were filled with office workers seeking a bit of fresh air and tourists gawking at the concrete jungle they found themselves in.

Ty headed east on one of the less crowded streets, sidestepping random puddles, piles of trash, people with strollers, and the brave urban joggers. Wandering with no destination in mind felt apt, considering his career suddenly had no direction either.

He found himself at a dead-end street, looking out over First Avenue, the dated UN building sitting across from him. There was a whole world out there with shit going down in it, and he was stuck in fucking Chinatown. Ty longed for that feeling of purpose he had when he stood to pose a question to the trade minister, or when he spoke with a refugee woman frustrated with the state of her living conditions.

Ty had really thought Kenya and London were going to be his big breaks. He was perfect for that foreign correspondent position. But knowing that did fuck all when management couldn't see past the color of his skin.

Fuck them. He could do better. Wasn't that what he'd spent his whole life doing? Straight-A grades from a foster-system kid who'd been through three high schools in four years. Pulling all-nighters and working through the weekend as an editor of his high school newspaper to land himself a scholarship to Vassar College. Countless unpaid internships at community newspapers and freelancing until he built up a portfolio to pitch himself to the news stations. Then finally the networks. He thought he had made it.

So, he'd hustle some more. If that was what it took, then that was what it took.

Ty turned and headed back, head ducked as he started compiling a list of contacts he could reach out to.

"Tyler!"

He couldn't pinpoint where the shout came from at first. Then he noticed a wisp of smoke, and the source of the smoke leaning against a tree on the edge of the neighborhood park. Despite his bad mood, Ty broke out into a grin.

"Cameron Donnelly." He walked over. "We have to stop meeting like this."

Cameron stood with his legs crossed at the ankles, arms folded over his chest, cigarette dangling from his fingers. Maybe it was the additional weight he'd put on or maybe he'd gotten new clothes, but he was filling out that shirt and leather jacket in a way that made Ty's dick take notice.

Cameron took another drag of his cigarette. "You're in *my* neighborhood, so this is really on you."

"You live around here? I didn't know that."

An amused smirk played over Cameron's face, so much more expressive now without that scraggly beard. He even had a little cleft in his chin that Ty hadn't noticed back in Kenya.

"No, I work here. This is UN territory. Don't you know that?"

They were in Murray Hill where all the UN offices in New York were located. He did know that, but he'd been too preoccupied to connect the dots. "Right." He chuckled. "So, how have you been?"

Cameron dropped his cigarette butt on the ground and gave it a little step and twist with his foot. "Fine. You?" His head remained bowed as he pulled out a wrinkled pack and tapped another cigarette from it.

"Uh, yeah, I'm good." Ty didn't feel bad about lying straight to Cameron's face, especially not when Cameron shifted from foot to foot, looking guilty as hell. "Smoke break?"

Cameron's eyes met his, and Ty caught a glimpse of uncertainty and what felt like fear, before Cameron shifted his gaze down to his lighter. A quick click was followed by a burning crackle, and then a deep exhale as the air filled with smoke. "Yeah."

The fingers holding the cigarette trembled, and Cameron shifted again.

"You're sure you're okay?" Ty asked.

Cameron pulled at his bottom lip with his teeth, eyes darting around the street at anything that moved before finally landing on Ty, guarded and wary. They stayed there for a moment before he spoke. "Why do you care so much?"

That was a good question. Because it wasn't like they were seeing each other. Shit, they hadn't even exchanged phone numbers after hooking up at Davis's party. But that had been a week ago, and Ty would be lying if he said his mind hadn't drifted back to Cameron several times since then.

So, why did he care? Because Cameron looked like a skittish animal who had been through more than one soul ought to have experienced in a lifetime. "You left kind of suddenly last week," Ty said. It was a dumb excuse, considering he usually didn't like his hookups hanging around, but he'd felt a weird twinge of regret after he'd all but kicked Cameron out.

Cameron's gaze shot to his and held steady for a moment. "I had stuff the next morning."

Ty believed that about as much as he believed that Cameron was fine. His phone buzzed in his pocket, and when he pulled it out, Dani's name flashed on the screen. Fuck. He didn't want to talk to her now, but he did need to get back to the office.

"Hey, listen. What are you doing tonight?" He almost laughed out loud at the blatant skepticism in Cameron's eyes. "I'm asking if you want to grab drinks. Nothing else."

The skepticism dimmed, but only a fraction. "Sure," he said flatly.

"What's your number?"

Cameron gave it to him, if somewhat reluctantly, and Ty promised to text him about where to meet. When they shook hands, the roughness of Cameron's palms scraped against his skin, raw and unadulterated, like the man. As he walked away, Ty wondered if he had signed up for more than he could ever bargain for.

The nondescript door on Forty-first Street had the name *The Basement Bar* scrawled across the front. Cam hadn't liked that name when Tyler suggested it; he liked it even less when he opened the door to a set of dark, narrow stairs.

Backing away, he let the door swing shut, and reached into his pocket for his pack of smokes. Only two left of the second pack of the day. Going through the familiar motions of lighting up wasn't working like it used to, and even as the nicotine seeped into his lungs, he itched for something more.

The shaking limbs, sleepless nights, wavering appetite, and false alarms going off left and right—it had all been getting worse. Some days, it felt like he'd been dropped into the center of a giant whirlpool where everything spun in circles around him, slipping through his fingers and making him nauseous as he tried to orient himself.

Coming home was supposed to have fixed it, but instead he was retreating further into his dark place, away from the outside world and its constant spinning. Even now, the darkness loomed on the edges of Cam's consciousness, waiting to draw him into its comforting embrace.

"Hey, Cameron."

He jumped, his study of the glowing cigarette tip interrupted by the one man who seemed to stand counter to the spinning, and who kept showing up in Cam's life right when he needed something solid to hold on to.

Tyler was dressed impeccably, as always. The attraction Cam had toward Tyler was as strong as it had been in Dadaab, if not stronger for the fact that he could act on it now. In fact, it was one of the few things he *could* do something about, and the realization emboldened him.

"Hey." He inhaled another lungful of smoke and leaned into his attraction, letting his gaze linger on Tyler's lips.

Tyler grinned at him as he took the spot next to Cam on the wall. His lips curled into a smile that Cam felt in his gut. "So, are you still trying to maintain your field cred?"

"Huh?"

"The smoking."

"Oh." He'd forgotten he was holding the cigarette. "Um, yeah. Something like that."

"'Something like that'?"

Tyler and his goddamn questions. "It's a bad habit, I know." He took one last drag and extinguished the stub with the heel of his shoe.

"I don't remember seeing you smoking that much in Kenya."

"I smoke more State-side."

"Really?" Tyler cocked his head. "Why's that?"

Cam cursed himself for opening that line of questioning. "Let's go inside?" he suggested, trying to deflect.

"Sure." Tyler opened the door and led the way down the stairs.

As soon as he stepped through the door, Cam froze. A single light at the bottom of the steps illuminated the way. He took one step and gripped the handrail tightly, fighting the feeling of the walls closing in around him. His heart thumped harder until the rush of blood past his ears drowned out whatever Tyler was saying.

The door opened behind him, and the creak of the hinges broke through his deafening pulse. Spinning to the side, he pressed his back against the wall and almost tumbled down the stairs in his haste. But rather than men armed with machine guns, he was met with two women dressed in suits and high heels, smiling at him as they waited for him to move on.

"You okay?" Tyler's voice echoed from the bottom of the steps, bouncing around the narrow space, and Cam's head spun.

With hands running along both walls, Cam talked himself into putting one foot in front of the next, eyes trained on each step until he arrived at the bottom. The narrow hallway turned at ninety degrees and opened into a cavernous space, dimly lit and decorated like an old-fashioned library.

Leather-bound books filled the bookshelves, and the air carried the faint scent of old paper. Low leather couches and armchairs were arranged in groups, packed in close to maximize seating. Tea lights graced each table and wall sconces hung around the room.

The bar sat along the wall opposite to the entrance, lit by hidden lights so that it glowed from the inside out. On the far side of the room, a swinging door, designed to blend into the wall, led into the kitchen.

"We're sitting over there." Cam pointed to the empty pair of seats by the kitchen door.

Tyler turned to follow Cam's gesture. "Are you sure? That's by the kitchen."

"Yeah, I'm sure."

Tyler nodded at the hostess, who gathered a couple of menus and led them to the pair of armchairs sitting side by side with a low, round coffee table in front of them.

"Wait," Cam said as Tyler moved to take the chair that faced the front entrance. Tyler stopped, a question in his expression.

"What's wrong?" Tyler asked with a frown.

"Um, can I?" He nodded at the chair.

Tyler chuckled. "Yeah, sure."

The hostess handed them the menus as they took their seats, but Cam didn't register a single word she said to them. Sinking into the plush armchair, Cam's darkness settled down, and when Tyler's hand landed softly on his arm, he managed not to jump.

"What's going on?"

"What do you mean?" Cam frowned.

"I mean, this whole thing." Tyler gestured at their chairs. "You seemed . . . I don't know. And did something happen on the stairs?"

Cam's skin prickled. "It's standard operating procedure."

"For what?" Tyler's eyes widened and his mouth twitched.

"Field operations." He tried to push the darkness back further and focus on the now. "You always survey a new space for possible entry and exit points. Always sit close to one of them, never expose your back."

Tyler laughed out loud. "FYI, Cameron. You're not in the field anymore."

Didn't Cam know it? "Smoking isn't my only bad habit."

"And the stairs?"

It was hard to keep his darkness at bay with Tyler and his dogged persistence. They were thankfully interrupted by their waiter—Tyler handled the food. The only thing Cam wanted was the biggest bottle of whiskey available.

"So? The stairs?" Tyler asked when the waiter left with their order.

The words caught in Cam's throat as the darkness rose up again, and he didn't fight it as hard this time.

"Small spaces," Cam managed to croak out. "They make me uncomfortable."

"And the smoking?"

Jesus Christ, he never gives up, does he? "I don't know. I need it more here."

"Isn't it usually the other way around?" Tyler sat diagonally in his seat, elbow propped on the armrest, body leaning toward Cam.

The darkness edged in close, hovering all around him. There were things better left buried in his darkness, but with one look, Tyler zeroed in on the single opening in Cam's defenses and drew out his secrets, question by question.

Fatigue hit him like a train. Acting normal, pretending to fit in, fielding questions he didn't have answers to—the weight of it was heavier than the burden of responsibility he bore in the field. He wanted to drink, drown in his darkness, then bring Tyler home and take comfort in the mind-altering passions of sex.

"Cameron?" Tyler spoke low and thick, his lips curling at the corners.

He latched on to the sound of Tyler's voice rolling over his name, and let his lust take over.

"Why are you looking at me like that?"

His brain supplied images of Tyler naked, legs spread wide, begging for Cam to fuck him into the mattress. He chased that feeling of control over his own pleasure, the ability to give and take as much or as little as he desired.

He didn't notice when the waiter came back with their order. A glass appeared in his hand and he brought it to his lips for several satisfying swallows. The heat from the whiskey settled in his stomach, mixing with the heat from his growing lust.

"Shit." Tyler glanced away and shifted in his seat. "Here, eat." He shoved a plate into Cam's hand and pointed at the charcuterie board sitting on the table.

The food tasted like dirt on Cam's tongue, and he washed it down with what remained in his glass.

"Would you like another, sir?" their waiter asked.

Cam must have nodded because the waiter returned a few minutes later with another glass.

"Jesus, Cameron." Tyler kept peeking over at him and shaking his head. "You really don't play around, do you?"

"What do you mean?"

"I mean, when you turn it on, you really turn it on. It's like you flip a switch. One minute you're all brooding and damaged, and the next you become this sex machine. I can feel it radiating off you. Shit, you're going to make me jizz my pants."

Cam's lips twitched at the image of Tyler peeling off his soiled boxer briefs, wet with his come.

"Don't look at me like that. We're in public, for Christ's sake." Tyler chuckled. "How did I ever think you were in the closet?"

Mention of the closet was a bucket of cold water on Cam's raging libido. He tossed back several mouthfuls of his whiskey. He almost didn't taste it anymore, barely felt its burn. Catching the waiter's attention, he pointed at his nearly empty glass.

"And there you go again."

Cam frowned at Tyler. "What?"

"You flipped the switch again. Now you're back to brooding and damaged."

"I'm not brooding and damaged."

Tyler lifted an eyebrow at him. "Yes, you are."

Cam emptied his glass.

"You need a smoke, don't you?"

"Why do you think that?" His brain hadn't even registered his need until Tyler brought it up.

"You're rubbing your fingers together like you're itching to hold something." Tyler nodded to Cam's hand where it lay on the armrest.

Cam closed his fingers into a fist, willing the itchiness to go away. His darkness pulled tight around him, faster than he could stop it. The waiter came back with another drink.

"Hey." Tyler's fingers wrapped around Cam's wrist before he could bring the glass to his lips.

Cam stared at Tyler's hand, warm on his skin. Then more fingers on his chin, his cheek, turning his head until he looked into Tyler's eyes. He couldn't turn away, couldn't stop Tyler from seeing how uncomfortable he felt in his own skin.

"You want to get out of here, don't you?"

"Yes." With the simplicity of that single word came a spark of relief that grew when Tyler didn't question it, merely let go of Cam's captive hand.

"Go ahead and wait outside. I'll settle the bill." Tyler put a hand on Cam's shoulder and squeezed. "Don't leave without me."

There was no danger of that. Cam chugged his drink. He planned on ending the night with Tyler naked underneath him.

CHAPTER SEVEN

The minute they got to Cam's apartment, he headed straight for his stash, pouring them each generous fingers of whiskey, neat. He handed one glass to Tyler, pulled a new package of cigarettes from the cupboard, and went to his window overlooking the fire escape.

In the relative safety of his apartment, he embraced his dark place, his heart settling into a steady rhythmic thump, and his nerves dulling to a pleasant hum.

Tyler came to stand next to the window, hair falling over his forehead, one hand slipped casually into his pocket—a striking contrast to the disarray of Cam's life. It made Cam crave him more.

"Sorry about that back there." Cam's throat closed in around the words.

Tyler regarded him for a second. "You don't like crowds," he said, observant as always.

"I don't like people."

Tyler nodded unquestioningly. "But you weren't like this in Kenya."

"I hid it better in Kenya." And yet, he'd never sought the solace of his dark place so much when he was in the field.

Tyler's eyes narrowed like his journalist bullshit detector had pinged.

"Why aren't you hiding it as well now?"

If he had the answer to that question, maybe he wouldn't need to resort to his dark place so often. Cam stabbed his cigarette butt into the glass jar he kept by the window for ashes. When he went to finish his drink, it was covered by Tyler's hand.

Cam looked up and found he could see each individual black eyelash surrounding eyes that saw how deeply disturbed Cam was, and yet Tyler hadn't gone running in the opposite direction. His steadfastness called out to Cam like the beacon of a lighthouse as he drifted in the midnight sea. When Tyler led him to the couch, he followed.

Tyler sat sideways, facing him, close enough for his knee to bump against Cam's thigh. "Your apartment looks like your cabin from the camp."

His bare walls felt appropriate. There were boxes of his stuff packed away somewhere: books about aid and development, souvenirs he'd picked up in the various countries he'd worked in. But the idea of setting them all out as decorations set Cam on edge, as if his years of work were nothing more than window dressing and wall coverings.

But Cam didn't want to talk about his lack of artistic style. He set his hand on Tyler's thigh and slid it up to where he hoped he'd find the bulge of Tyler's cock. But Tyler intercepted him halfway. A thin thread of doubt wound through him at the realization that Tyler might have envisioned this night going differently. He tried to pull his hand away, but it was trapped between Tyler's palm and thigh.

"Hey, have you . . . have you thought about talking to someone about . . . you know, the stairs and crowds?"

A low-grade panic bubbled up in his chest at the mention of talking to someone about his crazy. His darkness rushed in to suppress it.

"What are you talking about?" he managed to croak in a voice that didn't sound like his own.

"You're drinking a lot and smoking a lot. It seems like . . . I mean, the transition back home can't be easy. Doesn't the UN do debriefs or counseling?"

He wrenched his hand out of Tyler's grasp and reached for his glass sitting on the table. Cam had brought Tyler home so they could tumble into bed, naked and sweaty, and lose themselves in physical sensations and pleasure. He didn't need lectures about how he couldn't keep his shit together.

"Hey." Tyler shot forward to help steady the glass that shook dangerously. "You okay?"

Cradling the tumbler, Cam brought it to his lips, where it clinked against his teeth as he sucked the alcohol down.

"I'm fine," Cam mumbled into the empty glass.

"Are you sure?"

Cam couldn't blame Tyler for not believing him. He barely believed himself. "I'm fine," he said again with more false conviction, accented by the thud of the glass set down heavily on the table.

Though he trembled at the core of his being, Cam met Tyler's scrutiny with a glare and dared him to suggest otherwise again. A wordless battle volleyed between them, and much to Cam's surprise, Tyler backed off.

"Okay," he said, his posture softening until he slouched into the couch. "I'm sorry I brought it up. I'll mind my own business."

The apology did little to ease the cocktail of hormones coursing through his veins, and Cam fisted his hands on his knees, willing his body into stillness.

"Hey, I'm sorry. Really I am."

Tyler grasped him by the shoulder, warm and solid, pulling him back before he drifted too far away.

He turned his head so he could brush Tyler's knuckles with his cheek. The physical touch was one of the few things he understood—real and tangible, it kept him anchored. Pursing his lips, he pressed one small kiss, and then another, to the parts of Tyler's wrist he could reach.

"Cameron."

Cam latched on to Tyler's forearm to keep him from taking his hand away. With his eyes squeezed shut, he focused on the weight of Tyler's hand, the smell of Tyler's skin under his nose. He needed this physical connection; he would do anything to keep Tyler here.

"Please," Cam whispered, sounding desperate even to his own ears.

Tyler didn't answer, and Cam opened his eyes to meet Tyler's gaze. "Please," he repeated. "Take me to bed."

Tyler's lips parted, and he lost that laser-beam concentration. Cam saw his opening and tugged Tyler close, groaning when their lips finally met. The kiss was as good as the last time—the perfect amount of pressure, the right amount of tongue. The kiss tasted better than all the whiskey Cam had drunk in the past week, and it filled him with the blissful numbness he sought so fiercely.

He buried his fingers in Tyler's silky hair and leaned in closer, kissing his way along Tyler's smooth jaw, no stubble even though it was late in the day. Then down his neck, until he latched on to a spot near the base where the waft of Tyler's cologne was the strongest. Tyler gasped as Cam increased the suction on the soft skin, the sound filtering through the growing haze of desire in his mind.

He rose onto unsteady feet, dragging Tyler with him. With hands tugging at clothing and mouths clashing against each other, they stumbled toward the bedroom. Cam shoved Tyler up against the wall and pinned him there. The rare sense of control coursed through his veins. Cam ground himself against Tyler, the hardness of Tyler's body next to his own sending his blood roiling in the most powerful way.

"Yes," Tyler hissed.

And, suddenly, there was too much clothing between them. Cam tugged at Tyler's shirt and fumbled at the buttons, getting nowhere until Tyler's hands closed over his own.

"Here, let me." He pushed Cam a step backward and set about undressing with that quick efficiency Cam so admired.

Cam watched, hands fisted, as each inch of skin was revealed. His fingers itched to take this beautiful man, press him down, and possess him. Tyler finished and approached. As Tyler worked the buttons of Cam's shirt and eased the fabric over his shoulders, Cam trembled for a different reason. The need to make Tyler his rose like an uncontrollable force inside of him. Cam reached for him but found air as Tyler dropped to his knees.

He unbuckled Cam's belt with a heated leer through dark eyelashes. Passion spiked in Cam's blood, feeding the desire to dominate and control. He buried his fingers in Tyler's thick hair and tugged—Tyler's eyes fluttered shut, and he let out a ragged exhale. Pulling Tyler's head back with one hand, Cam traced his thumb down the side of Tyler's cheek and then pressed it into Tyler's open mouth. Tyler's lips closed around it and sucked, his tongue bathing the pad of Cam's thumb as Cam pressed it deeper inside.

Tyler peered up at him, eyes unfocused but with enough surrender that Cam shook with the incredible sense of power. He tore his thumb from Tyler's mouth, the scrape of teeth against his skin sending a sharp spike of desire through him. To his great satisfaction, Tyler wasted no time in keeping his mouth occupied.

When the warmth of Tyler's mouth closed around Cam's cock, his knees nearly buckled, and he held himself up with fingers tight in Tyler's hair, the other hand gripping Tyler's shoulder. Tyler groaned around him, the vibrations low and resonant, and Cam's hips shot forward in his search for more. Tyler gagged a little, the sound almost as pleasurable as the swipe of Tyler's tongue along his length. Some small part of his brain warned him to back away, but Tyler's hands on his ass held him deep, then pulled him deeper.

"Goddamn, Tyler." Giving in to that base desire for domination, Cam fucked Tyler's face, pumping in and out of the warm, wet mouth, as Tyler held himself still and gazed up at Cam with hazy, lust-filled eyes. Tyler squeezed his ass, and a steady, low moan reverberated around his cock, encouraging him to pick up speed.

The view was nearly as good as the feeling of slipping in and out of Tyler's throat. The unflappable Tyler Ang was on his knees, eyes wild, hair in disarray, lips stretched thin while Cam used his mouth. It was almost enough to make Cam drive in hard and coat Tyler's tonsils with his semen—but no, Cam needed more.

He pushed himself away with such force that he stumbled back against the bed, and Tyler caught himself before he sprawled on the floor. He breathed hard, gripping the bedsheet under his hands to keep himself from grabbing Tyler and fucking him into the floor.

With a leer, Tyler wiped the back of his hand across his spit-slicked chin, and crawled up to Cam.

"Did you like face-fucking me?" Tyler whispered against Cam's ear, his chin still wet. "I thought you were going to come all over my face."

Full-body shudders ran through Cam at the image. He rolled over and pinned Tyler to the bed. Tyler wiggled his jaw side to side, working out the kinks; Cam grabbed it with one hand, holding it still so he could mimic the face-fucking with his tongue.

Tyler moaned into his mouth, emboldening Cam and affirming his control over their kiss. Cam ran a hand down the tapered side of Tyler's body and gripped the narrow hip with a strength that came from something not quite himself. *Tyler is mine*, the words echoed through his mind.

With great reluctance, Cam peeled himself away from the comfort of Tyler's body and scrambled over to the nightstand, where he had stashed a new box of condoms.

The image that greeted Cam when he turned back around seized him, stole his breath, and left him hungrier for the escape that Tyler offered. Tyler was on his knees, back toward Cam, looking over his shoulder with his lips parted and his arm moving in a way that left no doubt to what his hand was doing. The slope of his back called to Cam, and he ran a finger down the valley of Tyler's spine. Tyler gasped when Cam reached the bottom and continued farther.

The simple intake of air was like a shot of adrenaline to Cam's already hypersensitive system. He pushed Tyler forward until his chest lay flat against the bed, his ass in the air, presented to Cam for the taking.

Cam moved behind Tyler, his body flushed with the only thing that had felt right and good for weeks: his desire for Tyler. He let it direct his movements as he prepped Tyler with slick fingers and rolled the condom onto his own dick. When he sank into the tight warmth of Tyler's body, it was like he was finally back in control of some small part of his life.

He held himself still, savoring the feeling, knowing that it would be short-lived.

"Cam." Tyler arched, bringing Cam's attention back to the beautiful man bent over underneath him. "Fuck me, please."

Cam took the reins of his lust and drove it onward like it would be his saving grace. He snapped his hips sharply, and Tyler cried out, begging for more. Tyler's cries mixed with the *slap, slap* sound of skin against skin, all of it fuel for the need raging inside of Cam.

"Yes, right there." Tyler shifted, reaching down with one hand. "Oh god, I'm going to come." Cam tightened his hold on Tyler's hips, made slippery from sweat. He was right at the cusp too, so close to that ephemeral release he longed for.

Tyler tensed under Cam's hands, clamping down hard on Cam's dick and drawing his orgasm out from the pit of his stomach. Cam pitched forward, driving them both onto the mattress, and for a few moments, Cam floated in the freedom of his climax. The sweet bliss wiped out all the darkness, stilled all the spinning, and with Tyler in his arms, he finally felt at rest.

They were close, much closer than Cam had originally believed. He could hear them shouting, voices ringing out into the night air, no distinguishable words, but Cam understood what they were saying—he could feel it in his bones.

He threw one foot in front of the other as he ran, arms pumping, lungs dragging in air. He ran through the streets, through forested woods, through the expanse of deserts. It didn't matter what direction he took, or where he was going, all he needed was to get away.

But they were gaining on him, their footsteps shaking the ground until they reverberated through the soles of his feet. Metal clanged and clashed against pavement or gravel or trees, ringing as the sharp blades swung through the air. There were sticks too, thin wooden batons or metal pipes, the perfect length for swinging and hitting with maximum force.

They were almost upon him, but he couldn't stretch his legs any longer. They were going to catch him—their panting breaths were right behind him, their exhales on the back of his neck.

No!

Cam crouched on the ground, arms wrapped around his head as they overtook him, but nothing hit him except the rush of air as they raced past. He stood to his feet as they ran on, his heart still pounding heavily in his chest. But if they weren't chasing him, then they were chasing . . .

Ahead of the mob ran a solitary figure—a little girl or a young man, a woman with blonde hair or a grandfather with a cane—and the mob was gaining.

No! Cam took off, determined to get there before the mob. Catching up with them, he pushed them aside, grabbing their sticks and their machetes, using their own weapons against them. He kicked, punched, and struggled, but there were too many. They subdued him and then brought him along to watch.

Stop it! No! Leave them alone! His shouts were ignored as the mob descended upon the solitary figure, their blows landing squarely on their target. Their victim stood no chance, falling to the ground, arms raised in a feeble attempt at protection. The mob was relentless, raining blow after blow on the defenseless victim until they lay there, motionless.

Cam dropped to his knees as the attackers spat on the ground and sauntered off. Crawling over to the limp body, he prayed that help would arrive, that the life could be saved. But as his cheeks grew wet with tears, he bent over the lifeless form and knew he was too late.

"Cam!" Strong hands gripped his shoulders, pulling him from the body, and he struggled against them, not ready to leave.

"Cam! Wake up!"

"Wha—" Consciousness rushed at Cam with the speed of a bullet train, pushing him to the surface of sleep and breaking through while his body was still reacting to the dream.

It was dark and hot. The sheets were wet and tangled around his legs. He kicked at them, but they stuck to his skin. Next to him on the bed, Ty was shrouded in shadows, hair sticking up on end, arms reaching out for him.

Cam scrambled backward, falling off the bed and onto the floor. He didn't stop until he stood with his back against the wall, one hand out to keep anyone from getting too close.

"Jesus Christ, Cam." Ty still sat on the bed, running a hand through his hair. "Are you okay?"

He was in his apartment, in New York City. It had been more than a month since he'd returned home. He was home.

Only it didn't feel like home.

With shaking legs and one hand running along the wall, he headed toward the living room and the pack of cigarettes that sat by the window sill. His hands trembled so badly he couldn't get the lighter to spark.

He jumped when a hand closed around his own. Ty took the lighter from him and held the flame steady. The first hit of nicotine did nothing for the shakes—this dream had been too potent, too powerful for one lungful of smoke. Cam sucked again on the cigarette, pulling the nicotine forcefully from the tobacco until it coated his lungs.

A glass appeared in front of him. Ty held it out, a frown marring that perfect brow. Cam closed one hand around the glass, but it shook so much that a trickle of water escaped the rim. Ty took the cigarette from him, placed it gently across the top of the glass jar, and wrapped Cam's other hand around the glass too.

With both hands gripped as tightly as he could make them, Cam brought the glass to his lips and sipped. Much too slowly, his body transitioned from dream state to reality, and the shaking dimmed to a minor shiver. He shifted the glass to one hand and picked up his cigarette again.

Then a blanket was wrapped around his shoulders, and he was led over to the couch. Cam sank down into the cushions as Ty sat next to him, wearing nothing but his boxer briefs.

"You want to tell me what that was all about?"

No, Cam did not.

"You don't have to tell me now. But you're going to have to tell somebody at some point. You almost punched me in the face back there."

Shit. Ty was right.

Cam took a drag of his cigarette and another sip of his water, then clenched his jaw at the memory of it all. "It's a recurring dream."

"The same one from the plane?"

Cam nodded.

"What happens?"

The dream replayed in Cam's mind in fast-forward, rushing through the scenes before someone hit Pause right as the attackers reached their victim. Then the reel switched to slow motion, each blow swung in distinct clarity—he flinched as they connected.

"There's a mob chasing me. Except they're not chasing me. They're chasing someone ahead of me. I try to stop them, but I can't. They beat whoever that person is to death."

Silence rang loud in the stillness of the night, broken only by the faint crackling burn of Cam's smoke.

"Jesus Christ, Cam." Ty sat with one leg bent on the couch, his elbow propped against the back cushions, hand in his hair. "Are they always this violent?"

"Yes."

"And do you know the person that . . . dies?"

Cam frowned at the sense of familiarity he felt whenever he thought of the victim. He always tried to identify who it was. But the figure running in the distance always looked different, and by the time he got close enough, he'd never been able to put a name to the face.

"It's a different person every time."

"And you haven't seen someone about this? It sounds like something you should hash out with a therapist."

On the outside, Cam scoffed. But the truth of Ty's words struck a fear so pure that it drove him to his dark place.

"I'm serious. You need to talk to a professional about this. How long has this been going on?"

Shivering under his blanket, Cam stared at the burning end of his cigarette. He had never counted the number of months and years he'd been plagued by the dream. But they had been increasing in frequency during his last year in the field and hadn't let off now that he was State-side.

"A while."

"What the hell is 'a while'?"

He scowled, cowing further into his blanket. "A long while."

"Jesus Christ." Ty ran his hand over his face, then buried his fingers back in his hair. "Does anyone else know about this?"

"No."

"Not even Izzy? Or Cary?"

"No." Cam forced more emphasis into that one word, but even that small effort zapped whatever strength he had left. All he wanted was his comforting darkness to slow his racing heart, dull his nerves, and let him sink into its insulating familiarity. "Listen. It's late. Go back to bed."

"You're not coming?"

"I need another one of these." He held up the cigarette.

Thank god Ty didn't argue. "Where do you keep your sheets? I'm not sleeping on the mess in there."

"There's a linen closet in the bathroom." Cam's eyes followed Ty as he walked away, a silhouette fading into the shadows. Now someone knew. Cam wasn't really surprised at that. Of all the people who could coerce his secret out of him, Ty had both the skill and constancy to do it.

It took him longer than usual to light a second cigarette. By the time he made it back into the bedroom, Ty had finished changing the sheets, the dirty set lying in a pile on the floor, and was lounging against the pillows, his face illuminated by the light of his phone, lips angled in a pout.

Cam crawled onto the bed and settled himself in, one arm lying above his head as he stared at the ceiling. He felt Ty studying him, his gaze heavy on Cam's skin. It lasted for several moments before the light blinked out and the mattress shifted under Ty's weight.

"Are you going to sleep?"

Cam could hear the tiredness in Ty's murmur. "Probably not."

A minute passed in silence. "Wake me if you need anything, okay?"

Something light and curious reached into his dark place and squeezed his heart. He turned away from Ty and tried to ignore the slow, steady breaths of the man sharing his bed.

CHAPTER EIGHT

Ty woke the next morning with a hammer pounding in his head. He didn't remember drinking that much the night before, but with trying to keep up with Cam and then the middle-of-the-night incident, Ty supposed he shouldn't be surprised at the hangover.

There were voices in the living room, floating in through the closed bedroom door. A female one, upset, angry, objecting loudly enough that Ty cringed from where he lay in the bedroom.

"Shh!" That must be Cam.

"What? Why do I have to whisper?" Izzy—still not whispering.

"Because you're hurting my head!"

"Well, that's not my fault, is it?" Izzy again, marginally quieter. "Honestly, Cam, what is wrong with you? You look like shit!"

"People with hangovers generally look like shit."

"Most people aren't constantly hungover. Or drunk and on the way to hungover. You never used to drink so much."

"And you never used to be so annoying. Wait, no, you've always been this annoying."

"This isn't funny."

"Who's joking? I'm not."

Ty sat up slowly with a hand pressed against his temple. His clothes sat on the floor where he'd dropped them last night, next to the dirty sheets.

"I'm serious, Cam. I'm worried. And it's not only me. Mom's worried too."

"You talked to Mom about me? Great. That's exactly what I need."

"What choice did I have? She says you won't talk to her."

"Maybe because there's nothing to talk about!"

Ty cringed at the shout as he eased himself out of bed and grabbed his clothes. He shouldn't eavesdrop, but it wasn't like he could be blamed if they were yelling at each other.

A heavy sigh came from Cam. "I told you, Izzy, I'm fine. It's been hard adjusting back, but I'm handling it."

If what they were talking about had anything to do with what had happened last night, Ty wasn't sure Cam was handling it very well at all. After slipping into his jacket, he opened the door and strode down the short hallway, making as much noise as he could to warn them of his approach.

He found Cam by his window sill, cigarette burning in his hand, and Izzy standing a few feet away, arms crossed. She whipped her head around as Ty entered. Her eyes narrowed.

"Tyler Ang? What the hell are *you* doing here?" she demanded, her glare so remarkably like Cam's.

"Well, good morning to you too."

"Wait, is this how you're 'handling it'?" She directed this at Cam.

Cam looked like he wanted to crawl into a hole with his smokes and a bottle of whiskey. "Izzy . . ."

"No, Cam. I'm being serious here. You do not look like you're handling anything, unless you're talking about his dick." Izzy shoved her chin in Ty's direction.

"Whoa." Ty raised both hands, palms out. The last thing he wanted was to get dragged into the middle of a sibling argument.

By the window, Cam curled in on himself, his jaw ticking, brows drawn low over his eyes. Eyes that looked a little wild, like he was still suffering from the lingering effects of his nightmare.

"Maybe you guys should take a breather and cool off." Ty didn't like the way Cam's hand trembled as he raised the cigarette to his lips.

"No, you stay out of this." Izzy turned to him, hand waving in the air. "I've heard of your reputation, and that's not anything that my brother needs right now."

His reputation. What reputation? Ty's hackles rose.

"Jesus, Izzy. Not you too." The words were muffled behind Cam's hand across his face.

"Cary's told me all about you," Izzy continued, arms crossed again.

"Yeah?" Ty bit out, forcing himself to keep his hands by his side. *Stay cool. Stay collected.* "And what exactly did he tell you?"

A smidgen of doubt flashed across Izzy's face before she pressed her lips into a thin line and lifted her chin. "That you're a slut." She didn't sound entirely convinced, despite the sting of her words.

The cold shock of humiliation sliced through his veins. Yeah, he slept around. But everyone did. That didn't make him a slut. It took everything in him not to storm out of the apartment.

"Oh my god, Izzy." Cam straightened from his position by the window. "What the hell?"

"That's what Cary said."

"Who the hell cares what Cary said?" Cam's volume was rising now. "He can say whatever the fuck he wants. In fact, you can say whatever the fuck you want too. I don't give a fucking damn."

Izzy took a step backward at Cam's shouting, her eyes wide with a touch of fear. Despite her earlier accusation, Ty found himself stepping forward, putting himself between Cam and his sister to try to lessen the jolt of Cam's words.

Cam went on. "What does it matter who I'm fucking? Maybe I'm a slut too. Maybe it's not only Ty. Maybe I'm fucking every guy I can manage to pick up off the street."

Ty flinched at those words, even though he was pretty sure they weren't true.

"Maybe I'm trying to make up for all those years of living like a goddamn monk." The hand holding the cigarette stabbed the air in Izzy's direction. "You have to learn how to mind your own goddamn business sometimes. This is one of those times."

A quiet hiccup echoed in the silence left by Cam's rant, and before Ty could say anything to try to deescalate the situation, Izzy turned on her heel and marched out of the apartment. The bang of the door when she slammed it shook the walls, and Ty cringed.

Cam collapsed back against the window frame.

"Well, that didn't go very well," Ty said, which earned him a glare. "You probably shouldn't have yelled at her." Ty didn't want to examine why he was defending someone who'd called him a slut.

Cam stared vacantly out his window. "You should go." He said this quietly, as if he'd used up all his energy in his rant.

"Are you sure?"

Cam didn't look like he was in any condition to be left alone. His eyes drifted shut, and the sigh he let out sounded like it came from the deepest part of his soul, emptying him of everything he had in him. "Please. Just go."

Ty was a fast learner—he didn't need to be yelled at twice to know when to leave. "Call me if you need anything, okay?"

Cam didn't respond, and after a moment debating whether it was a wise move, Ty let himself out of the apartment.

As he waited for the elevator to arrive, his mind replayed the moments right after Cam woke up and before his brain caught up with the rest of his body. Ty had seen the look in Cam's eyes before. A long time ago.

It was one of his foster dads—he couldn't quite remember which one; he'd been young at the time. The man had been a giant hulking thing with big muscles and a bigger presence that dominated every room he entered. But it was his eyes that stood at the forefront of the vague memory—the vacant, wild look in those eyes, almost like he was possessed. It was the same look in Cam's eyes.

Ty's fuzzy memory recalled that the foster dad had been a veteran of the Gulf War; Ty hadn't understood it at the time, but it was obvious now that the guy had suffered from PTSD of some form. It wasn't any stretch of the imagination to assume that Cam had PTSD too. All those aid workers, always talking about field cred and trying to one-up each other with the horrifying shit they'd seen over the years. Ty doubted that Cam's nightmares and constant drinking would ever resolve themselves without professional help.

He rode the elevator down, crossed the lobby, and paused with his hand on the door when he saw Izzy on the sidewalk, arms wrapped around her midsection. She turned at the sound of Ty opening the door and quickly wiped at her cheeks, but that did nothing to hide the tears rimming her eyes.

"Hey." Ty approached with caution, stopping a couple of steps away.

Izzy glared at him from under damp lashes for a heartbeat before her shoulders sagged and her expression softened. "Hey."

"You okay?" Ty asked.

Her lips pressed together, and she straightened her back. "Yeah," she said in a none-too-steady voice.

A beat passed in awkward silence between them. Ty juggled the urge to console with the fact that she'd called him a slut.

"Is it true?" Izzy studied him with a furrowed brow.

"Is what true?"

"That he's sleeping around?" Izzy lifted her chin. "Is it true?"

"Are you sure I'm the one you should be asking?" Ty mimicked her pose, crossing his arms over his chest. "You know, since I'm a slut and all."

Izzy had the decency to flinch at her word being thrown back at her. "Sorry about that. I was out of line."

Ty took a deep breath and told himself to let it go. "I've been called worse."

"So, is it true?"

Ty let out a dry chuckle. "I wouldn't know for sure. But I don't think so."

"So, are you guys a thing?" She shifted to face him. With her arms crossed and feet hip-width apart, she looked like she was interrogating him, and doing a damn good job at it.

Was that what they were? A thing? What was 'a thing'? "I wouldn't say that."

"Then what? Fuck buddies?" An elegant eyebrow popped up.

Ty shifted on his feet, wondering why that term rubbed him the wrong way. "Something like that, I guess. I don't know. Maybe." Jesus, he'd lost his ability to string a sentence together.

Izzy studied him for a moment longer while Ty shifted again, feeling like a child being scolded. "He wasn't always like this, you know." Her voice had lost the hard edge of her questions, and she ran a hand through her mane, rearranging her hair around her shoulders. "He used to be the happy one, and I used to be the moody one. If you can imagine that."

She started down the sidewalk, and Ty fell into step next to her. "What happened?"

She flicked her eyes to him and then away, her lips pressed into a line. "He'd kill me if he found out I told you."

"You're a confidential source." Ty grinned, slipping into a familiar journalist mode. "Your identity is safe with me."

She eyed him again. It took her half a block to start talking.

"He'd been working in the field for maybe two years? Something like that. I'm not too clear on the details, actually. He's never told us the whole story. But . . . Look, he used to be this really out-and-proud guy, okay? He was the president of the gay-straight alliance at our high school, and he'd organize trips for everyone to go to the gay pride parade every year. All that stuff."

They came up on a Starbucks and, without asking if Ty was interested, Izzy headed inside.

"Triple, venti, half sweet, nonfat caramel macchiato, please." She rambled off the drink to the barista and pulled out her wallet.

Ty put a hand over hers, pushing the wallet back toward her purse. "Coffee, black," he ordered.

"Oh, thanks." She tucked a strand of hair behind her ear.

"No problem." Ty let his lips curl into his grin. "You were saying . . . Cam changed after he started working in the field?"

She nodded. "Not right away. It was after some incident with one of his local colleagues." With their drinks, they sat at an empty table in the corner. "I don't remember which country he was working in at the time, but one of his colleagues was gay. I think they became friends, but then . . ." Izzy peered at him and winced. "The guy died."

"Oh?" Ty frowned.

"Yeah." Izzy dropped her eyes to the coffee she held between her palms. Quietly, she continued. "He was beaten to death for being gay. I think it was his family or his community or something."

He sat back in his chair and forced himself to release his death grip on the flimsy paper cup. That was it. That would explain Cam's dreams.

She took a deep breath before raising her head, her eyes ringed with tears again. "Cam took it really hard. Knowing him—at least who he was back then—he might have encouraged the guy to come out, who knows."

He took a sip of his coffee. The hot, bitter liquid burned a comforting trail down the middle of his chest, distracting him from the weird pressure he felt there. "He was different after that?"

"Yeah." Izzy chuckled humorlessly and shook her head. "He got reassigned to a different posting after that. They wanted to get him out of the country, I think. Anyway"—she waved her hand in the air—"he basically had to go into the closet, which is ridiculous because Cam's never been in the closet. We all knew he was gay since, like, forever."

"And he's never had counseling for that?"

Izzy shot him an incredulous look. "Cam? Ask for help? Please, are we even talking about the same guy?"

She had a point. But that was the problem, wasn't it? Cam hadn't gotten help back then, and who knew how many more traumatic events he had lived through since? It was a miracle he was still semifunctional after all this time.

"Okay, listen." Izzy slid her coffee off to the side and put both elbows on the table, hands clasped together. "Maybe you guys are fuck buddies. Maybe you're more, whatever, it doesn't really matter." She pinned him with a hard stare. "But Cam's in a bad place right now, and he's blocked all of us out. You seem to be the only one he's let in, so if you do anything to hurt him, so help me god, I will track you down and end you."

Ty should have laughed and brushed off Izzy's threat, because he never expected to find himself as one of the few people in Cam's inner circle. Sure, they'd hooked up a few times, shared things with each other that Ty suspected they hadn't shared with anyone else in the world. But that didn't mean they were a . . . what had Izzy called it? A thing? So he shouldn't take the threat seriously, right?

Except he did. And he was sure that if Izzy had any doubts about his intentions toward Cam, she *would* track him down and end him. Whatever the hell that entailed.

"Look, I have to go." She stood and adjusted her bag across her shoulder. "Thanks for the coffee. And don't fuck up." She strode out of the coffee shop like she owned it.

Alone at the table, he took another sip of his dark brew and placed the cup down gently, before rubbing his palms across the top of his thighs. As much as he wanted to deny it, Cam was somehow inching his way into the space Ty kept between himself and everyone else. He could already feel it reacting to the presence of a new person trying to slip inside.

It was that goddamn vulnerability, the touch of wildness in his eyes, the hint of a deeply broken soul that Cam tried so hard to hide. Why the hell he'd chosen Ty to open up to, Ty had no idea. God knew, he wasn't all cuddles and warm hugs.

He stood and tossed his coffee in the trash. Out on the street, he flagged down a cab. As the cab pulled away from the curb, Ty reminded himself that he lived his life alone and independent, because he didn't need anyone else. But even as he reminded himself, he had a sinking feeling that things were about to change.

CHAPTER NINE

Two weeks later, Ty stepped out of the elevator and into the lobby of the American News Network building, still a little heady from his interview with Editor in Chief David Beretta. He'd studied for this interview, watched hours of ANN on TV, written up answers for every conceivable question they could throw at him. Even Dani had put in a good word for him.

The interview had gone well and Ty felt pretty pleased with himself. From the friendly smile on David's face, he was pretty pleased with Ty's answers too.

Ty stopped in the middle of the lobby. But what if he didn't actually like any of Ty's answers? After all, journalists were trained to keep their opinions to themselves; didn't Ty do exactly that every single day?

Fuck it. He pushed the doubt to the back of his mind and marched toward the doors. There was nothing more he could have done, and if it wasn't good enough for them—

The thought was cut short by the ball of nerves rolling around in his stomach.

No. It had to be good enough. Ty was made for that foreign correspondent job; he had the experience, the on-camera presence, the killer instinct needed for an international posting. They *had* to give him the job.

Forgoing a cab, Ty headed toward the Columbus Circle subway entrance and pulled out his MetroCard. He swiped himself through and meandered his way to the end of the platform to wait for the next downtown 1 local train to Chambers Street.

"Tyler?"

He turned at the sound of his name. The stranger was good-looking, bulkier than Ty, with the charming air of a boy next door. He was dressed in a sharp suit, probably tailored. The guy looked familiar, but Ty couldn't quite place him.

The stranger chuckled, tipped his head to the side, and squinted a little with a grin on his lips. It was cute, sexy even, but a little too much for it not to be a practiced move. Ty grinned, beating back a laugh.

"I'm Libor."

Oh right. Like the London Interbank Offered Rate. Ty remembered now. Some hookup from . . . he wasn't sure when—or where. They maybe had a good time?

"Hey!" Ty held out his hand for a shake. "Good to see you again."

Libor held on to his hand a little longer than necessary, and when he let go, his fingers trailed over Ty's palm. The glint in his eye erased any doubt about his intentions.

The train rolled in then, its deafening rumble obliterating any possibility of conversation. Good thing too; Ty didn't really understand his sudden aversion to the good-looking guy who wanted to pick him up. And he couldn't resist the urge to rub his palm against his thigh to erase the lingering sensation of Libor's fingers.

"So, Tyler. How've you been?" Libor was overly cheerful as they piled onto the train, pushed close by the press of commuters on the forever-busy 1 train.

"Good. Great. You?" For probably the first time in Ty's life, his brain blanked on questions to ask someone. He was always so good about finding something interesting about the person to discuss, but as he scoured his brain, he realized he had zero interest in well-dressed fuckboys who were only concerned about dicks.

Ty completely missed Libor's response, too stunned by the realization that people probably thought of him as a well-dressed fuckboy. Because up until Cam had turned up, when it came to men, he'd pretty much been concerned about nothing else but a guy's dick.

The twenty minutes it took for the train to traverse the length of Manhattan passed in a blur of Libor talking about god knew what, and Ty offering up the obligatory responses that implied he was listening.

Izzy had called him a slut and said he had a reputation. So what if he did? What was wrong with no-strings-attached sex between consenting adults? But the longer Libor spoke, with that practiced smile and smoldering eyes, the colder the blood ran in Ty's body. The thought of doing anything remotely sexual with Libor now made him sick to his stomach.

The train jerked to a stop at Chambers Street, and he couldn't get off fast enough, squeezing his way in between other passengers in search of the door. When Libor followed him, Ty almost told him to get back on the train. Instead, he bit his tongue and made a beeline for the exit.

"So, uh, what are you doing tonight?" Libor asked as they climbed the steps toward the sidewalk. "Want to grab a drink?"

Shit.

As they cleared the steps, Ty's phone buzzed in his pocket, and when he pulled it out, a text message was waiting for him from Cam. *You busy? Can I come over?*

Warm relief washed over Ty, melting the ice in his veins. He hadn't seen Cam since the confrontation with Izzy weeks ago, and he'd been too preoccupied with his job search to reach out. "Um, sorry." He waved his phone in the air. "I've got plans."

Understanding dawned on Libor's face as he stepped back and nodded. "Some other time, then."

"Yeah, some other time."

Libor did the little head-tilt-grin thing and disappeared back down the subway stairs. Ty let out a sigh as he tapped out a message. *I'm heading home now. Meet me there.*

Fifteen minutes later, Ty stepped off his elevator, turned the corner, and stopped short. His apartment was at the end of the hallway, and piled on the floor off to the side of his door was a heap of limbs that resembled Cam.

What the hell?

The heap of limbs stirred as Ty started down the hall, and after a split second of confusion, the moving mass focused on Ty's approaching form. He was too far away to read Cam's eyes, but if the tension in his shoulders was a sign of anything, Ty would guess that Cam was working on autopilot while his brain played catch-up.

He stopped a few feet away and waited until Cam's eyes lost their slightly wild look.

"How did you get here before I did?" Ty checked his watch. It was a little past seven.

A slight frown creased Cam's forehead. "I'm not sure."

That answer didn't engender much confidence in Ty. Had Cam already been here when he texted?

With several grunts, Cam attempted to haul himself up to standing. Ty caught his elbow as his back slid along the wall and his feet shuffled underneath. The bags under his eyes were so dark, it was like he'd gotten punched in the face, and the normal bright green of his irises was now noticeably dull. He'd also lost some of the weight he'd put on when he first got back to the States: his cheeks were starting to hollow again, and the arm under Ty's hand felt bony.

He was a wreck. Danger was written all over him.

Ty debated sending him away. Life was complicated enough with the job search, and who knew what kind of disaster Cam had brought with him. But then Cam blinked with those tired, weary eyes, and he remembered Izzy's words about how he was the only one Cam let in. Who was he kidding? Yeah, life was complicated, but Cam was already entwined in all of it. Ty couldn't send him away even if he wanted to.

Pulling out his keys, he went for the door just as Cam exhaled heavily, and Ty caught a whiff of alcohol on Cam's breath. The warm feeling he'd gotten after receiving Cam's text turned chill.

With practiced movements, he shrugged out of his coat, hung it up, then held out his hand for Cam's. It took Cam a second too long to pass it over, and Ty nearly snatched it from him.

"Want some coffee?" Ty headed for his kitchen cabinets.

"Got anything stronger?"

Cam stood in the middle of the kitchen, hands braced against the back of a chair so tightly that his knuckles were white. The buttons on his shirt were misaligned, and one tail hung loose from his pants.

He needed a haircut, a shower, and a close shave. He probably needed a good meal and about twenty hours of uninterrupted sleep. The last thing he needed was more alcohol.

"No, I don't." An unfamiliar anger laced his words with a steely hardness. Cam had the audacity to glare at him for that response. Well, that was too fucking bad. "You want coffee or not?"

"Fine. Sure."

Ty bit back a retort and reached for the drawer with the Nespresso capsules. The fragrant aroma of instant coffee beans did nothing to ease the fluster of irritation or the twinge of disappointment he felt about Cam's condition.

"Here." He handed a mug to Cam and went to plop himself down on the couch. Taking a sip of the steaming-hot brew, Ty closed his eyes and tried to channel calm.

They had texted back and forth in the week since Cam's unfortunate blowup at Izzy. Cam had reached out to Ty first to apologize. Then there were a couple of incoherent messages in the middle of the night, followed by more apologies the next day. Ty had been suspicious, but he hadn't had any proof. Now that Cam was in his apartment with his wobbly steps and bloodshot eyes, it wasn't difficult to figure out. Cam was getting worse.

"So, you want to tell me what's going on?"

Cam sat down on the edge of the couch with a thud, a bit of his coffee spilling over the side of his mug. Ty turned away from the sight of Cam licking his hand and then his tongue trailing up the ceramic surface.

"There isn't anything to talk about," Cam mumbled into his mug as he hunched over it.

"Then why are you here?" Ty's annoyance made the words sound harsher than he'd intended.

Cam threw a look over his shoulder. His eyes were vacant, with a touch of desperation, and the way they moved down Ty's body left very little doubt as to Cam's intentions. A rock formed in the pit of Ty's stomach, and his skin crawled with a grimy, dirty feeling.

He never used to be one to turn down a booty call—hell, he was usually the one to initiate them—but here he was, about to do that twice in one day.

Cam's gaze held steady, and Ty scowled back. Their staring contest heated the air around them, as if simply by looking they were exciting the electrons in the room. Then Cam put his mug down on the table and shifted on the couch so he was leaning back next to Ty, close enough that Ty suspected he would make a move. *Don't do it. Please, don't do it.*

Ty squeezed his eyes shut as Cam lifted a hand. The backs of fingers brushed lightly against his cheek, gentle, almost caring, reaching past Ty's defenses and stirring a part of him normally kept hidden under many thick layers of confident aloofness.

The fingers left his cheek and settled on his shoulder, warm and heavy, clashing with the cold that lingered inside. It was nothing more than a hand on a shoulder. Yet through that simple contact, Ty recognized a deep sense of loss so familiar and so intense that he wasn't sure if the feeling came from Cam or from himself. A thought occurred to him: maybe that was why he found it so difficult to say no to Cam—his hurt felt like Ty's own hurt.

Ty's hand floated up of its own volition and covered Cam's, his fingers curling so they were clasped together. Then he turned and pressed a kiss to the point where they were joined.

When he opened his eyes, he found Cam had shifted closer, close enough that the variations of green in his irises were visible. It was so hard to say no, to pull back and not give in to the physical gratification that Cam sought. But then Cam sighed, and the acrid scent of alcohol mixed with smoke registered in Ty's mind, reminding him why he had to say no.

The nightmares, the fear of small spaces, and people—that didn't look like the Cam Ty met in Dadaab. It didn't sound like the person Izzy described, either. Cam was hurt, Ty was sure of it, and he needed professional help that Ty couldn't provide.

"Cam, I know what happened." Against his better judgment, Ty had gone back to his office after Izzy's tell-all and done some research.

According to his bio, Cam had been based in Nigeria early in his career, so that was where Ty had started. After sorting through hundreds of newspaper articles and with liberal use of Google Translate, Ty came across a couple of articles about a series of gay bashings around the time Izzy had mentioned. One of them had been of a local UN volunteer; the man had died, but there was no mention of Cam.

"What do you mean?"

The change was so subtle, Ty would have missed it if he hadn't been holding Cam's hand. A stiffness replaced the lazy, languid way Cam sat on the couch. His eyes took on a sudden sharp focus.

"I know what happened in Nigeria."

Cam pulled his hand back, and Ty found himself rubbing his palm at the loss. Sitting up straight, with both feet planted on the floor, Cam leaned away from Ty, as if he was ready to bolt at the slightest provocation. "What the hell do you know about what happened in Nigeria?"

This was what Ty had been hoping to avoid, but there was little possibility that they could talk about this without it becoming a full-blown confrontation. The drinking, the smoking—it was all so obvious, Ty wondered how he'd missed the picture before this. A sliver of fear wound through him, laced with anger. He had enough on his plate, why did he have to be the one to deal with this?

"Your friend. Who died." He noted the lack of sympathy in his own voice and winced at himself.

"Did Izzy tell you?"

"I found some newspaper articles." Ty tried to shrug it off. Not a lie, but not a whole truth.

Cam shot off the couch and paced around the room, one hand stuck in his hair, the other on his hip. "You've been looking into me? What, like some sort of background check?"

Every step of Cam's pacing rubbed at Ty's ire. His journalist mask wasn't going to be strong enough to carry him through this encounter unscathed.

"It's far from a background check." Ty tried to keep his voice even, but from the way Cam paused mid-pace and pinned him with a stare, he must have picked up on the strain.

"What the fuck is it, then?"

His calm, collected façade cracked as his body reacted to the mix of fear and anger that had ensnared him. "The drinking? The nightmares? Is it possible that it's all stemming from what happened in Nigeria? You've never talked to anyone about it, have you?"

"Fuck you. Don't try to tell me what to do."

"Up to thirty percent of aid workers suffer from mental health issues, Cam. It's okay to ask for help. Especially with something as traumatic as Nigeria." Ty paused, knowing Cam wasn't going to like the next words out of his mouth. "It was personal, wasn't it?"

"What the hell do you know about what happened? About what it's like working out there? The things I've seen? The things I've fucking lived through? You and your polished loafers and pressed chinos in your fancy news studio, talking about the world like you have a fucking clue. I'll let you in on a secret, Ty"—Cam bit out his name like he was disgusted with it—"you don't have a fucking clue."

What remained of Ty's mask shattered. Cam might have been drunk and irrational and trying to provoke a response, but Ty's allotment of patience was exhausted.

"You're right, Cam. Maybe I don't have a fucking clue what it's like out there. But life can be just as shitty right here. Maybe I haven't worked in war zones, but it doesn't mean I haven't experienced my fair share of the crap life dishes out." Ty's voice shook, and his body vibrated with nervous, anguished energy. "In case you've forgotten, I've never known my father. My mother died when I was eight—old enough to understand I was abandoned and alone in the world, too young to do a fucking thing about it. And then the foster system? Constantly rotating through foster homes, getting beat by some foster parent who felt like taking their shit out on me? And starving because they didn't feel like feeding me? The derision from kids at school, from the fucking teachers—do you think that was easy? Do you think that was fun?"

Cam's face had lost what little color it had. Ty's point had been made, but the words wouldn't stop rolling off his tongue, exposing all the fragile truths he normally kept hidden deep inside.

"Everything I have—my polished loafers and pressed chinos—I fucking worked for, every single goddamn penny. And I'm still working my ass off to prove to entitled little shits that I deserve to be here. So, don't fucking tell me I don't have field cred."

His throat closed, making it difficult to breathe. His nails were digging into the palms of his hands, but he couldn't get his fingers to unclench. He had always prided himself on being a strong person, but then there were times like this where everything seemed to be impossibly out of reach. No matter how hard he had worked, or how far he had come, there was always more ladder to climb, higher levels to achieve. Lost in his own trial, it was a moment before he remembered Cam was still there, shrunk into himself, eyes distant and lifeless.

Shit. He hadn't meant to lose it like that.

"I'm sorry," Ty croaked, but Cam was already grabbing his coat from the closet. "Wait, Cam. Don't go." He chased after Cam and put his hand on Cam's shoulder, only to have it thrown off. "I'm sorry. Let's talk this through. I really think you need help."

Cam didn't bother putting his coat on and was already halfway out the door. "I don't need any fucking help. And I sure as hell don't need any help from you," he snarled as he slammed the door shut behind him.

Ty flinched at the bang. He should go after him and stop him before he did something stupid. Instead, Ty collapsed against the wall as the last of his strength drained from his limbs. Cam probably wouldn't listen to him anyway. Ty ran a hand over his face.

Fuck.

CHAPTER TEN

With a cup of coffee in hand, Ty sat down at his kitchen table and opened his laptop. He felt like a student again with his weekends dedicated to homework, except this time homework was trying to find a new job.

In fact, it was worse than Ty's first job-hunting experience straight out of school. The job market was bad for journalists these days. Too many young graduates willing to work absurd hours for no pay. Ty didn't mind the long hours, but he wanted the pay.

Out of the dozens of unread emails, one caught his eye. It was from a grad school friend who he'd reached out to earlier this week. As he clicked on the email, he told himself not to get his hopes up.

After the standard greetings and pretending to care about what the other person had been up to during the past several years came the good stuff: Behind the Veil was hiring. Behind the Veil—Ty had heard of them before. They were a startup investigative journalism outfit that put out a podcast series last year. They'd gotten great reviews and a bit of a fan following if Twitter was to be trusted.

Ty clicked on the link to the job posting. They wanted to transition to video episodes and they needed a bigger research team. Was that something Ty could do? He hadn't done any investigative journalism since grad school, but he remembered enjoying it. Chasing down leads, digging through documents—it was hard, tedious work, but there was always that euphoria after cracking open a case.

This would be a sideways move if anything. And the pay was decent, but not great. Ty read through the job description again, trying to imagine himself in that role. What the hell, he figured. ANN hadn't gotten back to him; he should assume the worst.

Ty shot a thank-you note back to his friend and went to find the *Behind the Veil* podcast on his phone. Right as he picked it up, it rang. Unknown caller. He tapped the Answer button.

"Tyler Ang."

"Ty, it's Izzy. Is Cam with you?"

He frowned at the unexpected question. "No, why would he be?" He'd tried calling a couple of times since their unfortunate blowup a week and a half ago, but Cam hadn't answered. At this rate, he very much doubted he'd hear from the man anytime soon. He told himself he wasn't disappointed about that.

"Shit." She sighed into the phone.

Ty frowned at her tone, alarm bells going off in his head. "What's wrong?"

Her hesitation only made Ty fear the worst. "I can't find Cam. No one's seen him for two days."

Ty's brain kicked into high gear, and he stood to pace around his kitchen. He started compiling a list of places to look, people to call. "You've checked with all his friends?"

The memory of Cam seeking comfort from Ty flashed through his mind. He'd turned him down, so maybe Cam had gone to seek that elsewhere. His gut clenched at the idea of Cam with someone else.

"Of course I have." It was clear she thought that was a stupid question. "Cary hasn't seen him and can't get him on the phone. And I'm calling you. So, no, he isn't with his friends."

"There's no one else?"

A pause. "Really? Have you seen him hanging out with anyone other than me, you, and Cary?"

She had a point. Ty stopped in front of his window and ran his free hand through his hair. "Have you checked his apartment? Maybe he's passed out at home and isn't answering his phone."

"Not yet. I was going to go over there after I called you." Her quiet hitch of breath tugged at Ty's heart.

Ty squeezed his eyes shut. Goddamn it, Cam. He wasn't even here and he was still burrowing deeper into Ty's personal space and taking up room. "Did anything happen over the past couple of days? Anything unusual?"

"Honestly? I don't even know what's unusual anymore." Ty could imagine Izzy waving her hands around in exasperation. "I spoke with him on Wednesday. He got upset when I tried mentioning a therapist again."

"Explain what you mean by upset."

Another pause. Longer this time. "He yelled at me again," she said, her voice flat with annoyance, but Ty could hear the unspoken distress. "And then he went on some rant about his boss wanting him to get help too, and . . . about you."

Great. He paced back to his kitchen table, where his coffee had grown cold.

"He makes it sound like we're all out to get him. Like going to see a therapist is tantamount to getting a lobotomy or something," Izzy continued as Ty stuck his coffee mug into the microwave. "Listen. I know this is a lot to ask, but . . . would you mind coming to his apartment with me? I think I'm going to need backup."

The microwave hummed while Ty turned the request over in his mind. "Izzy, I don't know if that's a good idea. We kind of . . . had a fight."

"So?"

"So, he hasn't returned any of my calls for the past week and a half. I don't think he wants to see me." Ty gripped the edge of the kitchen counter.

"Ty, I'm pretty sure all Cam wants right now is to drink himself into oblivion. He doesn't want to see any of us."

Izzy and all her good points.

The microwave dinged, and Ty stared at the stainless-steel box, his coffee waiting inside. Who was he kidding? There was no way he'd be able to sit in his kitchen and job search knowing Cam was out there somewhere, probably drunk and getting into trouble. Something changed in that moment, as Cam broke through his defenses and invaded his personal space. It felt inevitable, like every interaction they'd had over the past months had led to this moment.

"Okay, fine." Ty resigned himself to an afternoon of traipsing around the city. He left his coffee in the microwave and turned toward his bedroom. "I can meet you at Cam's apartment in forty-five minutes."

"Thank you!" Izzy inhaled loudly, as if she'd been dragged from the water and taken her first full breath of air.

"Don't thank me, yet. We still have to find the bastard."

The building superintendent didn't want to let them in. But Ty turned on his charm, and Izzy did that hair flip thing that girls did, and they somehow convinced the guy to let them into Cam's apartment. Ty wasn't sure what he expected to find when the super unlocked the door: maybe Cam passed out on his bed, finally getting some much-deserved sleep.

What they found made Ty's heart drop into the pit of his stomach. The minute the door opened, they were greeted by the stench of cigarette smoke, alcohol, and the musty, mildewy smell of dirty clothes. Next to him, Izzy gasped as she covered her mouth with her hand.

They ventured into the kitchen first, where dishes were piled high in the sink and take-out containers were scattered across the counter. The window in the living room was wide open, letting in gusts of cold autumn air that did nothing to clear out the stench. The glass jar of ash and cigarette butts lay on its side.

Random pieces of clothing littered the couch, the coffee table, the floor, and in the bedroom the sheets were in a tangled pile, half hanging off the bed. Empty liquor bottles were scattered throughout the apartment as if Cam had dropped them wherever he happened to finish the last sip. From behind her hand, Izzy made little half-gasp and half-sobbing sounds. When Ty put a comforting hand on her arm, she turned to him and leaned her forehead against his shoulder.

"Oh my god, Ty, what happened?" she whispered.

He shook his head, arms around her shoulders. "I don't know. But if this is what his apartment looks like, I can't imagine what state he's in."

"We need to find him."

He couldn't have agreed more.

"You guys are going to clean this shit up, right?" Ty had forgotten about the super, who stood at the bedroom door with his hands on his hips, glaring around the apartment in disgust. Ty didn't blame him. "'Cause we can evict him for shit like this, you know."

With a quick squeeze on Izzy's shoulder, he made sure she was steady on her feet before ushering the super back to the front door and out to the elevators.

"Yeah, we'll clean it up. Don't worry about that." Ty dug into his pocket for his wallet. "Listen, the family is going through a tough time, and we'd appreciate your discretion in this matter." He pulled out a fifty. "We need a couple of minutes here, and then we'll get out of your hair. Thanks so much for your help."

He stuck out his hand for a shake, the fifty tucked neatly inside. The super smiled as he clasped hands with Ty. "Yeah, sure. We all go through tough times. As long as the place is cleaned up, we're all good. You hear me?"

"We'll hire professional cleaners. There won't be a trace of the mess."

With a nod, the super got into the elevator, and Ty made his way back to Cam's apartment.

God, Cam. What the fuck happened? Where the hell are you?

He thought back to the last time he'd seen Cam, wild and lost. Ty went to the window and pushed it shut, cutting off the cold November air. He righted the toppled glass jar but left the ashes spilled over the windowsill. Izzy was still in the bedroom, crouched down and examining something in her hand.

She didn't look up when he came in. "It's Cam's phone." She had it plugged into its charger, and they waited in silence as it booted up again. As soon as it connected to the network, messages started popping up on the lock screen, most of them from Izzy, a few from their mom and Cary. The last were the ones Ty had left earlier that day.

"It doesn't look like he's checked his phone for the past few days." Izzy scrolled through them. "Shit."

"What about his work?" Ty cast about for another phone. "Do you think he would have shown up at the office?"

"I don't know." Izzy stood and left the charging phone on the nightstand. "I tried the UN switchboard yesterday, but the number they put me through rang and rang. I can't imagine him being functional like this, though."

"Yeah, I agree."

"Fuck." Izzy turned and went back to the living room, picking up clothes as she went. "I don't know where else to look. I was really banking on him being here." She dropped the clothes in a pile on the couch and dug her fingers into her red mane. She turned to Ty, eyes blazing. "And how can you be so calm?"

"Who says I'm calm?" Ty frowned, crossing his arms over his chest. He felt far from calm. He felt . . . There was no one word to describe how he felt, but it wasn't entirely unfamiliar. The sense of confusion was distinct, as was the frustration laced with anger. The last time he'd felt like this, he'd only been a child, faced with the incomprehensible concept of losing his mother; being an adult apparently did nothing to diminish the strength of those emotions.

"Well, you look too fucking calm for all of this." Izzy strode out of the living room, and Ty followed her into the kitchen, where she began collecting empty bottles and setting them at the end of the counter. "I'm over here freaking out and cleaning. I never clean! And you're standing there, cool and collected, and—" She braced her hands on the edge of the counter and hung her head forward.

"Hey." Ty went over and put a hand on her arm again. "I know you're worried. I may not show it, but I'm worried too."

"Yeah." She shrugged him off and went to stare at the dishes in the sink.

An idea popped into his head: there was one place he could check. "I've got some contacts in the police department. I can give them a call and see if they've picked him up somewhere."

Izzy spun around, her hair flying over her shoulder. "Like arrested? You think he might have been arrested?"

Ty raised both hands, palms out. "I don't know, but it's a possibility. To be honest"—he dropped his hands—"it might not be the worst thing to happen."

Izzy's frown deepened, and Ty was struck by how similar her mannerisms were to Cam's. She opened her mouth to say something but was interrupted by the ringing of a phone.

"Shit." Izzy dug into her bag and pulled out her phone. "Yeah?" She went back into the living room with the phone pressed to her ear.

"Shit, sorry. I forgot the time." Her tone changed from apologetic to annoyed. "Well, I'm having a bit of a family emergency here, so— Yeah, yeah, fine, I get it. Give me, like, twenty minutes. I'll be there."

She strode into the kitchen, stuffing her phone back into her bag with more force than necessary. "I've got to run to a shoot. Princess no-name model is having a hissy fit about being kept waiting."

"You go. I'll get in touch with my contacts and let you know if I hear anything."

"Yeah? You sure?"

"Yeah, go do your thing. I'll take care of it."

Izzy smiled, a small tilt of the lips. Then, before he could anticipate it, she stepped in close, put both hands on his shoulders, and leaned up to plant a kiss on his cheek. "Thanks, Ty. We owe you one."

He nodded, and she disappeared out the door. He went back into the bedroom and checked on Cam's phone. It was still charging, so he left it on the nightstand.

Instead, Ty pulled out his own phone and scrolled through the contact list until he found the number for his police contact.

"Hello?"

"Hey, it's Tyler Ang. I've got a favor to ask."

There were voices off in the distance, whisperings that edged closer and threatened to invade his dark place. Cam burrowed down further, seeking the depths where nothing could penetrate the heavy cloak of black that enveloped him. But the depths were thinning, the voices grew louder, and Cam found himself floating to the surface.

Cold underneath him, cold pressed against his side. Something bright shone into his eyes, and something hard dug into his back. Groaning, he tried to bring his arm up to cover his eyes while he rolled over. The movement was miscalculated, and suddenly he found himself falling. It lasted for only a second before he hit the solid, unforgiving floor.

He groaned again. His limbs and joints ached, and his head pounded like some alien was trying to escape from his skull. He tried an experimental blink, and his vision filled with flashes of gray, blurry with white light around the edges. He tried it again, and after a second a concrete floor materialized underneath him. Where the hell was he?

With weak limbs, Cam tried to push himself to sitting, only to fall back against the narrow ledge of a bench behind him. He winced as it hit him across his back.

"Good morning, sleeping beauty." The low rumbling voice was familiar, but Cam couldn't even tell what direction it had come from, never mind label it with an identity.

A loud clang reverberated off to his right, and he flinched away from it, covering his ears from the assault.

"You going to get up? Or are you planning on spending another night in here?"

Another night? What the hell? Cam covered his face with his hands, rubbing at his eyes and scratching at the stubble that bordered on a beard. Oh god, he felt like shit. "Fuck off."

"Oh . . ." The low rumbling voice had an equally low and rumbling laugh. "He lives."

Cam squinted against the harsh lights and dared to peek up to the right where he thought the voice was coming from. Though his vision was still fuzzy around the edges, the long, jeans-clad legs of Tyler Ang were unmistakable, as were the narrow hips and broad shoulders covered in a tight gray T-shirt under a tailored wool coat. The hair was its usual coifed perfection, and those lips curled in an amused grin. Amused at him, Cam's half-functioning brain noted, as he sat on the floor of a . . . was this a jail cell?

"Where the hell am I?"

Ty let out a chuckle. "You don't know?"

Cam shot him his best glare. "Would I be asking if I did?"

"You're at the Twenty-fourth Precinct." Ty's statement was decidedly void of amusement. "Do you remember how you ended up here?"

Cam hung his head and tried to pull up his last coherent memories. Some of them came in flashes: a police car, a park bench, stumbling out of a bar. Then further back there was a phone call with Izzy and ordering takeout at his apartment. None of them were complete memories though, more like a sense of déjà vu that he had been there once upon a time.

"I'll take that as a no." A couple of footfalls echoed across the cell. "Come on. Let's get you out of here."

A gentle hand settled under his elbow and, after the initial flinch at the unexpected contact, he recognized the long fingers and warm grip. He let Ty haul him to his feet, and had to lean against the other man during the few moments it took him to find his footing.

"Easy there," Ty whispered. "You all right?"

Cam took a deep breath and inhaled Ty's cologne, that musky scent reminding him of the nights they'd spent together, the feeling of Ty underneath him. Then Ty was holding him at arm's length, forcing Cam to be in the now and stand on his own two feet.

"Hey, you okay?" Ty's eyes showed worry and concern as they peered into Cam's own.

Was he okay? Cam glanced quickly around the jail cell he'd woken up in, and noticed a police officer hovering beyond the iron bars with a set of keys in his hand.

With a voice that was hoarse from god knew what he'd done, Cam said, "I don't know."

Ty's lips twitched. "Well, that's a start."

Cam let himself be led out through the police station. Ty spoke as they walked. "You've been in here since last night. The police found you passed out on a park bench and you were 'incoherent'—was the word they used. Said you threw up in the back seat of their cruiser; they're pretty pissed about that."

Cam grunted. He didn't remember that part.

"Here. Sign this." Ty handed him a clipboard with some papers on it. There was a big *x* at the bottom of the page, and Cam obediently scrawled something that resembled his name across the line.

Ty took the clipboard from his hand and replaced it with Cam's wallet. He hadn't even noticed that it was gone. He patted his pockets for what else he was missing. "My phone?"

"You left it in your apartment." Ty handed it to him. A tap on the home button revealed a bevy of missed calls and unheard voice mails, but the thing was fully charged.

"My keys?"

Ty eyed him with a slight grimace. "Can't help you with that one."

"Ah, shit."

"Yeah." Ty tugged on his arm. "Come on. Let's go."

Out in the brisk November air, Cam pulled his coat tighter around him. The wind made his headache worse, and the cold seeped into his aching limbs. Ty flagged down a cab and held the door open while he slid into the back seat.

It was only when Ty gave his Tribeca address that Cam realized they weren't going back to his apartment. Newly resurrected memories of empty liquor bottles and take-out containers flashed through his mind. Maybe it was better he didn't go home right away.

They rode in silence, Cam staring out the window as streets, cars, and trees passed by. A whole world out there, separated by a mere window and car door. And yet it might as well be another galaxy, it felt so unattainable and impossibly far away. Cam squeezed his eyes shut. He might walk those streets, but he would never *belong* on those streets.

His darkness was uncharacteristically silent. It was still there, occupying that same corner of his mind. But it didn't call to him, didn't beckon. What in the world it was waiting for, Cam didn't know.

He took a deep breath and then let it out. In his mind, he reached out to the darkness, only to snatch his figurative hand back. The darkness was easy, familiar, comfortable. But going there aroused as much fear as it did relief. How much longer could he wallow in the oblivion it offered?

Cam forced himself to open his eyes and look at the harsh world outside his window. He might not like it, but that was where he was.

Once in Ty's apartment, Cam sat down heavily on one of the chairs at the kitchen table. The pounding in his head had worsened, and the erratic starts and stops of the cab ride hadn't helped.

"Coffee?"

"Yes, please," Cam muttered, holding his head in his hands.

"And here. Some Advil."

"Thanks." Popping two pills, Cam put his head back into his hands and waited for the medication to kick in. By the time Ty set a cup of coffee in front of him and he'd taken a couple of sips, his brain had cleared enough to start putting coherent thoughts together. "Was I charged with anything last night?"

Ty chuckled from across the kitchen table. "They let you off with a warning. You can thank me for that, by the way. I had to call in favors."

"Oh." Cam stared into his mug. "Thanks."

He took another sip of the coffee, the warmth of the liquid slowly chasing away the cold that had taken up permanent residence in his body during the past several weeks. "How did you find me?"

"You can thank Izzy for that one."

Cam flicked his eyes up, careful not to move his head too suddenly. "Izzy?"

"Yeah, she called me earlier today and said you were missing. Apparently, she'd been looking for you since yesterday morning."

He sighed. He was never going to hear the end of this.

"We went to your apartment." Cam stiffened at Ty's pause. "It's not pretty."

Yeah, that description fit with what little Cam remembered.

"Then I reached out to my police contacts to see if they'd come across you at all." Ty waved his hands across the table, palms up. "And here we are."

"And Izzy?" Cam almost didn't want to know.

"She had to run to a photo shoot." Ty's lips crept into a grin. "But don't worry. I've already told her you're here."

Cam grimaced. "I wish you hadn't."

"Losers can't be choosers. I think I'm going to enjoy her laying it on you."

Yeah, Cam could imagine. He took another sip of the coffee. Maybe it was the caffeine or the medication, but the pounding in his head was growing a little softer and he could rotate his joints without feeling like he was going to fall apart.

"Do you mind if I use your shower?" Even Cam could smell the stench wafting off his body, and he wondered how Ty managed to bear it.

"Yeah, come on." Ty led him to the bathroom and handed him a set of towels. "I'll dig up some extra clothes for you. Leave what you're wearing on the floor."

"Thanks."

It was a relief to climb in under the warm spray. As the water washed over him and rolled in streams down his skin, the last of the aches and pains eased, and with them something deep inside of him broke.

Tears mixed with water as Cam braced his hands against the cool tiles. But his legs weren't strong enough to keep him upright, and he collapsed against the wall, slid down to the floor, and wrapped his arms around his knees.

With each drop of water that hit his body and each tear that flowed from his eyes, another piece of him broke apart, revealing the raw, uncensored version of himself underneath. It was painful exposing his inner self to the light of day—a pain that transcended the physical, yet manifested in a tangible ball in the middle of Cam's chest.

That part of himself held all the things Cam thought he'd lost out in the field—his innocence; idealism; desire to make an impact, influence the world, be significant—only to find they were all still there, hidden deep inside. But now that they were uncovered, it felt like he was in danger of losing them all over again.

A knock at the door announced Ty's entrance, and although Cam's brain told him he should get up off the floor, his body wouldn't cooperate.

"Cam?" Ty called out in the steam-filled room. "Are you okay?"

"Yeah, I'm . . ." *Sitting on the floor of your shower, crying over my lost innocence.*

Ty opened the shower door, unperturbed by the water suddenly drenching the rest of his bathroom. "Are you all right?" He crouched down to Cam's level, water soaking his T-shirt. "Do you need help?"

Cam shook his head. "No, I . . ." *Needed to let the water wash it all away.* "I need a minute."

"Okay. I put clean clothes on the toilet seat. And a new toothbrush and razor by the sink. Take your time." Ty crouched there for a moment longer before he nodded and let Cam be.

With hands braced against the tile, Cam hauled himself up from the floor inch by inch. His head spun when he reached standing, the air thin with steam. When the room settled again, he quickly soaped himself down, noting a hint of something he associated with Ty in the body wash he'd found in the shower.

The towel was lush against his skin, and the clothes Ty had left him were the most comfortable set of sweats and T-shirt known to man. They smelled freshly laundered, but beneath the detergent, Cam could also detect a little bit of Ty.

His reflection in the mirror made him wince: tired, hungover, like a piece of road kill run over too many times. Rubbing his palm across his scruff, Cam debated keeping it. He'd seen a lot of people sporting beards these days—nothing quite like the behemoth he had in the field, but maybe something short and neatly trimmed. Would Ty like that? He dismissed the errant thought. After a brush of his teeth, he went back outside.

Ty was sitting at the kitchen table, typing away at his laptop with his lips in that adorable little pout. "Feel better?"

Retaking his seat, Cam wasn't sure how to answer the question. Physically, he felt better, cleaner. But mentally, he was fucked up. He settled for a shrug.

"So, you want to tell me what happened?" Ty closed his laptop and set it aside, attention focused solely on Cam.

He owed Ty an explanation. The problem was, he had no idea where to start. How did he explain his darkness without coming across like a complete madman?

"I have this . . . darkness." Yep, he sounded crazy.

"A darkness?"

Cam took a deep breath, held it in his lungs, and then let it out in shaky spurts. His hands found the cup of coffee that still sat on the kitchen table, its contents now cold. He held on to the mug as if it physically grounded him to this world. "Yeah, it's quiet there, comforting. It takes me away from the rest of the world and I don't have to deal with it all."

"What do you have to deal with?"

"All of it. Everyone, everything. Demands. Expectations." Cam stared down into the cold coffee. "The darkness doesn't ask anything of me."

A moment passed in silence before Ty spoke again. "I'm not sure this darkness is such a good thing." His hands were folded, one on top of the other, on the kitchen table, and he spoke with a steady, gentle cadence. "Hiding never sounds like a solution."

Cam winced because it was true, but that didn't make it any easier to hear.

"You know I think you need to see a therapist, right?" Ty went on. "Izzy does too."

Cam nodded. "So does my boss."

"Have things been bad at work?" He didn't sound surprised.

"Yeah." Cam rubbed his hand over his face, and then it went back to the mug. "It's been pretty bad."

"In that case, you'll see someone?"

Cam sighed. It didn't feel like he had much choice anymore. No, he had a choice. But the alternative was unacceptable.

"Um." Cam's heartbeat quickened with his next question. "You said my apartment was a mess, right?"

"Yeah." Ty had the decency to look apologetic when he had no need to. "I did try cleaning up a bit, but . . ."

Cam opened and closed his mouth a couple of times before he managed to get the words out. "Can I stay with you tonight?"

Ty's lips curled into a smile, no oozing charm, simply a curve of the mouth that put Cam's erratic heartbeat at ease.

"And, um . . ." Cam dared to continue.

"Yeah?"

"You wouldn't happen to have any smokes, would you?"

Ty shook his head with a look of defeat, and Cam felt his own lips curl up of their own volition.

"If you're up for it, we can take a walk down to the bodega on the corner."

"Can we get some food while we're at it?"

"Anything you'd like, sleeping beauty."

Cam grimaced. Yeah, he was never going to live that one down.

CHAPTER ELEVEN

"When you woke up in the jail cell, how did that make you feel?"

Cam scowled and gritted his teeth, tracing his finger along the piping of the gray upholstered armchair. It'd taken a few days to get a meeting with human resources and then another week or so before the UN-approved therapist had availability. He'd managed to stay away from alcohol during that time, and some small part of him hoped the UN would leave it at that. But no luck. He'd already promised Izzy, Ty, and Teresa that he would see someone, so he was seeing someone, but that didn't mean he had to like it.

"Like shit."

From her matching armchair across a low coffee table, Dr. Jacqueline Brown smiled politely at his curt response. She probably got a lot of those. "And what does 'shit' feel like, exactly?"

Cam sighed. It was going to be one hell of a long hour if she kept asking him to elaborate when he didn't know what answer she was looking for. He glanced around the room, as if the answer might be written on the pale-gray walls, or the floor-to-ceiling bookshelf, or the fake plant in the corner. For a place purported to help those with mental health issues, the therapist's office looked kind of bleak.

"Like everything hurt: my head, my body. Everything."

"And what about your emotions?" Dr. Brown was calm and casual, as if this were nothing but small talk over a cup of coffee rather than digging through Cam's psyche.

"What *about* my emotions?"

She clicked her pen open and wrote something on her notepad, the tilt of her head sending her braids cascading over her shoulder.

"Mr. Donnelly." She regarded him with her big brown eyes and wide, friendly smile, hands folded neatly over the notepad. "I know it can be hard to talk to someone about these things, especially someone you've only recently met. So, let me lay out some ground rules before we go any further. I can only help you as much as you want to be helped. And if you want help, that means talking about your feelings. I know, I know." She raised her hand to preempt any protests. "Feelings can be difficult to talk about. But that's what we're here for. I want to know what you're feeling—your emotions—and how those feelings are informing your decision making and behavior."

She paused, and Cam waited for her to continue.

"Do you think that's something you can do?"

He certainly didn't *want* to do it. But *could* he do it? Cam thought back to waking up in the jail cell, Ty finding him on the floor of the shower, the way Izzy's eyes had teared up when she made it over to Ty's apartment later that night. His brain couldn't fully comprehend why they cared, but they wanted him to do this. So, perhaps . . . perhaps for them, he could do it.

The words caught in his throat. He reached for the water sitting on the table next to him. The cool liquid helped, but he couldn't stop the thought that the stinging bite of alcohol would have been more effective. He held the cup in his lap, gripping it with both hands, and studied the way the edge of the water tilted up as it made contact with the side of the glass.

"I felt scared." He sounded raw and broken in a way he didn't recognize.

Dr. Brown nodded. "Scared of what?"

"I don't . . . feel like me, anymore." The darkness called out to him with a prickling sensation rippling across his skin. His fingers ached from their grip on the glass.

"How do you feel right now?"

It was daunting to admit out loud what had been slowly driving him insane from the inside. The words resisted him. "I feel . . . the darkness. It's getting closer."

"The darkness? Tell me more about the darkness."

"It's . . ." Cam squeezed his eyes shut. "It's a safe place. No demands, no pressure. I can just be."

"Hm, demands and pressures. Can you elaborate? What do you mean by that?"

"It's . . ." Cam blinked, and when he reopened his eyes, Dr. Brown was scribbling on her notebook. "A lot rides on me being able to do my job well."

She lifted her head, hands folded across her notepad. "Such as?"

"Lives." He hadn't known he was going to say the word, but the moment it slipped out, he felt a physical blow at that raw spot deep inside, past where his darkness lurked. "If I don't do my job, people die." Cam said it like it was a revelation, like puzzle pieces clicking into place. Sucking air into lungs that had momentarily forgotten how to work, he lifted his gaze to find Dr. Brown with that same pleasantly stoic expression on her face.

"Does that apply to both your job here and the job you had in the field?"

"Yeah, yes, of course." His heart beat a rapid thump in his chest.

"And when did you start experiencing this darkness?"

"A while ago."

"Days? Months? Years?"

"Years. Many years."

Dr. Brown scribbled some more before continuing. "Do you remember the first time you experienced the darkness?"

Cam frowned into his glass. It was a part of his life one day, like a freckle that he never noticed developing, and it didn't matter because he had a million freckles, so what was one more? "I don't know."

"How about your earliest memory of the darkness?" she asked. "Close your eyes and think back. Last year? The year before? Keep moving backward until you arrive at the first time you *remember* encountering the darkness."

Silence settled over them as Cam scrolled back through years and years of memories. He'd been in the Congo, and his team had been held up at gunpoint for a couple of days; afterward he'd gone drinking at a local expat bar and woken up in his bunk with no clear recollection of how he'd gotten there.

Then in Chad, the situation on the ground had been rough, and someone returning from an R&R trip had brought back some decent whiskey; they'd finished the entire bottle over the course of an evening.

Uganda was emergency after emergency, and half his staff had caught some weird bug and had to be evacuated—his first R&R trip in almost a year had been spent in a drunken haze, and he'd returned to work more drained than when he'd left.

And then, of course, there was Nigeria.

Cam opened his eyes. He didn't want to remember Nigeria. Already his heart was racing and his lungs were empty of air.

"What is it?" Dr. Brown asked. "Mr. Donnelly?"

He sucked in oxygen with a shaking breath. "Listen, I've seen a lot of shit out there. So if we're talking traumatic experiences, I've got plenty to choose from. When did this whole darkness thing start? I honestly couldn't tell you. Maybe between the third and fourth funeral I went to for kids who died because of malnutrition or inadequate health care? Maybe the first gun fight I got caught in? Who knows."

"Okay, you've seen a lot of shit, as you say." Dr. Brown was infuriatingly calm. "Take me back to the first one, and we'll go from there."

Cam gritted his teeth. "Seriously? You want to go through all of them?"

She cocked her head. "If that's what it takes."

He released his death grip on the glass to run a hand over his face, only to find that the glass trembled dangerously.

"Mr. Donnelly?" She was patient but stern.

He didn't want to talk about the first one. He could talk about every single one after that, but he didn't want to talk about that one.

"I know this is hard, Mr. Donnelly. But if you don't talk about it, it's going to fester. Isn't that how you got to be in the situation you're in now?"

Fuck Dr. Brown and her logic.

With shaking hands, he put the glass back down on the table and leaned forward, bracing his elbows on his knees, fingers rubbing his temples. He wasn't sure his voice would cooperate, even if he wanted to talk.

"I . . ." He cleared his throat. "I was, uh, based in Nigeria." In his mind, he could see the UN office, picture the guard by the entrance. "About eight years ago, I think." Images of all the people he'd worked with floated by, like old pictures in a photo album, until he landed on the one. A young man with a shy smile. He'd been earnest, friendly, and inquisitive. "He was a local volunteer. His name was . . ."

It hovered at the tip of his tongue but fizzled out before the memory could be formed into a sound. He went back to it, digging around for the young man's name, testing random vowels to see if they fit the empty space the name once occupied. No—he had to remember the name, he couldn't have forgotten it. Guilt settled on him, thick and heavy, and he buried his face in his hands.

"Don't worry about the name for now," Dr. Brown said. "It'll come back to you. Tell me what happened to this man."

Pieces of memories, dusty with age, materialized on the pages of the photo album; snippets of places and conversations flitted past as he flipped through. "He was gay. It was dangerous to be gay in Nigeria. We talked about that a lot. He confided in me."

He turned the page. "I was very vocal about being gay back then. I'd gotten some warnings." Cam remembered the looks he got sometimes from random people he didn't know, and that tingle of fear that ran down his spine. He remembered the conversations with his country director, which he'd dismissed as backward and old-fashioned.

"I went looking for him one day." He paused and searched through the pieces of memories. "I don't remember why I was looking for him. There was a group of men crowded together on the street. That's not too unusual, but something felt wrong."

The next pages of the album were blank, black holes where no memories existed. Then a few pages later, the memories came back. "I don't know what happened." Cam pushed himself upright, hands gripping his knees. He was still in Dr. Brown's office, but he didn't see the shelves of books or the gray couch along the wall. He didn't see her sitting opposite him, observing him, with a slight frown creasing her forehead.

The darkness called to him, wanting to pull him away from the memory and leave it where it was buried. It would be easy to give in, to let the darkness wash it all away. But then he'd forever be the disgraced alcoholic aid worker getting picked up by the police because he passed out on a park bench somewhere.

He held it off. "I remember my pants were wet at my knees from where I was kneeling beside him. His fingers were bent out of shape. I was afraid to touch him, in case I injured him more. Not that it made a difference in the end."

He remembered the soul-deep anger and how he wanted to take a baseball bat to the men who'd done this. He might as well have been the one wielding the weapons that had killed the young man who had confided in him. He remembered the conversations about coming out and how every word he'd spoken was essentially a death sentence.

Cam collapsed back into the armchair, heels of his hands over his eyes.

"Aduba Okeke."

"Excuse me?"

"The man's name was Aduba Okeke." How could he ever have forgotten? Aduba, racked with nerves when he approached Cam to talk about his sexuality. His eagerness to volunteer, to help in whatever way he could. His dream of becoming a UN aid worker one day.

Cam gave up the fight and let himself sink into the darkness. His skin crawled and tremors shook his limbs. He needed a glass of whiskey and a cigarette in his hands.

"Mr. Donnelly." Dr. Brown's sounded far-off and muffled. "Mr. Donnelly. Cameron, listen to my voice."

Did he want to listen to her voice? Maybe he wanted to stay here, where it was safe and dark and insulated.

"Cameron, focus on the sound of my voice and follow it back to me."

He turned toward it warily, but took a tiny, tentative step in its direction.

"I'm right here. We're in my office, in Midtown, New York." She was a little closer now, a little clearer. "We're talking through some things, and I know it's difficult, but we're going to get you through this, okay?"

Cam took a breath and the darkness slipped off him to wait in the curtains. He blinked, and when everything finally came back into focus, the office suddenly looked a lot brighter than it had moments ago.

"Cameron, are you with me?" Dr. Brown leaned forward in her chair, notepad discarded.

His hands still shook and his skin still crawled, but he was here. He nodded.

"Good. We're going to get you through this."

Ty was early to the restaurant and asked for the table next to the kitchen door. He took the seat with his back to the front door, then turned sideways to watch for Cam over his shoulder.

It had been more than two weeks since he'd brought Cam home from the police station only to find him huddled on the floor of the shower, rocking back and forth. His eyes had been haunted and filled with so much emotion Ty couldn't understand it all. The image played over and over in his mind, and no matter how many times he pushed it aside, it kept coming back.

And every time it played, he'd get the feeling again, the one he'd had in Cam's apartment that reminded him of times he didn't want to dwell on. The feeling got stronger with each replay of Cam on his shower floor, and with it, random snippets of memories of his mom: the way she tucked him under her arm as she read to him; the smell of burning in the kitchen which meant they'd be ordering pizza for dinner; the look in her eyes as she tried to smile through the pain.

The bell on top of the restaurant's door jingled and pulled Ty from his thoughts. Cam scanned the room, eyes darting from table to table before finally returning to settle on him. He looked so much better than the last time Ty had seen him. He still had bags under his eyes, but they weren't as dark as before; his cheeks didn't look sunken in, but maybe that was because of the short, neatly trimmed beard.

Ty tilted his head as he pondered the new look. The beard wasn't bad; the man bun Cam had had in Kenya was a deal breaker, but Ty could get behind a nice beard.

As Cam made his way to their table, he unzipped his winter coat, revealing a pair of snug-fitting jeans and a graphic tee with a picture of a bulldog and the caption *I bite*.

"Nice T-shirt," Ty said as Cam slid into the empty chair.

"Huh?" Confusion crossed Cam's face, and he looked down at his chest. "Oh, Izzy. She threw out all my old clothes when I moved back. I didn't really have a say in any of the new stuff."

"She's got good taste."

Cam leaned both elbows on the small table between them, hands clasped. "Better than me."

Questions about the last two weeks lined up to roll off Ty's tongue, but he ignored their poking and let the silence stretch between them. In the past, the silence had at times been awkward, full of uncertainty and apprehension, but it seemed different now, and Ty had never quite experienced anything like it before. A comfortable silence, one he was loath to break. How strange.

"Thanks for meeting me." Cam's gaze dropped to his hands.

"No problem." Ty dragged his chair closer to the table, and his knees bumped against Cam's. "Sorry," he said as he felt Cam pull his legs back.

Cam let out a short breath and smiled—it wasn't quite forced, but not quite natural, either. "It's okay."

The waitress approached. "Hi, guys. Welcome to the Anchor. Is this your first time here?" She set down glasses of water as she rattled off the special brunch items. "I'll give you a moment to look at the menu."

As the waitress walked away, the tension eased noticeably from Cam's shoulders.

"How are you doing?" Ty asked.

Cam cocked his head to the side and paused before answering. "I've been worse."

Ty turned in his seat so he could cross his legs at the knees out from under the table. "That's not very encouraging." He rested one elbow on the table.

"Yeah, well . . ." Cam trailed off as his eyes shifted around the restaurant.

A beat passed in silence. "Izzy said you went to see a therapist."

Cam's eyes shot back to him. "You've been talking to Izzy?"

Ty half winced. "More like she sends me messages randomly without any prompting. She's honestly the best source I've ever come across—valuable information and I never even have to ask for it."

Cam shut his eyes with a sigh and shook his head. "Goddamn Izzy. She can never keep her mouth shut."

"She's worried about you."

"I know." Cam glared at him, but there was no anger. "Yeah, I've been seeing someone; got referred to a therapist through the UN."

"They didn't issue any disciplinary action, did they?"

"Well, there's the therapy. That feels disciplinary." The wry little smile on Cam's lips told Ty that was supposed to be a joke. "They're calling it a 'workplace injury,' so I guess I got off easy. HR gets progress reports from the therapist, and I have to go to these status check-ins every month."

"That doesn't sound too bad."

Cam shrugged. "Could have been a lot worse. My coworkers all stare at me like I'm a crazy man."

They locked eyes for a moment before both breaking out into grins. It was surprising to see a bit of Cam's humor, self-deprecating though it was. But it felt a little fragile around the edges, as if Cam wasn't sure how to embrace that side of himself, or if he was allowed to.

The waitress came back with two coffees and took their brunch order: French toast with fruit for Cam, eggs Benedict for Ty. When the waitress left, Cam did that open-and-close thing with his mouth. With fingers tracing the handle of his coffee mug, Ty waited for Cam to form the words he wanted to speak.

"Thank you." His voice was thick when he finally spoke. "For bailing me out at the police station."

Cam's eyes met his, and Ty noticed that they were once again the bright clear color he remembered from their first few meetings. Green eyes that were defensive and vulnerable in turn, a window into a complex soul that had caught Ty's imagination and wouldn't let go.

Behind all of Ty's time-toughened defenses, his personal space was shifting, changing shape to accommodate Cam inside. It felt weird, having someone inside, but it also felt nice—a little too nice.

"You're welcome."

Cam smiled at him, the same one he had for the kids in Kenya, for his family on the flight home. And now . . . for Ty? He swallowed around the weird lump in his throat and broke eye contact before taking a sip of his rich, hot coffee.

"So, how's the therapy going?"

Cam dropped his gaze to his coffee before he also took a sip. "It's fine. It's . . . hard." He leaned away from the table. "It's a lot of talking about feelings. But I got a dog. He's called Busker."

"You got a dog? From therapy?"

That smile again, the one that lit up his eyes. "Yeah, some old mutt from the Humane Society. He's about as messed up as I am. Half-blind and slobbers everywhere."

Ty grimaced at the description. "He sounds horrible."

"Yeah." Cam cocked his head. "He'd drive you insane."

Ty suppressed a shudder at the thought of dog slobber all over his apartment.

"Anyway, Busker was a homework assignment." Cam paused as the waitress returned with their food.

The aroma of freshly fried ham mixed with the acidity of hollandaise wafted up from his plate, and Ty's mouth watered at the beautiful presentation before him. He picked up his cutlery and immediately sliced a neat slit into his poached egg, the yolk running out and soaking through the English muffin underneath.

It took him a moment to notice that Cam was frowning at his plate. "Is it okay?" Ty asked, nodding at the French toast.

Cam's gaze shot up quickly, then back down. "Yeah, everything's fine." He picked up a fork and poked at the artfully piled fruit.

Ty cut off a piece of English muffin, ham, and egg; piled it all on his fork; and placed the entire thing in his mouth. Across from him, Cam cut his French toast into different-sized chunks, selected the smallest one, and nibbled at it.

"So, homework?" Ty asked as he compiled another forkful of food. "Tell me more about that."

Cam gave a half shrug with one shoulder. "Not much to tell, really. I have to keep a journal." He scrunched up his face and directed it at his plate. "And write down what I feel every day."

"Does it help?"

Cam pushed his food around a little more before giving another half shrug. "I don't know. It's exhausting, though." He dropped his fork and reached for his coffee.

"And the dog? How is he homework?" Ty placed his cutlery down, each balanced symmetrically on either side of his plate.

"He's supposed to make me feel better." Cam's lips curled at the corners. The mention of the dog seemed to help lighten his mood. He sat up straighter, as if shaking off invisible weights.

"Looks like he's doing his job."

Cam glanced at him, eyes wide with a hint of surprise. "Yeah, I guess he is." The look on his face was a little dreamy, and Ty felt a sudden pang of jealousy of the dog.

He took a sip of his coffee and picked up his cutlery. Jealous of a dog, how ridiculous. Assembling the various components of his food, he took a bite and chewed with a little more aggression than was necessary for poached eggs.

On Cam's fork was a piece of strawberry, and he pushed it around in the pools of maple syrup. Once it was fully coated, he slipped it off the fork onto the edge of the plate and stabbed a ball of cantaloupe to repeat the process.

Ty watched for a moment. "You don't have to pretend to eat if you're not hungry."

Tension rippled across Cam's shoulders, and the fork clanged where it dropped onto the plate. Cam looked around the restaurant, eyes once again darting from the door to each table and then back to the door.

Ty lowered his fork and followed Cam's gaze. There was nothing out of the ordinary: casual diners and harried waitstaff. "What's wrong?"

"Nothing. Sorry." Cam shifted, scraping his chair across the floor, and then put an elbow on the table to cradle his temple on his fingers. His eyes slid shut, and he let out his breath in a huff.

Ty said nothing. He held his coffee between both hands, elbows braced lightly on the tabletop, and waited. It was a couple of moments before Cam came back to him, and when he opened his eyes, they held that vulnerability that had so drawn Ty to him.

"Sorry, it comes and goes, and I haven't figured out what triggers it yet." Cam sat up straight again and stared at his food as if it had done something to offend him.

"What do you mean?"

"This reaction." Cam waved a hand in the air, then dropped it on the table. "And my appetite. Or rather, my lack of appetite. It's fine one day and I'm eating full meals, and then the next I can't even swallow one bite. Dr. Brown says it's part of my whole . . ." He waved his hand around again.

PTSD? The journalist in Ty wanted specifics, but he stopped himself. "And what does he say you're supposed to do about it?" Ty put his coffee back down but didn't pick up his fork.

"She's a she. She said I should try to eat at least something every day." Cam rubbed his hand over his face. "If I can maintain my weight, she'd rather focus on other things first."

"So, do you want to try to finish your food?" Ty braced his hands on his thighs.

Cam stared at his plate for a moment longer before looking away, a little sad and defeated. "Not really."

Ty grabbed the cloth napkin from off his lap, dabbed his lips, and dropped it on the table next to his plate. "Then let's get out of here." He waved to the waitress and asked for the bill.

When he turned back, Cam was staring at him incredulously. "Seriously? But you're not finished, either."

"That's fine." Ty smiled as Cam eyed him suspiciously. "Really, it's fine. Why don't you go wait for me outside?"

"But the bill—"

"I've got it." Ty waved him off.

"But you didn't get to finish your food."

Ty surprised himself, reaching across the table and grasping Cam's hand. "I ate about ten more bites than you did. I've got it." He nodded toward the door. "Go wait for me outside. You probably need a smoke, anyway, don't you?"

Cam narrowed his eyes at him but didn't argue. Then his gaze dropped to where their hands lay on the table. Right when Ty moved to pull his hand back, Cam flipped his around and held on. It was a simple gesture, but Ty's personal space shifted again and locked into a new formation with Cam firmly on the inside. When Cam peered up at him, the bustle and hum of the restaurant faded to nothing.

"Here you go, sir. You can pay up at the counter." The waitress broke through their moment, and Ty dragged in a breath.

"Thanks." He took the little clipboard and then gave Cam's hand one last squeeze. "Go, I'll be out in a minute." He waited as Cam weaved his way through the tables and exited the door before he went to pay for their uneaten meal.

He was in uncharted territory. Letting Cam inside his personal space was one thing—new and terrifying but something he could deal with—but that look they'd shared was about more than personal space. Cam was moving way beyond that and rubbing up against the walls of his heart.

Cam at his worst had been difficult to turn down. But Cam all sobered up and actively trying to work through his PTSD was damn near irresistible.

Ty didn't step outside immediately after paying. Instead, he paused inside the door where he could see Cam with a cigarette in hand, blowing smoke into the chilly near-winter air.

Ty swallowed against his dry mouth. His personal space was precious, but his heart was off-limits. The problem was, he didn't know how to keep Cam out. Only one thing was certain: he was fucking terrified.

Outside, Cam glanced over his shoulder and spotted him through the glass window. Ty forced himself to grin and pushed open the door.

"You good?" he asked as he joined Cam outside, grin firmly in place.

"Yeah." Cam put his smoke out with the heel of his shoe. "Thanks for brunch."

"No problem."

They fell into step, walking along the sidewalk. "Listen," Ty started, his stomach churning with the ten bites of food he'd eaten. "Something came up at work, and I've got to pop in for a bit."

"Oh?" Cam peered over at him.

How had he missed the hint of auburn in those long lashes after all this time? Ty stopped himself before he swayed closer.

"Yeah, I'm really sorry. But I've got to go." Ty's heart skipped a beat at the confusion on Cam's face.

"Okay. Um, before you go, though." Cam dropped his head, his hands stuffed into his coat pockets. "I know it's a bit early, but I wanted to ask if you were doing anything for Thanksgiving."

"Thanksgiving?" Ty did a quick mental inventory; he was off for Thanksgiving, but he had to work Christmas. That is, if he still had a job.

"Yeah, uh, Izzy and I are going up to our parents and, um, would you like to come?" Cam nibbled at his lip and shifted from foot to foot.

The walls of his heart gave a little as Cam brushed up against them hard. "Um, wow, um, thanks. I, uh, I'll need to check my schedule to see if I'm working." The lie felt like ash on his tongue.

Cam nodded. "Yeah, sure, let me know."

"Yeah, I will. Sorry, I've got to go. I'll be in touch, okay?"

"Yeah." Cam leaned forward an inch, and Ty took an involuntary step backward, half turning to scan for a cab coming down the street.

As one rolled to a stop, Ty called out over his shoulder. "Thanks again."

Cam nodded at him and Ty ignored the way his eyes had narrowed, the beard-covered jaw clenched tight, and tension lined the shoulders. As he slid into the back seat of the cab, Ty forced himself to focus on his hands in his lap rather than peek out the window at Cam as he receded into the distance.

CHAPTER TWELVE

For two full days Ty debated whether he should turn down the Thanksgiving invitation. He was lying in bed, staring up at the ceiling when a text came through on his phone. His first thought was that Cam had texted him, but when he checked the message, it was from a number he hadn't bothered saving.

What's up? Crazy running into you on the train.

Libor. Looking for a booty call.

Ty was less than interested. He threw the phone back onto the nightstand and went back to staring at the ceiling.

Sleep evaded him as he turned over Cam's invitation in his mind. There was no logical reason not to go. His alternative was another holiday spent alone with takeout and Netflix. But going meant nothing, he told himself sternly. It was only Thanksgiving, for fuck's sake.

He was still trying to convince himself of that when exhaustion finally overcame him in the midnight hours. And when he woke up in the morning wrapped around a pillow, nuzzling it as if it had an auburn beard, he tried to tell himself that meant nothing too.

It wasn't until he arrived at his office that he finally gave in and admitted that it wasn't nothing. He could count on one hand the number of times he'd been invited to someone's house for Thanksgiving. Going to Cam's was definitely something, but he didn't know if that was something he wanted.

He sat at his desk, staring at his phone, with the string of messages he'd shared with Cam staring back at him. In that moment, memories of his mom rose unbidden from his subconscious: the two of them laughing as they chased each other around the park; her telling a silly joke as she lay weak and thin on the hospital bed. With his thumbs poised over the keyboard of his phone, Ty felt warm and comfortable, yet scared and out of control all at the same time.

It would be safer not to go. But then one more memory resurfaced: it had been close to the end, and she had squeezed his hand with a surprising amount of force. She'd told him to be strong, don't be afraid, fight and never give up.

For the first time in a long time, Ty wished she was still with him so she could tell him what the fuck to do. Except he already knew what she would have said.

So, he accepted the invitation.

He didn't see Cam again until Thanksgiving. Though, in the intervening week, Izzy had sent him several selfies with Busker, and even a photo of Cam with the dog. It'd looked like an unguarded moment: Cam crouched down and scratching the mutt behind the ears, wearing a look that screamed love. Ty had gone back to stare at that picture more times than he wanted to admit.

By the time Cam and Izzy picked him up on Wednesday night to drive up to Scarsdale, Ty wasn't sure joining their family for Thanksgiving was such a good idea anymore. It felt too much like meeting Cam's parents, which was ridiculous because he had already met them and this wasn't the sort of relationship where meeting the parents was a milestone. Or so he told himself.

To add to that, Scarsdale was in one of the wealthiest zip codes in the country, and Cam had once admitted that he'd gone to a fancy private school. Ty had spent most of his adult life pretending to be part of the upper crust of society, but Cam's family *was* the upper crust of society. Did he really think he'd be able to slip seamlessly into their lives?

Most of the drive was filled with Izzy regaling them with stories from her photo shoots. Ty chimed in a few times with antics from the newsroom. Busker lay on the back seat next to Izzy, snoring.

Cam was mostly silent, eyes trained on the road. His grip on the steering wheel looked a little too tight, but maybe Ty was projecting his own nervousness. As they got closer to the Donnelly house, the mood in the car shifted. Izzy ran out of stories, and Ty didn't feel like telling any more himself. He tapped his fingers against his legs while Cam's knuckles turned white.

When they finally pulled into a tree-lined drive that ended at a large gray-stoned house, the tension in the car was palpable. Cam parked behind a black Mercedes, turned off the engine, climbed out, and left the door hanging open. Busker lifted his sleepy head from his paws, and Izzy sighed in relief.

"Thank god," she muttered. "I don't know if I could've taken much more of that." She let herself out with Busker in tow.

Ty followed more slowly. His nervousness was stupid; he was good with people. He'd met dozens of people who had less reason to like him than Cam's parents. He needed to pull his shit together before he rubbed off too much on Cam and sent him into a tailspin.

He climbed out of the car and walked around to lean against the trunk, arms folded across his chest. Tension lined Cam's shoulders, and his hand trembled as he brought a cigarette up to his lips. And there was that scary warm feeling again, growing stronger with each passing day.

"You okay?" Ty asked when Cam finally turned around, cigarette butt crushed under his heel.

Cam's jaw ticked, and he studied the ground for a minute before meeting Ty's gaze. "I didn't warn you before, but my family's crazy. I mean, you've already met Izzy."

Ty raised an eyebrow. "What do you mean by 'crazy'?"

Cam shifted on his feet. "They're . . . I don't know, enthusiastic?"

"You've used that word to describe them before."

He shot Ty a quick glare. "That's because they are."

A grin tugged at Ty's lips, and his ridiculous self-doubt faded. This was Cam, and he knew Cam. Perhaps not in the same way Izzy and his parents knew him from a lifetime of being a family. But he knew Cam in the middle of the night, raw and exposed. It was both terrifying and comforting how much he was drawn to that Cam.

"Anyway, you've been warned."

Cam stepped close to open the trunk, and without thinking, Ty pulled him in between his spread legs. His hands landed on the small of Cam's back, and Cam's arms floated up to his shoulders.

They leaned into each other, forehead against forehead, as if drawn together like opposite ends of a magnet.

Ty exchanged his nervousness for Cam's tension, and like a double negative, they canceled each other out. Their breathing offset one another too; Cam breathed out as Ty breathed in, sharing the same air until Ty felt a little dizzy. He tightened his hold, and Cam shifted closer.

He didn't know who initiated the kiss. One minute they were breathing, and the next their lips brushed against each other, soft and gentle. Cam tasted like smoke and ash and all the forbidden things Ty never allowed himself to want. But now he'd gotten a taste, and he feared that one taste wouldn't be enough.

"Hey! Save that shit for the bedroom!"

Cam jumped at Izzy's shout across the drive, and Ty itched to tug him back. Instead, he stood and ran a hand through his hair to fix any stray strands while Cam grabbed their bags from the trunk. Once inside, they followed the voices to the living room.

Cam's parents were there talking with Izzy, and so was another person Ty had not expected to see: Cary Davis. That black Mercedes must have belonged to him. All four sets of eyes turned to them as they entered, and Ty slipped behind his professional mask.

"Tyler!" The older redheaded woman, whom Ty remembered as Cam's mom, jumped up from the couch and advanced on him with a bright smile.

"Mrs. Donnelly." Ty bent down to give the petite woman a hug. "It's so nice to see you again."

"Oh please, call me Wendy." She waved her hand in the air. "And it's our pleasure to have you over."

Cam's dad was next. "And I'm Bill, no formalities necessary here."

"Great to see you again too." He shook hands with the tall older gentleman, from whom Cam and Izzy must have gotten their height.

"And this is Cary Davis, a good friend of the family." Wendy gestured to where Davis sat in an armchair with a tumbler in his hand. "He went to the same high school as Cam and Izzy. Inseparable they were, the three of them."

"Oh, we know each other already, Wendy." Davis nodded at him, smirking. "Ang."

"Davis." Ty nodded back.

Izzy looked back and forth between them and rolled her eyes.

"Come, come!" Wendy ushered them forward. "Would you like something to drink? Bill, can you make sure the kids all have something to drink? Is anyone hungry? I can pull something together."

"No, Mom. We ate dinner before we drove up," Izzy said, scratching Busker's head. "But I could use a glass of wine, Dad."

"Cary, Tyler, how do you know each other?" Bill asked as he poured a red for Izzy.

Davis took a sip of his drink, his eyebrow cocked as if in a challenge.

Ty wondered if Davis thought he was treading on his territory. "We run in the same social circles down in New York."

"Oh, really?" Bill looked intrigued.

Izzy threw Davis some side-eye. "Cary throws some spectacular parties. He's kind of famous for them."

"Is that so?" Bill held an empty tumbler in one hand. "I had no idea, Cary. Tyler, what would you like?"

"Whatever you're pouring."

He took the glass Bill offered and hesitated for a split second, examining his seating options. A large sectional dominated the room, surrounded by a smaller love seat and an armchair. Everything was decidedly warm, from the throw pillows to the family photos on the mantel, to the textured rug that covered most of the floor. The place felt lived in, worn around the edges from years of gentle use.

Davis was already in the armchair, and Cam threw himself onto the love seat. Izzy was curled up in the corner of the sectional with Busker, and Wendy and Bill took the long end. That left Ty with the short end of the sectional, closest to Cam.

Wendy dominated the conversation, peppering Ty with questions until he told her everything there was to know about the newsroom. She gushed about having seen him on TV a few times, and then asked about all the famous people he knew.

When she wasn't busy petting Busker, Izzy jumped in on the conversation, shaking her head at her mother's questions and making snarky comments that Wendy waved off with a practiced, dismissive hand. Halfway through the evening, Bill and Davis turned into their own conversation about something Ty couldn't catch, and Cam shifted, stretching his legs out as he slouched into his seat.

"Oh, dear me." Wendy yawned. "I need to take my old self to bed." She stood and leaned over to kiss Izzy on the head. "You kids behave yourselves."

Then she moved to Ty and kissed him on the head too. He blinked in surprise, and Izzy smirked at him. Cam was next, and he bent forward to better accommodate his mother.

"Cam, dear. I assumed you and Tyler could share your old room, so I gave Cary the guest bed, okay?" Wendy placed her last kiss on Davis's head, seemingly oblivious to the uncertain glance Cam cast in Ty's direction.

She headed for the stairs with another yawn, and Bill followed her a moment later.

"Sorry." Cam sat up, hands on his knees. "I forgot to tell her. I can sleep on the couch if you'd like."

"Really? It's not like we haven't shared a bed before." Ty grinned, and his heart did a weird flipping thing when the corner of Cam's mouth tilted up.

"Come on, Cary. Let's go." Izzy stood, giving Busker a gentle nudge to get him off the couch, and tapped Davis on the shoulder.

"Why? I'm comfortable here." Davis made no move to uncross his legs and stand from his armchair.

"Don't be a dick. Come on." Izzy stole his drink from his hand and grabbed him by the elbow.

Davis threw Ty one last challenging look before he rose and trailed Izzy and Busker back to the kitchen.

"You're sure it's okay?" Cam asked. "I know out by the car and everything, but . . ."

Ty raised an eyebrow and chuckled. "Yeah. I'm fine."

Cam made as if to speak, but pressed his lips together in a slight smile at the last second. "Come on, I'll show you where everything is."

He was running again, this time on streets that wound through a concrete jungle. He ducked down this side street, and then up that avenue, but no matter how hard he ran or what direction he took, they kept chasing him. And they were getting closer.

Their shouts grew louder, the thump of their feet against the ground pulsing through Cam's veins, and the clang of metal against metal ringing out behind him. They were gaining, and he couldn't outrun them.

A risky glance over his shoulder showed them to be a lot closer than Cam had thought. Only a few feet away, barely enough time for Cam to raise an arm as he stumbled backward and fell to the ground. Then they were upon him, then moving past him, and not a single hand, not a single stick or metal pipe, brushed his skin as they passed.

Cam scrambled to his feet as they continued down the street, now chasing after a figure running in the distance. *No!* He took off, their positions reversed as he pumped his legs to catch up to the angry mob. Closing the distance, Cam fought with everything he had, because it was the right thing to do, because lives depended on it.

He fought, but they were bigger and stronger. There were more of them, and when they fought back, he knew he was going to lose. They restrained him, wrenching his arms behind his back until his shoulders felt like they would dislocate. Half marching, half dragging, they towed him to where the faceless victim had fallen to the ground.

The mob was on top of the poor soul, and all Cam could see were the feet kicking back and forth to little avail. *No! Leave him alone! He never did anything to you!*

Then he noticed the polished loafers and the hem of neatly pressed chinos. No, no, no. It couldn't be.

No! Get off him! Cam struggled against his captors, his movements sending sharp stabs of pain through his shoulders. One of the mob came over and punched him deep in his gut, and Cam collapsed into himself, gasping for air. Still, he struggled.

Don't touch him, you disgusting bastards! Next came a punch in the face, snapping Cam's head sideways. His vision blurred, and his mouth filled with the coppery tang of blood. *No. Stop.*

With no warning, his arms were released, and he fell to the ground. Unable to move fast enough to catch himself, he collapsed face-first into the concrete, smashing his cheekbone and breaking his nose. His shoulders throbbed in pain, and it felt like a million spears stabbing his arms as blood flowed back into his limbs.

Grimacing, Cam forced himself up onto all fours with shaky arms that he couldn't yet fully control. He drew himself, inch by excruciatingly slow inch, toward the body that lay prone and still on the ground ahead of him. *No. Please. Not Ty. Please let him be okay. Please.*

The loafers were scuffed and the chinos were stained and torn. The baby-blue polo shirt hung loose, ripped halfway up his chest. Underneath, the normally smooth, silky skin was broken and bloody. His arms lay in awkward, unnatural positions, fingers crooked, bone sticking out.

And his face. Oh god, his face. Cam's eyes stung, the wetness on his cheeks joined by a fresh flow of tears.

Patches of thick black hair were missing. A gash split one eyebrow into two. Both eyes were swollen shut. His lips were busted and bleeding, and his nose, once straight, was now crooked.

No, oh god, Ty. Cam kneeled over the lifeless body, longing to pull the man into his arms and never let go, yet afraid to touch him. Grazing a hand gently along the once-smooth skin of Ty's face, a pain blossomed in Cam's chest that hurt far more than any of his physical injuries. No, Ty couldn't be dead, not when he finally found him. The baby-blue fabric darkened with drops of tears falling from Cam's eyes.

No. Cam cried into Ty's still shoulder. *No. No!*

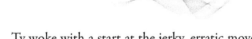

Ty woke with a start at the jerky, erratic movements shaking the bed. Next to him, Cam thrashed in his sleep, caught in the throes of a nightmare. Sitting up, Ty ducked a flying fist, grabbed Cam's arm by the wrist, and held it down.

"Cam!" He shook the sleeping man's shoulder. "Cam! Wake up!" He shook it a little harder.

"Ty!" Cam sat up with a jolt, wide-eyed and chest heaving. He scanned the room in a panic until his eyes landed on him. "Ty, oh god, Ty."

Cam reached for him and traced his hands over Ty's forehead, his nose, and his cheeks.

"Hey, yeah." Ty held on to him as Cam leaned in close and brought their foreheads together. "That's me. I'm here."

"You're okay," Cam whispered, so quietly Ty almost didn't hear him despite their proximity.

"Yeah, I'm okay. I'm totally fine. It was all a dream."

Cam leaned back a few inches, the wildness still visible in the moonlight spilling from the window. His fingers floated over Ty's face again, lingering along his jaw, pressing against his lips. He held up Ty's hands, studying each finger and pressing kisses to the knuckles. Cam's touch was delicate, almost reverent, and the examination turned Ty inside out with a potent desire to smooth Cam's brokenness.

"You're okay," Cam said, a little more clearly this time.

Ty nodded.

"It was a dream." It sounded like Cam was speaking to himself.

He took hold of Cam's hands and brought them to his chest. "Yeah, it was a dream. Was it *that* dream?"

Cam nodded, chin dropping low.

"Was . . . was *I* the victim this time?" Even saying those words gave Ty a chill deep in his bones.

Another nod and the hands held against Ty's chest flattened, pressing against the spot where Ty's heart thumped with increasing speed.

"Hey." Ty put a finger under Cam's chin to bring his head back up. "I'm here. It was a dream. Nothing happened, and I'm fine."

The wildness had faded some, but it still gave Cam's eyes that out-of-control look. As the adrenaline from the dream wore off, Cam began to shake—Ty could feel the tremors through Cam's hands. He laid them back down onto the bed and pulled the covers up tight. With Cam's head cushioned on his shoulder, Ty held him, as if he could squeeze the shaking right out of him. Cam's arms snaked around Ty's midsection and held on.

Slowly, Cam's breathing evened out, but neither of them slept.

"Tell me about the dream," Ty whispered into the night.

Cam didn't respond right away, a slight hitch in his breathing the only sign that he had heard the question. Then he shifted in closer and spoke with a voice that sounded as haunted as his eyes had looked.

"It's the same as always." He spoke quietly, his breath warm on Ty's shoulder. "I'm running and they're chasing me. They get ahead of me, and I try to fight them off. This time they held me back. But I can see who's on the ground."

"Me." Ty's heart did a quick *thump thump*.

"Yeah. Wearing your fucking chinos and loafers."

The corners of Ty's lips curled up, though he told himself it wasn't funny.

"Did I die?" His throat closed around the words, his body not wanting to entertain the idea even as his brain sought clarification.

Cam nodded, his beard-covered cheek rubbing against Ty's T-shirt.

Nothing else needed to be said. Cam dreamt about him; that must mean Cam cared about him.

Cam began tracing some pattern with his finger right in the middle of Ty's chest. The path of that finger blazed like fire, branding Ty in an elemental way. It hurt and made him feel alive all at the same time.

Ty closed his hand over Cam's, their fingers entwined as they held each other in the cocoon of blankets. He cared about Cam too, but that meant his life would be forever changed. He wasn't sure he was ready for that.

CHAPTER THIRTEEN

It wasn't until the next day, under the bright November sun, that the enormity of Cam's childhood house really dawned on Ty. Each of the four bedrooms had their own en suite bathrooms, the first floor had twelve-foot ceilings, and the backyard deck stretched for miles before ending with an in-ground swimming pool. And this was considered modest for the neighborhood.

Each room Ty entered bore obvious signs of the full, vibrant childhoods Cam and Izzy had had there. Pictures of them and their parents at varying ages hung on the walls. Many of them included Davis too. Magazines that bore Izzy's photography lined a bookshelf. The three-car garage held old bicycles and toboggans.

Cam and Izzy—and even Davis—moved about the house with complete ease, as if this was what a home should look like. And why shouldn't they? This was what they knew home to be. Except this didn't look anything like what Ty knew home to be.

The spacious rooms contrasted with the tiny closets Ty had grown up in, fighting others for the privacy of the bathroom. The single picture he had owned was of his mother, young at the time, holding a baby Ty in her arms. His entire life and all he possessed had fit into one suitcase, which he'd hauled around from one house to the next until they all blurred into the same monotonous set of walls and doors.

Busker woofed from behind him, giving Ty warning of approaching bodies.

"Hey."

Ty turned at the greeting. He'd been studying some family photos displayed gallery-style in the den. Cam was standing in the doorway, hands in his pockets, relaxed and calm, no tension in the shoulders, no ticking of the jaw.

Ty's heart skipped a beat simply from being in the same room as him. The air between them vibrated, like there was some sort of invisible tether, drawing them inextricably closer. Ty didn't want to examine it too closely, or put a name to it.

"Hey," Ty answered.

"Dinner's almost ready." Cam nodded toward the kitchen where Davis—of all people—had spent the day helping Wendy with the Thanksgiving meal.

Ty nodded but made no move to join the rest of the family. He'd gone into the kitchen earlier. Davis and Wendy danced around each other in the kitchen as if they'd practiced the routine a million times. In the living room, Izzy and Bill shouted at the football game on TV. Ty was an outsider observing them through picture-perfect windows; he was loath to stain the images with his presence.

"Oh god, what are you looking at?" Cam came farther into the room, scanning the pictures on the wall.

Ty grinned at the way Cam winced at pictures of himself. "You were a cute kid."

Cam grunted. "My mom always goes crazy with the pictures. She still has boxes and boxes of them stashed in storage somewhere."

"That must be nice."

He got a curious glance from Cam. "Yeah, it was nice, I guess." A beat passed in silence, heavy and filled with unsaid words. "Come on. They're waiting."

The dining room was set like a scene out of a television show. Garlands of colored leaves hung around the room, decorative gourds sat in pretty piles on the table. Dishes of varying sizes filled the rest of the space, and the family was already gathered with two chairs empty.

Everything looked and smelled delicious: green bean casserole, mashed potatoes, cranberry sauce, stuffing, and of course, the turkey. It had been ages since Ty had a Thanksgiving dinner; he'd certainly never had one as decked out as this one.

"This meal is amazing, Wendy," Ty said as they passed the dishes around the table. "Thanks for putting it all together."

"Oh, you're welcome. Cary and I pretty much have it down to a science now, we've been doing this for so many years." Wendy smiled and scooped a spoonful of mashed potatoes onto her plate.

"It's mostly Wendy. I only do what she tells me," Davis said from where he was sitting across the table from Ty.

"Nonsense, you're one-half of the team. You were even kind enough to drive up a day early to go grocery shopping with me." Wendy reached over and swatted him lightly on the shoulder. "So, Tyler, I'm curious, where are you from?"

Ty paused in the middle of chewing on a piece of succulent turkey. Wendy wore a wide, open expression. His stomach churned as he swallowed his food—*here we go again*. "I grew up in New Jersey."

"Oh, but where are you *from*? Before America?"

Cam and Izzy spoke over each other.

"Mom—"

"You can't ask things like that."

"What?" She surveyed the table, appearing genuinely oblivious to the insensitivity of her question.

Ty put his fork down and wiped his mouth with a napkin. It was always this question. As if his being here, in this country, having lived and worked and contributed to society, wasn't enough for him to be American. "I'm American. I was born in New Jersey and grew up there. I moved to New York when I started working."

"Oh, and what about your parents?"

"Oh, my god, Mom—"

"Stop—"

"Wendy—" Bill chimed in this time too.

Ty could tell Davis was trying hard not to smirk.

"They both died when I was young." Ty suddenly didn't have an appetite anymore.

"Oh, dear, I'm so sorry." Wendy reached over and placed a hand on top of his, her concern and sympathy earnest. But Ty had a distinct feeling that she still didn't understand her family's objections to her questions. "That must be terrible not knowing where you're from."

Her words were a bucket of ice water dumped over his head. "I'm from the US," he said with more force than was likely appropriate.

"Jesus Christ, Mom," Cam muttered under his breath.

Wendy nodded, but plowed on as if nothing was amiss. "So, then, do you have any Thanksgiving traditions, Tyler?"

Next to him, Ty felt Cam tense even more. Around the table, everyone except Bill had stopped eating. He needed to change the direction of this conversation—the last thing he wanted was to ruin Thanksgiving. If Wendy wanted answers, he would turn on the charm and give her some damn answer, even if it killed him.

"No, Wendy," Ty said, forcing a grin on his face. "I don't really have any traditions. I grew up mostly in the foster care system, so Thanksgiving or any of the holidays were never really happy times for me. Now, I take the opportunity to work, you know, when everyone else wants time off." He picked up his fork again and loaded it with some turkey. "It's worked out for me so far, but I'm glad I'm able to spend Thanksgiving with you this year."

"Cam, how's therapy going?" Izzy jumped in before Wendy could speak again, and suddenly all eyes were on Cam.

The veins stood out in sharp relief on the backs of Cam's hands, and Ty feared that Cam would shatter the glass he was clutching. The glare Cam threw in Izzy's direction would have leveled her had she not been his sister. As it was, she stared back, eyes wide with a message that even Ty could understand.

"It's fine," Cam bit out. Busker woofed from where he sat under the table. The tilt of Cam's lips bordered on painful. "I got a dog, obviously."

"But why did you get this one?" Davis asked with a glass of wine raised halfway to his lips. "He's so mangy."

Cam shifted his glare over to Davis. "Shut up."

Davis cocked an eyebrow as he sipped at his wine.

"Guys." Bill set down his fork with a thud. "Can't we get through one dinner without everything devolving into a soap opera?"

Ty snuck a glance around the table; all the members of the Donnelly family, Davis included, wore slightly guilty expressions. So maybe things didn't always go so smoothly with their big, happy family. And yet, even with the drama that waxed and waned at the dinner table, it felt . . . like a family. For the first time in his life, Ty learned to miss something he never thought he lacked.

"Hey, if you want to stay here for the weekend, we don't have to drive back tonight." Ty zipped up his weekend bag and straightened.

Across the room, Cam threw stuff into his backpack. He paused with a rumpled T-shirt in his hand. "Don't you have to work tomorrow?"

"Yeah." Ty shrugged and slipped his hands into his pockets. "But I can always jump on the train tomorrow morning."

Cam regarded him, eyes probing, and Ty did his best to keep his face neutral. It was getting harder and harder to separate his feelings from his expressions.

"I don't mind." Cam stuffed the T-shirt into his backpack. "There's only so much of their crazy I can stand. Besides, Izzy's driving back with Cary, so it's not like she needs me."

"Don't you miss the crazy?" Because Ty would if it were his to miss.

Cam took a step toward Ty, but it wasn't only a step; it felt like an invitation to something more. "I have enough crazy in my life. I think I need something a little calmer, more stable."

Ty swallowed around the lump that formed in his throat. He wanted to take a step too, but his feet were stuck to the floor. After a moment, the corners of Cam's lips tilted up and his head dropped as he turned back to his backpack.

"Let's drive back tonight," Cam said with a touch of the authority Ty remembered from the days when Cam ran entire refugee camps. The tone held a promise that maybe things would work out, but Ty wasn't sure how much he should believe it.

He grabbed his weekender and slapped his thigh twice. "Come on, Busker. Let's go." The old, half-blind dog staggered to his feet and plodded along beside Ty. Slobbery he might be, but he shared some key qualities with his owner—he had an uncanny way of working himself into Ty's heart.

They had barely pulled out of the driveway, with Busker snoring in the back seat, when Ty's phone buzzed in his pocket. He took it out—it was Dani.

"Hello?" Ty answered. "Hey, Dani."

"Hey, Ty. Happy Thanksgiving." Wherever Dani was, it was noisy in the background.

"Yeah, happy Thanksgiving to you too."

"I'll make this quick. I'm at this Thanksgiving thing, and I was talking with David Beretta." The background noise dimmed as if she'd moved down the hall or into the next room. "And he said that the guy they had tapped for the foreign correspondent position suddenly backed out."

"Seriously?" Ty's heart rate kicked up a notch.

"Yeah, so that leaves you at the top of their short list."

"Wow, okay. What happened to the other guy?"

"Not sure, but David was pretty pissed." Someone shouted her name in the background. "Listen, I've got to go, but wanted to give you a heads-up, okay?"

"Yeah, sure. Thanks for letting me know."

"No problem. Bye."

Ty hung up the phone and stared at the screen for a minute, Dani's news not fully sinking in. The job could be his; it could really be his.

"Who was that?" Cam's profile was open, curious.

"Danielle Myers. My editor." In all the excitement leading up to Thanksgiving and then the stress of meeting Cam's family, Ty had forgotten to mention he was looking for a new job—one that would take him halfway around the world. His stomach sank at the realization.

"Is everything okay?" Cam's hands were on the steering wheel, alternately gripping and releasing.

"Yeah," Ty said, pausing before he continued. "It's about a new job."

Cam flicked his eyes momentarily to Ty and then back to the road. "Oh, yeah?"

"But it's not with CBN. It's with ANN."

Another eye flick in his direction. "Yeah?"

"It's a foreign correspondent position." He took a deep breath. "It's based in Abu Dhabi."

Cam's eye flick lasted longer this time, almost too long before he turned back to the road and corrected his steering to avoid taking them into the next lane. After two beats, he continued. "Is it a contract position?"

Ty opened his mouth to speak and found he didn't like the answer he had to give. "No, it's permanent."

A couple of more beats passed in silence. "Oh."

Then the silence stretched, long and thick, broken only by the snoring dog in the back seat. The longer it hung there, the more difficult it was to break.

"You never told me you were looking for a job." When Cam finally spoke, it was soft with a hint of defeat.

Ty turned and found Cam's jaw ticking, his hands tight on the steering wheel. He suddenly felt like he had lied, that he had somehow tricked Cam into thinking he was someone he was not. "No, I didn't. You've had a lot on your plate."

Cam hands gripped tighter, and the steering wheel shook with the tension, sending the car weaving back and forth on the highway. "What's wrong with the job you have now?" He sounded almost strangled.

"What's *not* wrong with it?" Ty let it out all a little too vehemently. "They've got me locked into working the Chinatown neighborhood, and they won't admit it's because they're racist. They said they liked the work I did in Kenya and with the trade talks, but that's not enough for them to consider me for a foreign correspondent position. They have the audacity to say they need my skills at the local level. Yeah, well, apparently, the only skill they value is the color of my fucking skin."

Ty sucked in air as his heart beat out a rapid rhythm in his chest.

"You're just going to leave?"

Ty pinned Cam with an incredulous look. "I said they refuse to promote me. What choice do I have?"

His jaw ticked, his brow knitted together. "Right. Of course you should leave. Not like there's anything keeping you here, is there?"

Ty snapped his mouth shut. He didn't have anything keeping him here, not technically. Yeah, they had sex a few times, he'd met Cam's parents, and he'd held Cam in his arms last night, but that didn't mean they were anything, did it? Was he supposed to throw away his dreams because Cam had come waltzing into his life with those big puppy-dog eyes?

The car felt too small and suffocating. Ty cracked open the window, hoping the cold air would cut through the thickness of his anger.

"I *am* going to leave. Because *I* know when my time is up, when I've outlived my usefulness and I should move on." He regretted the harshness of his words even as they were coming out of his mouth, and hoped Cam didn't catch his implication that Cam had stayed in the field too long.

Cam's head snapped around so fast Ty thought they would swerve into the eighteen-wheel tractor trailer in the next lane. Cam course corrected in time, but by then the awkwardness between them had exploded into palpable hostility.

"You mean how I didn't leave the field? I had a fucking job to do," Cam bit out, growling through clenched teeth. "People depended on me. I wasn't about to shirk my responsibility because it got hard."

Ty scoffed. "What responsibility do I have to anyone but myself?"

The question festered like an infected wound in the middle of Ty's chest. The rational answer only poured salt onto it, the sting making it difficult to breathe. In the back seat, Busker stirred, whining once or twice before settling back into his slumber, and Ty wished he could escape as easily as the dog.

The rest of the drive was quiet. His answer—he had no responsibility to anyone—ran on repeat in his mind until the words didn't sound like real words anymore. Cam might have found a way into his life and was threatening to tear down the walls of his heart, but Ty's obligation was first and foremost to himself. His responsibility was to build a successful career, defy all the people who said he couldn't, and be the person his mother would have been proud of. He couldn't afford to get sidetracked by a vulnerable, damaged soul.

By the time they pulled up in front of Ty's building, he almost believed it.

"Thanks for inviting me to Thanksgiving." Ty schooled his features, slipping behind his professional mask.

Cam's stare was hard. He wasn't buying the act. "You're welcome. I hope you enjoyed it."

A little bit of Ty's fight melted away. He had enjoyed it, and he would cherish the brief glimpse of family he'd gotten, even if it wasn't in the cards for him.

He unbuckled his seat belt and pushed open his door. With one foot on the pavement, he turned. "Thanks for the drive back."

"You're welcome." Fatigue painted Cam's words and the droop of his shoulders. It was late, and they'd had a long day, but the weariness was from more than needing a good night's rest. An invitation to come up was on the tip of Ty's tongue—fuck responsibilities, the future, and anything that lay beyond the next sunrise.

But before Ty could speak, Cam dropped his eyes. "I guess I'll see you around."

It felt like more salt in his open wound. "Yeah," he managed to squeak out. "See you around."

The car pulled away before he was even halfway to the front door of his building. He stopped, turned, and watched as it disappeared into the New York City traffic.

CHAPTER FOURTEEN

"Tyler, thanks so much for coming in to talk with us."

"It's my pleasure." Ty shook hands with the three people seated across from him in plush, bright-colored armchairs. The one in the middle—the only one wearing slacks and a button-down—was Sanjay Reddy, the guy Ty had been exchanging emails with.

The one on the right was an Asian woman, young, likely straight out of college, wearing ripped jeans and a T-shirt that said *Nevertheless, she persisted*. The one on the left was a black man, late twenties maybe, also in jeans, but with a Brooklyn Nets hoodie on.

This was by far the strangest interview Ty had been to, but ANN had yet to extend an official offer, so he was hedging his bets.

"As you can see, we're a little unconventional here at Behind the Veil," Sanjay said, gesturing to the office space.

"I noticed." Ty grinned, turning on his charm. The woman gave him a half smile, but she didn't look amused. The other man's expression barely twitched. Tough crowd.

"You don't have much investigative journalism experience in your portfolio," Sanjay said.

"You're right." Ty widened his grin. "I don't."

He launched into his prepared answer for why his lack of experience in that area of journalism would not be a hindrance to the team. What followed was a lively discussion about the merits and drawbacks of investigative journalism, its purpose, and its limitations.

By the end of the forty-five minutes, Ty felt like he had attended a college seminar rather than a job interview. His brain swam with ideas, full to overflowing, and he was primed to go for another forty-five minutes. They all stood, Abby, Sanjay, and Rich, each shaking his hand before they walked him out to the lobby.

As he climbed into his cab, Ty reached for his phone. He pulled up Cam's number and was about to hit the Call button, when he stopped himself. They hadn't spoken since Thanksgiving a week ago, and the longer the radio silence lasted, the harder it was to reinitiate the conversation.

The energy thrumming through his veins faded to a dull hum, and he leaned his head back against the seat, staring out at the passing traffic. They were behaving like teenagers, neither one willing to admit what they were feeling. It was stupid, but every time his thumb hovered over the Dial button, he couldn't bring himself to tap it. And with each passing day, the pain in his chest grew a little bit sharper.

Cam was walking down the hall toward his office, coming back from a smoke break, when his desk phone started ringing. Jogging the last few feet, he grabbed the handset off the cradle. "Cameron Donnelly."

"Hey, Cam." Teresa came across the line, loud and clear.

"Hi, Teresa. How's it going?" He sat against the front edge of his desk, extending his legs out in front of him.

"How are you?"

Cam winced. Ever since his meltdown, Teresa had been asking him that question every time they spoke. "I'm fine, Teresa."

"You're sure?"

"Yes, I'm sure. Thank you." She was worse than his mother.

"Good. Have you read the latest coordination report from Doro Camp?"

Cam scanned his desk for the coordination report from South Sudan. Shifting some papers around, he dug up the report he'd read earlier that day. "Yeah, I've got it here. They really need to get their shit together on the ground."

"Yes, they do. We need someone with more experience down there to get things straightened out."

He tossed the report back into the pile of papers. "I agree. They're too close to the situation to be objective about what needs to be done."

Teresa didn't reply right away, and the hesitation sent a wave of prickles over his skin. "Did you have someone in mind?" he asked, though he didn't want the answer.

The phone line picked up the sound of Teresa's sigh before she answered. "A few names came up. Yours was at the top of the list."

He gasped as his darkness rushed at him so fast he wasn't able to hold it off. He hunched over at the waist, free hand braced against the desk. Teresa continued to speak, but Cam couldn't hear her over the sound of blood rushing in his ears. He needed to sit down. He needed a smoke. Fuck that. He needed a drink.

"—wouldn't ask this of you if we thought there was another way."

Cam struggled to remember the coping techniques Dr. Brown had given him, but in the moment, he couldn't piece them together while fighting off the darkness and trying to listen to Teresa.

"Yeah, Teresa, um, I need to call you back," Cam managed to squeeze out, his throat tight as his darkness tried to pull him away. "Yeah, sorry, I'll talk to you later."

He hung up without waiting for a response and shot out of his office back toward the elevator. His hand dug into his pocket where the package of smokes still sat, and he reminded himself not to squeeze it too hard. *Can't smoke the cigarettes if they're all broken.*

The elevator couldn't arrive fast enough, and when it did, Cam gave silent thanks that it was empty. Falling back against the wall, he closed his eyes and breathed. In, two, three. Out, two, three. He imagined a bright spot in his mind, somewhere in the distance, and told himself to walk toward that. One step at a time, heading toward the brightness, even as his darkness clawed at him.

When the elevator finally dinged and the doors slid open, Cam was not any closer to the brightness, but he hadn't let the darkness overtake him either. That was a good sign. Out on the street, the first couple of drags on his cigarette helped to soothe the prickling sensation across his skin, and he needed a couple of more before he felt like the darkness was temporarily satiated. It sat in the background, fully present and in his mind, but keeping a distance so he could sort this out on his own.

With his back against the cold concrete wall, eyes closed against the pedestrian traffic, Cam tried to recall what Teresa had said. Doro

Camp in South Sudan was a mess. The entirety of the newly formed country was a disaster, and the instability made it impossible for the aid community to provide a safe environment for refugees.

From what Cam had read about the conditions on the ground, they had two options: pull out completely and leave millions of people with a veritable death sentence, or send in a more experienced team to help gather more resources together. Those were his choices: leave people to die or go back into the fray.

He fumbled for his phone. Pulling up his contacts, he first scrolled to Ty and then stopped and stared at the name on his screen. Ty had no responsibility toward him, he had made that very clear. Cam was a fool to hope for anything more in the future.

Gritting his teeth, he scrolled past Ty's name and found Dr. Brown. He had an appointment with her later this week, but maybe she could squeeze him in last minute.

"When Teresa told you they were going to send you back out to the field, how did that make you feel?" Dr. Brown asked, pen in hand, notebook balanced on her lap.

Cam fiddled with the piping on the upholstery of the armchair he sat in. He should have known that would be her question, but the answer didn't come any easier. "I think I was afraid?"

"Okay. Why were you afraid?"

Cam had asked himself the same question the night before as he sat curled up on his couch, but none of the answers felt right. He wasn't afraid of the danger, or the people, or the type of work, though demanding it was. "I don't know."

"What about your darkness? Did it make an appearance?" Dr. Brown tilted her head forward, elbows now braced on the arms of the chair, hands steepled in front of her mouth.

"Yeah." Cam nodded. "Right away."

"Tell me about that. What was the darkness reacting to?"

Cam thought back to yesterday and how he had managed to keep the darkness at bay long enough to finish out the day at work. But when he got home, the darkness had come rushing in like a surging wave, drawing him down into its sweet oblivion. He'd drunk last night. The first time in several weeks. The hangover he'd woken up with was another confirmation that he needed help.

He shook his head. "I don't know. But I don't want to go."

She didn't respond for a moment, and Cam didn't know what else to say. He didn't want to go, because . . . The puzzle pieces began clicking into place, like smudged glasses wiped clean so he could see clearly again.

"Is it because I'd be forced back into the closet?"

Dr. Brown raised an eyebrow. "Is it?"

He tested out the idea in his head before speaking. "I don't want to have to watch what I say, where I look, constantly checking over my shoulder for someone who is a little too interested in me, because there's always someone trying to out me." Cam bent forward, elbows braced on his knees. "A lot of the communities we work in are very traditional and conservative. Few are accepting of gay people. There are consequences if I'm outted, not only for myself—I can leave anytime. But for the people around me, especially the local LGBT people who aren't able to leave, it's dangerous."

He paused and Dr. Brown stepped in. "That's a lot of responsibility you carry, keeping everyone around you safe in addition to yourself."

Cam rubbed his hand over his face and spoke into his palm. "I feel like I've barely relearned how to be myself. I'm finally getting my fucking life back together. I can't afford to lose it all again."

And then there was Ty, who had consumed his thoughts as much as the prospect of going back out into the field. He had been there as Cam spun out of control and pulled him back onto solid ground. What right did Cam have to expect him to give up his dreams? Especially if Cam wasn't going to be around either?

"What are you thinking about now?"

Cam glanced up, momentarily lost in his thoughts. "There's a guy." Saying it out loud was like confessing to a crush for the first time. He shifted back in his seat, rubbing his palms against his thighs.

"Someone you're seeing?" Dr. Brown's consistent nonjudgmental expression was what Cam usually liked about her, but sometimes he wished she would react so he'd know if what he was feeling was normal.

"Yeah, but not really." Cam frowned as he searched for the words to describe what he and Ty were supposed to be. "He's probably leaving too." He let out a heavy sigh. "He might get a job in the Middle East."

Dr. Brown nodded. "And how do you feel about him possibly leaving?"

Cam lifted a shoulder and let it drop. "We haven't made any promises to each other." The sadness he felt at those words surprised him.

"How do you feel about that?"

It always came back to his damn feelings. "I'm not thrilled about it."

"Does he factor into how you feel about going back into the field?"

Phrased that way, a new option materialized in Cam's mind. Would he give up the field if Ty gave up the new job? His heart hammered at the possibility. "I don't know."

CHAPTER FIFTEEN

Ty knocked, then stepped back, almost expecting to be hit by the same stench as the last time he'd stood there. But this time, when the door to Cam's apartment swung wide, there was only the faint scent of takeout.

"Hey." Cam was dressed in sweats and a hoodie, hair still damp from the shower he must have taken, and feet bare on the wooden floor. Desire curled so hard and fast in the pit of Ty's stomach that he braced his hand against the doorframe for a moment.

"Good timing. The delivery guy just left." Cam held the door open, and as Ty moved past, he got a whiff of a soapy-clean scent. Forget takeout, Cam seemed more appetizing than food.

He followed Cam into the living room, where the takeout bag was still wrapped up and sitting on the coffee table.

"Thanks for ordering food." Ty draped his coat over a chair before settling down next to Cam. He sat a little closer than was needed for eating dinner, his body drawn to Cam in a way that echoed the hollowness Ty had felt over the past days.

"Yeah, no problem." Cam pulled boxes from the bag, followed by chopsticks in their paper wrappers and fortune cookies.

Ty took the box that was handed to him and opened it. White rice with beef and broccoli. Chinese food, and it was as foreign to him as some of the things he'd eaten in Kenya. When Cam handed him a pair of chopsticks, Ty grinned apologetically and reached for the plastic fork instead.

Cam's eyes shifted to the chopsticks in his hands and back to Ty. "Oh, sorry. Was Chinese food a bad idea? You said to order anything in your text, but I didn't really think . . ."

Ty forced himself to broaden his grin because it was so stupid. "It's fine."

"Are you sure?" Cam frowned at him. "We can order pizza instead or something."

"No, no, it's fine." Ty pushed the food around with his fork. "I don't mind Chinese food. Not my favorite, but every once in a while, it's fine."

Cam broke apart a pair of chopsticks and rubbed the ends together like he'd been doing it all his life. Then he positioned the two wooden sticks between his thumb and forefinger and dug in to his box of chicken of some sort. "You don't like chopsticks, though?"

Ty shrugged as Cam picked up a piece of chicken and popped it into his mouth with no hesitation. "No, not really. I mean, I know how to use them. I prefer forks."

They ate a few bites in silence, Ty with his eyes trained on the contents of his box. All week, he'd tried to convince himself that his life was his own and he didn't owe Cam anything. But the more he'd doubled down on the idea, the emptier he had been. He hadn't felt quite that alone since the days right after his mother's death.

"Listen." He stuck his fork vertically into his rice. "About that drive back from your parents' place." Cam's eyes were on him, but Ty kept focused on the oil glistening on his food. "I'm sorry about how I reacted. I should have told you about the job thing earlier."

"It's okay." Cam stopped eating too and laid his chopsticks flat across the top of his box. "I overreacted too. And you were right. I've been caught up in all my own shit. Sorry."

Ty opened his mouth to object because he had asked to come over so he could apologize, not so he could get an apology. But the words he'd rehearsed stuck in his throat.

Cam lifted an uncertain gaze to him, a line of tension tracing the press of his lips and the tilt of his shoulders. Cam had always been so honest and vulnerable, even when it got ugly, yet Ty couldn't even get a prepared speech out without the couple pieces of beef and broccoli he'd managed to eat turning into rocks in his stomach.

He put his box of food down. "You know I grew up in the foster system." Ty stared at his hands hanging between his knees as he spoke.

"I learned from an early age that I had to fight for myself because no one else was going to fight for me."

The cushion dipped as Cam scooted back on the couch.

"I switched homes fairly often and switched schools a lot too. No one thought I'd make anything of myself. I was always the poor foster kid with no parents, no support system, no stability. They wrote me off. So, I got used to doing everything for myself."

Ty peered over his shoulder at Cam, settled against the cushions. His hair had dried all mussed, and it didn't help that his fingers were currently buried in it as he braced his elbow along the back of the couch. He looked at ease in a way Ty had not seen recently, eyes bright and alert, jaw soft, lips plump.

He scooted back until he mimicked Cam's position, facing him. "That's all a really long way of saying I'm not good at having other people around to do life and stuff with." Ty dropped his gaze, picking nonexistent lint from his pants.

"I get that."

Their eyes met and locked, reading between each other's lines. Ty's fingers itched to pull Cam toward him, to hold him and feel their combined weight sink into the couch. He longed to sync up their inhales and exhales and breathe the same air. His need for Cam was so great that he shifted an inch backward in an attempt to clear his mind.

"So, um." He cleared his throat. "I, uh, got a couple of job offers."

The stiffening of Cam's shoulders was subtle. "Right, Abu Dhabi." Cam's voice sounded tight too.

He nodded. "It's with ANN; it's very prestigious. The position is foreign correspondent, which is what I've wanted to do since journalism school." It was Ty's dream job, which was why he couldn't understand why he wasn't more excited about it.

"You said you got a couple of offers?"

"Yeah." He pushed off the back of the couch and sat up straighter. "The other one is with this investigative journalism outfit called Behind the Veil. You should see these guys." Ty chuckled at the memory. "The shop is staffed by millennials—there are beanbags in their office. But they really know what they're talking about, and I think they're moving in a good direction, not only the journalism side of it, but also the business side."

"So, what's the catch?" The stiffness eased from Cam's shoulders, and he wore a tiny smile. Ty returned it with one of his own.

"No catch." He lifted his hands in a shrug and dropped them back into his lap. "I've never worked in investigative journalism. They cover primarily domestic news. And, honestly, it doesn't pay as well."

Cam was silent for a moment, seeming to ponder the question on both their minds. "Which one are you going to go for?"

Ty took his time answering. "I don't know. The choice should be obvious, but . . ." He tilted his head, and the angle brought him closer to Cam, close enough to see the rings of different shades of green in his eyes. He stared until Cam closed his eyes and didn't open them again. "What's wrong?"

Cam shook his head, then turned so that he sat with his back flat against the couch. "I might be leaving too."

"What?" Ty shot forward, fingers curling into the couch cushions as all thoughts of his job prospects vanished. "When? To where?"

"Maybe in a few weeks? Maybe next month? They haven't decided on a deployment date yet." Cam's eyes were still closed, and his jaw ground together. "It's our mission in South Sudan. The situation is bad there; they need someone with more experience."

"And they want to send you?" Ty moved closer until his knee bumped against Cam's thigh, and he put a hand on Cam's leg.

Cam peeked out from under long auburn lashes. "Yeah."

"But why you? Don't they have other people they can send?"

"I guess not." His mouth twisted. "Besides, I'm the best."

From what he'd witnessed in Kenya, he had no doubt Cam was one of the best. But this was wrong; Ty knew it in the marrow of his bones. "You're only starting to get better. Is it such a good idea to put yourself back in that type of situation?"

Cam nodded, his jaw ticking. "Yeah, it could be dangerous. 'Triggering' is what Dr. Brown called it. But she also thought it might help me face my demons."

"What? Fuck what Dr. Brown thinks. What does your gut tell you?" Ty leaned in a little bit closer and waited while Cam gathered his words.

"My gut is confused."

"Don't go." Ty surprised himself with the vehemence of those words. Cam blinked at him curiously. "I mean . . ."

When Ty didn't finish the sentence, Cam cocked his head, eyes narrowed. "What did you mean?"

"I mean . . ." What kind of hypocrite was he to tell Cam not to go when he had been talking about moving to Abu Dhabi himself? Who was he to ask Cam to stay and wait for him? "I don't think facing your fears is as helpful as finishing out your sessions with Dr. Brown."

Cam held Ty's gaze for a second before dropping them to his hands clasped in his lap. "Yeah, you're probably right."

Despite the truth in his words, they weren't what Ty really felt in his heart. Maybe he was selfish and a hypocrite, but he couldn't help the sense that it was all slipping through his fingers. He had spent a lifetime hashing things out alone, with a single-minded focus on his career. It was about to graduate to the next level, and he suddenly learned what it was like to have someone. The irony made the loss of what they could have been all that more potent.

He leaned sideways on the couch and propped his arm so he could comb his fingers through the freshly dried auburn hair, downy soft. Cam tilted his head, turning into Ty's hand, and his heart lurched at the small movement.

Cam had worn away at the walls of his heart and found a way inside, but it was too late. He was likely moving to Abu Dhabi, and Cam would likely go to South Sudan. And all this was a brief taste of something Ty could never have.

Ty curled his fingers more tightly into Cam's hair, and Cam's lips parted in response, soft, plump things that felt so good between Ty's teeth. If this was all the time they had left, he wanted to make the most of it, to fill up his reservoir to last him a lifetime.

"Cam." He put all his longing into that one syllable and hoped Cam would understand all the unspoken emotions behind it.

When Cam reached for him, fingers trailing along his collar, then fisting his shirt, Ty followed him. The touch of their lips was like a first kiss, and perhaps it was—their first kiss with all their multilayered masks thrown aside, exposing their true selves underneath.

They lay back on the couch cushions, lips unhurried but desperate. Their lumps and bumps and the sharp angles of hips and knees and elbows poked into each other in the most comfortable way. This was a real person and a real connection that was as flawed and fucked up as he was.

Ty delved his tongue into Cam's mouth, tasting the slight spice of the chicken, and further underneath a faint hint of the last cigarette Cam had smoked. It reminded Ty of that first night, on the plains of Kenya, with the two of them in the inky-black darkness.

He hadn't known it then, but sharing a smoke had been the beginning of Cam's slow, steady assault on the barriers around Ty's life. Now Cam was inside the most vulnerable part, and Ty clung to him, unwilling to let him go.

Ty rubbed his cheek against Cam's, loving the contrast between his skin and Cam's beard, the way they scraped against each other to create flames unlike any Ty had ever experienced. He pushed at the soft fabric of Cam's clothes to find bare skin underneath—nakedness along Cam's chest, his waist, his hip. The fact that Cam wore nothing—not even boxers—under his sweats did a number on Ty's insides. If he had known this when Cam answered the door, they might not have made it past the front hallway.

He moaned into Cam's mouth, fed by a need to manifest physically what had happened between them emotionally. He needed to feel Cam inside of his body, pushing into him, becoming one. Ty tried to pull away, but Cam's hands on his ass kept him right where he was. It sent a thrill through Ty, knowing that Cam was as reluctant to part as he was.

"Bedroom," Ty whispered against the column of Cam's neck, nipping and licking as Cam tightened his hold. Finally, Cam released him, but only long enough for them to stand upright, and Ty found himself in Cam's arms again.

It felt like too much sacrifice to be apart for anything more than a few seconds. They had navigated through a maze of wrong turns and false starts to find the real versions of each other, and they couldn't afford to lose even one moment.

Their teeth clashed together and their feet stumbled over each other, but they steadied themselves with hands that grasped and clung to whatever body part they managed to hold on to, until Ty found himself pushed against the bed. He sat down with an oomph.

Ty pulled Cam between his legs and then ran his hands along Cam's sides, pushing his sweatshirt up until Cam tossed it over his head. Ty took in Cam's body, skin marked by the effects of his oscillating weight, a couple of ribs that stood out a little too much for Ty's liking, the trail of auburn hair down his stomach. He ran his fingers over all of it, feeling all of it, leaving nothing untouched.

When his wandering hands were caught by Cam's, Ty glanced up and the expression on Cam's face stopped his heart. Underneath the raw vulnerability was a touch of wonder, and it took Ty a second to understand that it was directed at him—no one had ever looked at him like this before, like he was someone worthwhile, like he had something valuable to give.

He pressed his cheek against the heat of Cam's skin, his arms wrapping around Cam's back to hold him close. Right under his ear, Cam's heartbeat was steady and solid. Funny how he always thought of himself as the one who had his shit together. But, right then, it was Cam's strength that Ty leaned into.

He would have been happy to sit on the bed all evening with Cam standing between his knees, his face pressed against Cam's skin and Cam's fingers twirling in his hair. But Cam's chubby poked against his collarbone and the scent of musk drove him onward. With his tongue, he followed the deep-red trail of hair, planting kisses lower and lower, pushing Cam's sweatpants out of the way. He kissed the base of Cam's cock, feeling the organ fill and rise against his lips, and losing himself in the essence of the man.

Ty stopped thinking then, letting his desire guide him in his quest to commit every inch of Cam to his memory: the taste of Cam's pre-come, salty and sharp; the weight of Cam's length on his tongue; the tightening of Cam's fingers in his hair when he gagged on the head of Cam's dick.

"Fuck, Ty."

He relaxed his throat and let Cam have free rein as spit ran down his chin. He loved Cam like this—in charge but slightly out of control of his desire. He loved surrendering himself to Cam's passion and releasing the death grip he usually had on life. It was a freedom he hadn't known existed before Cam.

"Shit, I'm going to come like this," Cam warned.

Cam tensed under his hands, and Ty slowly eased his mouth off even as Cam's hips tried to bury his cock back inside. A string of spit hung from the head of Cam's dick, connecting to his mouth, and Ty took great pleasure in the shudder that shook Cam's body as he licked up the spittle with one last flick of his tongue.

Cam bent over and shoved his tongue inside Ty's mouth, pushing him back onto the bed. Ty sighed into the attack, welcoming Cam's weight and sinking into the mattress. Cam needed to take; Ty needed to give.

Cam fumbled at his belt, and together they rid Ty of his clothes, kissing interrupted only by necessity. The roughness of Cam's hands on his body awoke nerves that normally lay dormant; he felt alive under Cam's touch. Then those hands were on his ass, squeezing the muscles together and pulling them apart. A single finger slipped down Ty's ass crack and circled his hole.

"I want this," Cam growled at him, the finger rubbing the sensitive skin around his hole. "I want to be in here."

"Yes." Ty more than wanted it; he needed it like he needed air and water and food.

When Cam tried to pull away, Ty kept him there for one more swipe of tongue, one more nip on the lips. Cam wasn't away for long—only long enough to grab a condom and lube—but Ty welcomed him back into his arms like he'd been away for ages.

Ty shifted, spreading his legs wide to give Cam access to his body, but Cam set a hand on his hip and squeezed.

"There's a little something I've been wanting to do first."

Ty's breath hitched at the mischievous glint shining in Cam's eye.

"Turn around," Cam ordered, tapping Ty's thigh and moving out of the way.

He hesitated for a split second, wanting to ask what Cam had in mind. But Ty buried that part of himself that constantly searched for answers, and surrendered to Cam's lead. Flipping himself around, he lay back down, one leg on either side of Cam's knees, pillow hugged to his face.

Cam's hands landed softly on the backs of his thighs, kneading the muscles, then up to his ass cheeks. A stream of hot air blew across his opening, and Ty froze—Cam wouldn't, would he?

The first lick sent sparks shooting through his body.

"Jesus Christ," Ty muttered into the pillow, his hips tilting up to give Cam better access.

The second lick had Ty fighting against a flood of sensations; the third had him trembling and lost. Ty loved rimjobs, but this was no ordinary rimjob. This was Cam, turning him inside out with a flick of tongue, forcing feelings on him that Ty had never wanted to feel: exposed, transparent, wanton.

The scratch of Cam's beard went much deeper than the sensitized skin against which it rubbed; he felt it in his soul, sanding him down until Ty couldn't take any more of the exquisite torture. With weak fingers, he grasped Cam, tugging him up so Ty could feel covered by his body. Cam didn't disappoint, planting kisses along Ty's spine as he moved. By the time Cam's teeth bit lightly into Ty's shoulder, Ty could no longer form the words to ask for what he wanted.

Cam's kisses along his shoulder, up his neck, down his jaw, were a salve to his soul, giving him strength where he had none left.

"Cam," he managed to whisper, and he was rewarded with the delicious sting of Cam's teeth marking his skin.

Cam shifted on top of him, but Ty was too strung up to register much more than the cool smear of lube against his ass and the quiet crinkle of a condom being opened. Then Cam was back and a blunt pressure sought entrance into his body.

He moaned again, his body relaxing to welcome the sweet stretch of Cam's dick sliding into his ass. Once Cam bottomed out, they held themselves still, their heavy breathing syncing as their bodies melted into each other. Cam's hands found Ty's, and their fingers entwined—cheek against cheek, back against chest, legs as entangled as their fingers. Something shifted inside of Ty, not only the adjustment of having a dick in his ass, but the reality that they were different now.

He gasped at the first movement of Cam's hips pulling back, his heart lurching at the realization that their time was limited. The down thrust of Cam's hips slamming home reinforced the thought: the little miracle that had hatched in their mismatched relationship was going to be short-lived. Emotions so strong that Ty had no name for them coursed through his veins, heightening every sensation Cam lit up in him.

He cried into the pillow, glad to bury his face rather than reveal it to Cam. Every run of Cam's cock over his prostate, slam of Cam's hips against his ass, and hot exhale of Cam's breath against his ear fueled the sense of loss growing in Ty's soul.

"Fuck, Ty," Cam muttered, the simple words heavy with desperation that rang true to Ty. They reverberated through him, setting his spine tingling and triggering his orgasm from someplace so deep his body turned itself inside out.

"Fuck," Cam muttered again and, after a few more thrusts, he groaned through his own orgasm.

Ty couldn't move, and not only because his limbs were languid and his brain was fried. He had never been so thoroughly fucked, physically and in that secret part of his heart that he never opened to another person. When Cam pulled out and collapsed to his side, Ty felt the loss like a hole had opened in his chest.

CHAPTER SIXTEEN

Cam sat at the kitchen table, cup of coffee cradled in his hands as Ty zipped up the last of his luggage. He was leaving later that evening, flying out to Abu Dhabi, via Amsterdam. Cam's fingers clenched around the mug. He should have had a second cigarette before coming back up with their takeout, but he'd been reluctant to waste even a single minute he had left with Ty.

"That's about it." Ty stood with his hands on his hips. He surveyed the room before turning back to Cam.

Cam's heart skipped a beat as their eyes connected, and then it skipped again as Ty headed over. It had been doing that a lot lately. Often when Cam least expected it and couldn't brace himself for how much it hurt. It didn't help that they'd been together almost constantly since they made up after their fight on Thanksgiving. If they weren't at work, they were at one of their apartments, ordering takeout and having sex. Cam had brought Christmas dinner leftovers from his parents' house to Ty's office when he had to work the holiday. They had turned down Izzy's and Cary's invitations to New Year's parties and opted to stay home on the couch with Busker in between them.

It felt like they'd been trying to squeeze in as much time together as they could. But now it was already January, and it didn't feel like enough.

Ty pulled a chair over and sat down next to him, close enough that their legs automatically tangled together. "Hey, you okay?"

No, he wasn't. "Yeah." Cam tilted his head toward Ty. "You're the one moving halfway around the world."

Ty dropped his eyes to the table and traced his finger along the edge of the surface. "How did your session with Dr. Brown go yesterday?"

It had been a hard session. A lot of back and forth as Dr. Brown coaxed his feelings out of him. "It was fine."

Ty's gaze bore into him, disconcerting as always but now with the comfort of familiarity. "You're still set on going to South Sudan?"

Cam took a shaky breath. That was the other thing he'd hashed out with Dr. Brown. "Yeah. We settled on the three-month idea."

"That's good. Only three months in the field. And you're doing Skype sessions with her, right?"

Cam nodded.

"And then I'm back in three months too, so we'll be together again." Cam wasn't sure who Ty was trying to reassure.

The way Ty laid it out there, it seemed so simple. Short stints away—him in the dredges of a war zone, Ty in the opulence of wealth—and then back to New York like nothing had happened.

Except the war zone might kill him. And Ty's return would be temporary. And what would they do after that?

Cam knew this was goodbye. They'd both known for weeks now.

Ty leaned in, and Cam let himself be caught for a kiss. There went his heart skipping a beat again, and the sharp stab of pain that came along with it. Cam squeezed his eyes shut as they rested their foreheads together, the words fighting to get out as he forcefully shoved them back inside. No, he refused to ask Ty to stay, despite everything in him itching to grab Ty and never let him go.

Cam pulled away, a little shaken, and reached for the bag of food on the table. They ate their deli sandwiches and pickles in silence. Or rather, Ty ate while Cam picked at the pastrami and dipped and re-dipped the same fry in ketchup.

"You're not okay," Ty said.

"I haven't been okay in a long time, haven't you heard?"

"Cam."

He put down the sandwich he'd been shredding and wiped his hands on a napkin. "No, I'm not okay. But I will be eventually, right? That's what Dr. Brown says, at least."

"That's not what I'm talking about." Ty's forearms were braced on the table, and he leaned toward Cam with that intense, I'm-worried-about-you look. "I mean, you're not okay with this, with me leaving."

"And you're not okay with me going to South Sudan," Cam shot back.

They stared at each other across the corner of the kitchen table. Ty was right, but Cam was also right—there was no way to win an argument when both sides were right. Ty sat back first, and the standoff fizzled with all that they had left unsaid in the past weeks.

"Why don't you want me to go?"

Cam didn't answer right away, unsure what kind of answer Ty was fishing for. "I never said I didn't want you to go."

Ty scoffed. "Don't bullshit me. You don't want me to go, like I don't want you to go to South Sudan."

He tightened his jaw and closed his eyes, the words of his heart battling with those of his mind. His mind won out. He looked straight at Ty. "No."

Ty threw him a glare. "No what?"

"No, I'm not going to say what you want me to say." Cam raised his hands, palms out, as if that would stop the direction of their conversation.

"I want you to say what you're thinking."

"But you already know what I'm thinking, don't you? Because you're the journalist and you can parse my words and read between the lines. You've got me all figured out—you have ever since Kenya, haven't you?"

The words spilled out without Cam knowing what point he was trying to make, fueled by the unease and fear that normally resided in his darkness. He hadn't wanted to make their parting a thing. They both knew how this would end, and they were adults. They could pick up whatever pieces of their lives remained after today and move on.

Ty shook his head and stood, throwing the scraps of their food back into the delivery bag. "I don't know what you're talking about."

Cam glared at him. "Don't you?" He stood and followed Ty into the kitchen. "You want me to say that I've changed my mind and that

I won't go to South Sudan. You want me to tell you not to go to Abu Dhabi, to ask you to stay here, so we can be together. Isn't that what you want?"

Ty stood at the sink, back to Cam, with hands braced against the edge of the counter and head hanging forward. Cam knew he was right because *he* wanted to say those words too. He went on. "But I'm not going to do that. I'm not going to be the guy who asks you to give up your dreams just for some relationship."

Ty pushed away from the counter, turned, and rolled his shoulders, then planted his hands on his hips.

"And you're not going to be that guy, either." Cam's heart did that beat skipping thing as he stood a few feet away from the man he loved. Cam had admitted that to himself one Monday morning as he slipped past Ty in the bathroom while they were getting ready for work. He had put a hand on Ty's waist as he reached for the toothpaste, and in that moment, it'd all clicked. That was also when he promised himself he wouldn't ask Ty to stay.

Ty's eyes were hard as he gazed back at him, his lips pressed together in a firm line. Ty looked like he wanted to argue, but Cam could tell he wouldn't. "Goddamn it, Cam, it's not *just* some relationship for me." Ty's voice sounded raw.

"It's not *just* some relationship for me, either." He forced himself to loosen his jaw. "But that doesn't change things."

Ty took three steps toward him, grabbed the back of his neck, and pressed their lips together in a hard kiss. It was bruising, like Ty was trying to impress his mark onto Cam, and Cam kissed back, eager to leave a mark of his own.

When they broke apart, panting and hearts racing, Cam had to instruct each of his fingers to release their desperate grip on Ty's back. He forced himself to take a step back, and then a second step until Ty was out of arm's reach. He didn't trust himself not to latch on and never let go.

Ty stood with his hands stuffed into his pockets, shoulders hunched over. His eyes were shut, but after a moment he opened them and straightened his posture. "We better get going, then."

The cab ride to JFK airport was silent. They held each other's hands in a death grip while they gazed out their windows, attempting to appear nonchalant. Cam didn't know if the cab driver could feel the stress in the air between them, but Cam could, and it was so thick, he could barely breathe. He helped drag Ty's suitcases to the check-in counter, his heart cracking a little more with each step, knowing that they were inching closer and closer to the end.

By the time they reached the security doors, Cam's prickling was back in full force, his skin sensitive even to the fabric of his sweater. They stood inches apart. Cam didn't want to say goodbye—it felt too final.

"This isn't goodbye," Ty growled at him.

Cam pressed his lips together. Of course Ty would know what he was thinking. "So, I'll see you later?"

Ty nodded. "I'll message you when I get to the other side."

Cam tilted his head for a kiss. This one sweet, gentle. Ty said it wasn't a goodbye, and for the duration of that kiss Cam let himself believe it.

He took a step back, giving Ty room to walk away. With his leather duffel thrown over his shoulder, and a silver hard-cased carry-on, Ty headed toward the security doors. He stopped right before he went through, turned, and waved. Cam's heart skipped a beat, and then Ty disappeared through the doors.

Cam stood there, alone, and counted to thirty-five before he let himself walk away. First stop was outside for a smoke—maybe two. As his nerves settled, the call of his darkness echoed around the edge of his consciousness. Ah, fuck it. Cam put out his second cigarette and started for the train back into the city. It was a special occasion—he would indulge his darkness tonight.

Cam stepped off the plane onto the dry, dusty runway at the Doro refugee camp in South Sudan and was met by the burning heat of the scorching African sun. It hit him like a wall, dense and suffocating, rendering his lungs momentarily useless. Around him, people swarmed, rushing the cargo plane and shouting over the roar of the engine, eager to unload the shipment of much-needed supplies.

He stepped off to the side, getting out of their way, and gave himself a moment to acclimatize. It was always like this when he came off a flight from Europe. He shut his eyes and turned his head toward the sun, letting its rays seep into his pores until the very core of his being glowed with its molten fire.

When he opened his eyes again, his skin buzzed with the frenzy of activity around him; he had always interpreted that as excitement, but this time it felt eerily like the prickling that heralded his darkness.

His darkness—the security blanket he didn't want to use. Even now, it sat in the corner of his mind, waiting.

He hoisted his backpack over his shoulder, the weight of his laptop a reminder that he wasn't facing this alone. Dr. Brown had agreed to Skype sessions, and Ty had demanded them too. And the bottle of whiskey Cam had stuck into his giant duffel bag at the last minute wouldn't hurt either. Three months, he could do this; he repeated the mantra he'd created for himself.

Grabbing his stuff, Cam headed toward the line of trucks that sat off to the side of the runway. As he approached, a familiar blonde came around the cab of a Land Cruiser.

"Hey, boss." The Australian wore a big smile, ponytail bobbing as she jogged the last few steps.

"Patsy." Cam dropped his bags and gave her a hug. "So good to see you. I was skeptical that they would let you come after I requested your transfer."

"Eh, well, Robinson's got things sorted, so Dadaab will survive without me for a few months."

Cam hoisted his bags into the back of the Land Cruiser and mentally slipped into a role that felt both familiar and foreign at the same time. "What's the situation report?"

"Inventory is a mess. They can't keep track of what they have." Patsy slid into the driver's seat as Cam hopped into the opposite side of the cab. "Doesn't help that security is almost nonexistent. Raids on supplies at Dadaab are nothing compared to what they're describing here."

"Great. Sounds like paradise." Cam sighed. His brain churned to build a list of things that needed to be done, slowed by the rust that formed from months of lack of use.

"Oh, come on, boss. This is the life!" In any other setting, Patsy's laugh would have been contagious, but Cam could only manage a smile.

The drive to Admin Block was short, and Patsy showed him around before taking him to his cabin. She left him to settle in after letting him know about the team meeting later that day.

Staff cabins were the same no matter which refugee camp they were in. Some might be larger, some were smaller, but they all held that same barebones, slightly despondent aesthetic. Cam had never noticed it before; now it stood out to him like a sharp stick in his side.

He dropped his stuff in the corner and pulled out his laptop. No internet connection in the cabins meant he'd have to go to the common areas to get onto Skype. The thought of venturing back out into public made him want to pull out the bottle of whiskey.

Instead, he dug around for his cell phone and checked that it was connected to the local cell towers. The beauty of Africa was the leap-frogging of technology—food and shelter might be in short supply in some places, but cell phone reception blanketed the entire continent.

He pulled up Ty's contact and tapped out a message, but his thumb hesitated over the Send button. Ty had dragged a promise out of him to text when he arrived. Yet, sending it now felt like checking in, like they were a thing.

He dropped the phone onto the bed, message unsent. They had texted back and forth during the week between Ty's shipping off to Abu Dhabi and Cam's own departure to Doro. It had been nice to maintain the connection, almost as if nothing had changed. But that was in New York, and now he was in Doro—and things had changed.

The same arguments repeated themselves in his head: it was unhealthy and unfair to use Ty as a crutch; he needed to figure this out on his own. And yet the pull was unmistakable, even in the middle of Africa with Ty miles away on another continent.

Maybe he *should* pull out that whiskey. Fuck it. Cam grabbed the phone, hit the Send button, and dropped the phone on the bed again as if it burned his skin.

The connection was slow but the message went through. Seconds ticked by. Then an incoming message appeared on the screen.

Glad you made it! How was the trip?

Cam let out the breath he'd been holding. He grabbed the phone, now the lifeline he needed to keep his head above the suffocating heat threatening to drown him. Things *were* different now, but not in the way he'd expected.

The career he'd built had been fueled by pure determination and stubbornness. But maybe New York had made him soft, or maybe it was Ty. But determination and stubbornness alone weren't going to get him through the next three months. As he watched the progress bar inching along the screen, Cam clung to his lifeline as fiercely as he dared. Three months. He could do this.

CHAPTER SEVENTEEN

Cam ran between two rows of tents, his feet hitting the hardened dirt, the dew-drenched morning air in his lungs. His thighs burned from the pace he kept, but he didn't let up, savoring the acidity building in his muscles. He ran, his mind focused on the rhythm of his breathing, the thump of his footfalls, and the pulsing of his heart as it kept time.

This felt normal, this running through camp in the early hours of the morning. The camp's residents stared at him, not yet accustomed to seeing the crazy white man running past their tents without an emergency or a destination. Children whispered to their moms and giggled behind their hands; he'd have to find candy somewhere in Admin Block before he came out again.

He slowed to a walk as he approached the dirt road separating the wider camp from Admin Block and strolled across to the gate guarded by a UN peacekeeper. He raised his hand in greeting and made to turn toward his cabin when the peacekeeper yelled and flagged him down.

"Sir, were you outside Admin Block?" the peacekeeper asked, and Cam glanced pointedly back in the direction he'd come from.

"Uh, yeah. You saw me cross the road, right?" He pointed to where he'd emerged from the closest row of tents.

"Sir, it is not permissible to be outside of Admin Block without a peacekeeping escort." The peacekeeper frowned in disapproval.

Cam scowled. "Is that the standard operating procedure here? I was only going for a run."

"I understand, sir. But it is standard operating procedure. No one must leave Admin Block without a peacekeeping escort." The guy wasn't kidding.

"Since when? Is security really that bad?"

"Yes, sir." The peacekeeper nodded, face solemn. "It is very bad. Militia groups are active in this region, and the fighting is intensifying. It is not safe to be without armed escort. It is for your safety, sir."

Well, fuck. Cam gave the guy a terse nod and turned away, feeling like a suffocating blanket had been dropped on his head. So much for the stress-relieving run. His skin prickled at the thought of not being able to escape, to hand out candy to kids and engage in one small piece of normalcy. His darkness called, and Cam fought the urge to give in to its enticing invitation.

He had a shit-ton of meetings to coordinate, community leaders to empower, and missing inventory to investigate. As alluring as his darkness was right then, he couldn't afford to indulge. He gritted his teeth and reached into his pack for a smoke. Nicotine would have to do for now, but as it flowed through his veins, it barely took the edge off the biting hunger for his darkness.

He leaned heavily against the wall next to the door of his cabin, eyes squeezed shut, jaw clenched. He could do this. He had to do this. Just one day. Patsy could help if he needed some time to himself. He could skip dinner and skim off a little more of that bottle. And then he could crawl into the uncomfortable cot and give in to his darkness.

Cam forced himself to walk at a reasonable pace into the main administrative building, backpack slung over his shoulder, hoping to find the common work room empty and the internet connection strong—neither were guaranteed. He was already fifteen minutes late for their Skype date, and Ty didn't have much time before he had to go on air.

The common office shared by temporary staff was thankfully deserted and Cam pulled his laptop out at the desk set farthest from the door. The ethernet cable slid into its socket with a click.

"Come on, come on," he muttered as the laptop chugged away, attempting to connect. Seconds ticked by as the dots blinked to the left and then to the right. He tapped his fingers against the table and bounced his knee as he waited for the line to be established. When his Skype contact list finally loaded, he clicked on Ty's photo, the polished one that ANN had taken a couple of weeks ago. Pale blue rings emanated from Ty's photo, smiling at him, as Skype dialed across the internet.

"Come on, pick up, pick up."

The screen froze suddenly, then a burst of static came through his headphones, and then Ty was there with his perfectly made hair, dressed in a sharp suit, lips curled up in a grin.

"Hey." The low rumble filled Cam's ears and made its way deeper, where it curled around his heart.

He wanted to smile back. Hearing Ty's voice was probably the single best thing from this entire day, but it didn't make Cam feel better, it made him feel worse.

"How's it going?" Ty asked, his face filling Cam's screen, but something looked different.

Cam cocked his head to the side and leaned in for a closer examination. "Are you wearing makeup?"

Ty's forehead furrowed. "Shut up." The sound filtering through Cam's headphones didn't match up with the image of Ty's mouth moving. "I'm going on air in about fifteen minutes. I should be on set already."

"Shit. I'm sorry." Cam scratched his beard, itchier now that he was letting it grow out. "Camps don't really run on predictable schedules. I got back here as fast as I could."

"It's okay." Ty grinned, and Cam's heart skipped a beat. Crazy how it was still doing that. "Tell me how your day's going."

Cam stopped himself from swearing and bit back a sigh. He glanced at the closed door and lowered his volume. "It's like every other shitty day." He leaned an elbow on the desk and stuck his fingers into his hair to prop up his head. "We're trying to figure out what the fuck's going on with the supplies inventory. Shit goes missing, and it's not obvious where the leak is. We've already got twenty-four-hour guards at the warehouse, but either the guards are in on it or stuff is getting stolen elsewhere."

A frown lowered Ty's brows as Cam spoke. "Have you done background checks on the guards?"

Cam shook his head. "We don't have resources for that. Not that it would help. The military police have been tasked with general camp security, but the local population is so interconnected here that everyone's related to everyone somehow. I'd bet a million bucks that every single one of those guards is connected to some sort of armed militia group."

"Don't do that. You don't have a million dollars."

Cam's lips curled of their own accord, despite his sour mood. Voices drifted into the room, and Cam eyed the door. They grew louder then softer as people passed by. He let out the breath he'd been holding. "Anyway, how are you?"

"Good. This place is ridiculous. I swear there's some chocolate maker in the city who's raking in the cash. The past four parties I've been to all had fucking huge chocolate fountains." Ty shook his head.

Chocolate fountains. At four different parties. Meanwhile he was dealing with militia raids on humanitarian supplies. Ty felt farther away from him at that moment than ever before—separated not only by land and sea, but by experiences so vastly different that Cam couldn't hope to relate. His darkness inched closer.

"How's your, uh . . ." Worry marred Ty's brow. "How are you hanging in there?"

Cam didn't want to talk about that. It was easier to keep his head down and ignore it until his three months was up. "Um . . . it's, uh . . ."

"Have you spoken to Dr. Brown?"

"Yeah, I have." Cam shifted in his chair and readjusted the angle of his screen.

"And?"

"And I'm fine. I'm dealing with it," he bit out.

"Cam?" There was no way Ty believed him.

He squeezed his eyes shut for a moment, seeking out his darkness, yearning for its quiet comfort. "Really, Ty. I'm fine. It could be a lot worse."

Ty's frown deepened.

"Ty, you're almost on," came a voice in the background.

Ty glanced over his shoulder. "Shit. I'm sorry. I've got to go." He adjusted his tie in the camera. "Skype tomorrow?"

Cam shook his head in short, abrupt movements. "Going to be out all day tomorrow. Maybe the day after. I'll let you know."

"Okay." Ty opened his mouth, and the screen froze for several seconds before his next words came through. "Take care."

"You too." The connection went dead almost before Cam could finish speaking.

He closed the laptop with a little more force than was necessary and ripped the headphones from his ears. The darkness descended as the dichotomy tore at him. Chocolate fountains; fucking chocolate fountains.

His hands shook as he packed up his laptop and stood on unsteady feet. He needed a smoke, a whiskey, and a bed—in that order. He didn't remember walking back to his cabin; he put one foot in front of the other and held on tight to his backpack until he reached the relative safety of privacy.

The first drag of the cigarette brought the darkness wrapping more tightly around him, drawing him deeper. His lungs filled with nicotine until the cigarette burned to the butt, and then he went inside for the alcohol. Swigging straight from the bottle, he stumbled onto the floor beside the bed. The alcohol was warm as it trailed down his esophagus, and he hugged the bottle to his chest, sinking into his darkness. *Fucking chocolate fountains* was the last thought he had before he let unconsciousness take him, right there on the floor next to the bed.

Cam stared at his contact list, waiting for the little green bubble to light up next to Ty's photo. They had been missing their Skype dates all week. Either Cam couldn't make it back from some meeting, or Ty was caught up in work or a party. If Cam was honest, he wasn't really expecting Ty to make it to this one either—Ty apparently had a lot of parties to go to.

The door to the common office space opened, and Cam jumped in his seat, heart rate shooting through the roof, hands gripping the sides of his laptop in case he needed to use it as a weapon. A blonde head popped through, and Patsy smiled when she spotted him.

He forced himself to breathe and stretch his fingers, trying to relieve the pressure in his joints.

"Hey, boss." Patsy shut the door with her foot and came over with two beers in hand. "Sorry, did I startle you?"

"It's okay." His heart raced as he tilted the screen of his laptop down and took the bottle Patsy held out to him.

"Is that Tyler?" She nodded at the laptop as she plopped into a nearby chair. Patsy had wrangled the relationship status out of Cam early on when he kept disappearing for Skype dates, and then wouldn't let it go after she found out the mysterious boyfriend was the hot journalist they'd both met all those months ago.

"Supposed to be." Cam shrugged and took a swig of the watered-down brew. "He's running late."

Patsy nodded. "Must be hard, eh? Being back out here when you've got someone waiting at home for you."

"He's not at home."

She shook her head and waved it off. "Same thing. You know what I mean."

Cam readjusted his screen and ran the cursor around to keep the screensaver from kicking in. "Yeah, I do."

Patsy shredded the label off her beer bottle, and as Cam watched, a thought suddenly occurred to him. "How much longer do you want to be out here for? Especially, after . . . you know."

At Patsy's surprised expression, it dawned on Cam that he didn't usually ask these types of questions of his staff. A fresh wave of guilt hit him at the thought of having been so wrapped up in his own shit that he hadn't noticed his staff struggling through some of the same things he'd experienced.

"After all the shit we've seen?" Patsy asked as they stared at each other, her words weightier after the tragedies they had both witnessed over the years, over the past few days. "I don't know." She shrugged and went back to shredding the label. "I guess until I can't do it anymore. Isn't that what everyone does?"

"Yeah, but I wouldn't recommend it."

She ran her thumb back and forth across the glass bottle, understanding written across her face. "Don't know what else I would do instead," she said with a dry chuckle.

She had a point. Not a huge market for transferable skills that included negotiating their way out of checkpoints, rationing people to within an inch of their lives, and praying that the donor gods pulled through before everyone starved. "Come work for me." The idea made so much sense, Cam was surprised he hadn't thought about it before.

"In New York?" Patsy laughed out loud, but Cam didn't get what was so funny. She sighed with wistfulness. "Sure, boss. I'll let you know when I'm ready to throw in the towel."

Cam's laptop beeped with an incoming call.

"I'll leave you to lover boy." Patsy smiled as she stood and let herself out.

Cam waited until the door clicked shut before he accepted the call.

"Hello?" His screen showed only Ty's profile picture, the polished headshot from ANN.

"Hey," came Ty, crackling over the line. "Sorry, I'm at this party, so I can't do video." He let out a long exhale, and Cam wasn't sure if the tiredness he heard was fatigue or the quality of the call exaggerating the sound. "These fucking parties."

"More chocolate fountains?"

"I wish. Strippers this time."

Cam sat back, putting distance between himself and his laptop as if Ty sat inside it. "Oh."

"Yeah." Another rush of air blew over mouthpiece.

"Sounds like a hard life."

Ty barked out a chuckle. "Trust me. I'd rather be over there with you."

"No. You don't want to be here. No one wants to be here." He eyed the door as if someone might burst in at his comment.

"Tell me."

Cam sighed. He didn't want to tell Ty. He wanted to forget all of it and go back to those days when it was the two of them in New York, living life together. Cam's darkness swirled around him, and he drew it closer, taking another swig of his beer as he sought out that safe place.

"It's getting dangerous here."

"Dangerous how?"

There was no good way to explain the way the air rippled with nervous anticipation, how every new face looked suspicious, how bracing himself for bad news was a regular part of his day. How did he tell Ty that his darkness wasn't in the background anymore, it was around him almost constantly, and he welcomed it because it was safer than the crazy shit happening out there?

Cam squeezed his eyes shut. "They found two guards shot dead the other day. Single bullet holes to their foreheads. One still had his eyes open when they found him, apparently. This was right outside Admin Block."

"Shit."

Yeah, shit was right. He sank deeper into his darkness. "They're getting more brazen. Things are escalating."

"The militia groups?"

"Yeah." Cam rested his face in both hands, elbows braced on the desk.

"Shit."

The line was silent, but Cam could practically hear Ty thinking, his mind running through options and alternatives. But what was the point? Things were fucked up, and it was beyond Cam's ability to un-fuck them.

"What are the security protocols there? I mean, at what point do you evacuate due to security concerns?"

"Ha." Cam scoffed. "The security protocol is *Don't die.*" Even from across the miles, Cam was sure Ty was glaring at him.

"Have you talked to Dr. Brown about any of this?"

Fuck. He hadn't spoken to her in several weeks. She'd been on vacation, and then he'd been putting it off. He took another swig of his beer and set the bottle down harder than he needed to.

"You've still been doing your Skype sessions, right?" Ty's question landed like the accusation it was. "Cam? Hello? You still there?"

"Yeah, yeah. I'm still here. Scheduling sessions with her has been . . . difficult, with the time difference and everything. Look. I'm fine. I'll be okay." He slouched down into his chair and crossed his arms around his stomach.

"You don't sound okay." A beat passed before Ty spoke again, quietly. "I'm worried."

Cam's heart skipped a beat. "Don't be," he said, equally quietly. "I'll be fine."

Ty huffed into the phone. "The more you say that, the less I believe you."

"Well, what do you want me to say?" Cam shifted forward, leaning toward his laptop. "That people are getting murdered? That there are entire villages of people showing up every day because they've had their homes burned to the ground? That most of those people are children because their parents have been slaughtered? That the staff aren't allowed to leave Admin Block without armed escort—"

Static burst into his headphones, nearly deafening him, and Cam yanked his earbuds out. Skype showed that he was offline now—the connection must have been lost. "Fuck!"

He picked up his laptop and shot to his feet with it gripped tightly in his fingers. But instead of smashing it across the concrete floor like he wanted, he forced himself to put it gently on the desk and slowly unfurl his fingers. His hands shook, his heart raced, his skin prickled. His darkness was taking over, and he needed to get out of here.

He downed the last of his beer and then slammed his laptop shut. Keeping his head down, he made a beeline for his cabin, his darkness drawing him away from consciousness with every step he took. The door was barely shut behind him before he slid down the wall into a heap on the floor, shivers running through him despite the heat of the early evening.

He dragged himself to where he hid his whiskey in the closet and took a couple of shaky sips, some precious liquid spilling out the sides of his mouth. Ty wanted to talk security protocols. Well, this was Cam's security protocol: succumb to his darkness because that was the only way out of the hellhole he had willingly crawled back into.

The darkness pulled hard, and he welcomed it. He drew his knees up as he leaned back against the wall, and fell into the peace that came with unconsciousness.

"Hello? Hello! Cam?" Ty took the phone away from his ear. The screen showed the line had been disconnected and Cam wasn't online anymore. He tried dialing him anyway, but the call wouldn't even ring. "Fuck!"

He paced the narrow hallway outside the stupid party he'd gotten dragged to, hands planted on his hips. Cam's last words rang in his head: people getting murdered, militia groups on the move, armed escorts for the staff.

"Hey, Tyler." The door at the end of the hallway opened, and Ty's new coworker, Neal, popped his head out. "What are you doing out here? Come on, the strippers are giving lap dances!"

Ty put all his anger and frustration into his fake grin. "Not my kind of strippers."

Neal frowned and cocked his head, stumbling against the door and pushing it open. Blasting music from the party rushed into the small space. "What do you mean?"

"Never mind." Ty shook his head and waved him off. "I'll be back in a second. Need to make a phone call." He held up his phone.

"Workaholic!" Neal accused him as he tried to pull the door shut. "Need to play more!"

Ty glowered after him. Playing more was the last thing he needed or wanted to do. He checked his phone again, and Cam was still offline. He tapped out a quick message, hoping Cam would get it before the end of the night, and then steeled himself.

The party consisted of about twenty guys, all at varying degrees of piss drunk, scattered about the hotel suite while three topless girls shook body parts in their faces. Glasses and bottles decorated every surface.

Ty didn't know how they managed to keep up with the parties in this city. If it wasn't drunken debaucheries like this, it was formal galas with the wives; but either way, there was some sort of festivity nearly every night of the week. Ty was exhausted, and he'd only been here a month.

He went and poured himself a drink at the bar; one more and he could probably slip out without his bureau chief noticing. With glass in hand, he stood by the window. If there was one thing the party had going for it, it was the view. At the top of the latest shiny hotel, the room overlooked the rest of the city, blinking in lights. Ty gazed out onto the nightscape, but he didn't see a single thing. His hand sat in his pocket, fingers curled around his phone as he willed it to ping with a message from Cam.

Please, be safe. His heart lurched as he remembered the last video call they'd managed. Cam's beard and hair were growing out, uneven in places. His eyes sunken in, ringed with dark circles, and the bright green of his irises were a dull, bland color. He'd lost a lot of weight—a frightening amount in such a short time.

Cam wasn't fine, Ty knew that. He knew that Cam knew that. That goddamn sense of responsibility and unfounded guilt was going to kill him from the inside out, but there was nothing Ty could fucking do about it, and that was killing *him* from the inside out.

He rubbed the heel of his hand up and down the middle of his chest, trying to ease the tightness that constricted his lungs. It was an unsettling feeling, like an unwanted cloak was suffocating him, and no matter how hard he tried to shake it off, it only pulled in tighter.

Until a few months ago, he'd never given a second thought to being in a relationship; it figured that he'd go and fall in love with a guy who had the most dangerous fucking job in the world. Ty drained the rest of his glass and set it down on the closest flat surface he could find.

A quick glance around the room showed that everyone else was otherwise preoccupied, and he made his way to the door. He didn't care if they saw him leaving; he was done with this party.

The elevator ride was insanely fast, and his ears popped a couple of times on the way down. Striding through the lobby, he headed straight for the line of taxis waiting to take their drunken expat passengers back to their gated community homes. The taxi pulled away, and the lights from the hotel faded into the distance. This must be what Cam's darkness was like: like he was moving away from the light and into the dark.

Ty's heart lurched again, and he pressed his hand to his chest. He would never get used to caring for someone so deeply that it hurt.

The taxi drove past a streetlight, and Ty caught his reflection in the momentary glare in the window. He didn't look any different from six months ago, and yet he felt like another person. It dawned on him that a year ago, even six months ago, he would have loved this life: working hard during the day—international superstar journalist—then playing hard at night, with all the drinking, partying, and drugs.

But look at him now: sneaking out of parties so he could go home by himself and pine after his boyfriend. He rubbed a hand over his face. *Come on, Cam, message back already.* But nothing. No message pinging his phone. No green bubble next to Cam's name.

The taxi pulled up to his place, and after paying the driver, Ty let himself inside. After shrugging out of his suit jacket, he opened his laptop and logged on to Skype. Still no Cam. With a cold beer out of the fridge, he settled onto the couch to wait. If he had to wait all night, he would wait.

Three beers later, he was still waiting. And as his eyes drifted shut, the bubble next to Cam's name remained gray.

CHAPTER EIGHTEEN

Cam had a death grip on the door handle as the armored vehicle drove over another pothole in the dirt road leading back to camp.

"Ow, damn it." Next to him, Patsy sat in the middle seat, rubbing her head after it collided with the roof of the vehicle.

"Sorry, madam," the peacekeeper from Bangladesh shouted over his shoulder from behind the wheel. "I am picking the smallest ones."

"Jesus Christ, these roads," Patsy muttered under her breath, raising her hand barely in time to protect her head from another collision with the roof.

Cam couldn't have agreed more, but he didn't respond. His darkness was around him, a thick haze that was difficult to see through, difficult to hear anything behind. All he could do was grip the door handle and wait until they got back to Admin Block so he could go hide in his cabin.

He closed his eyes, trying to block out the rumble of the engine, Patsy swearing next to him, and the snoring of Osman, their interpreter, who sat on the other side of Patsy. His heart raced in his chest, his skin was on fire, and streams of sweat poured off his temples, down his neck, down his back.

In his mind, Cam pictured Busker—whom Izzy had temporarily adopted—with his scraggly mix of black, gray, and white fur, ungroomed and falling over his eyes. The dog lying on the couch with one paw hanging off the edge. How he would pad over and put his big, heavy head on Cam's lap. The wet, sloppy kisses Busker gave—the first one he gave to Ty that had Ty cursing and wiping his face with the back of his hand. How Ty pretended to be annoyed with the dog but kept sneaking him pieces of food when he thought Cam wasn't looking.

He held on—they were almost there.

The vehicle dipped right as the front wheel drove into another pothole, and then suddenly they were airborne. Shouts rang out, and Patsy fell against him as he slammed against the door. Pain exploded in his head, a white blaze that shot through his body and emptied his lungs.

They flew through the air for ages, and when the vehicle hit the ground, it felt like a hundred tons of bricks landed on top of him, crushing every bone in his body. The world rocked to a stop, and all Cam knew was pain. Pain in his chest, in his lungs as he struggled to breathe. In his ears where the only sound was a loud ringing. In his head, behind his eyes, along every inch of his body.

Something moved on top of him: Patsy. Oh god, Patsy. Osman. The peacekeepers. Ty. Busker. Izzy. His parents. His darkness swirled but didn't close in around him, its promise of numb oblivion frustratingly out of reach.

Hands pushed and pulled at him. Muffled voices were drowned out by the ringing in his ears. He tried to open his eyes, but they seemed sealed shut. More hands, pulling his arms, dragging him sideways. Pain shot through his leg. A wretched, guttural shout sounded from somewhere close by. His lungs couldn't suck in oxygen fast enough.

Hands on his ankles and more pain exploded in his leg, along his shin, right below his knee. But they kept dragging him. He tried to grasp on to something to steady the jostling, but his hands met nothing.

Something pointed scraped along his back, and another ear-curdling shriek rang out. A sharp line of pain blossomed diagonally from shoulder to hip. When someone's arm landed across his shoulders, he lurched away from the stinging contact.

Suddenly he was airborne again, hands under his armpits, hands under his knees. And still that shout of pain followed him as they carried him away. They didn't go far, though it felt like an eternity. They put him down on a cold, hard surface. A warm soft mass pressed against his right side, and he tried to see what—no, who it was, but the little he could see in his right eye was nothing more than blurred shapes.

More hands held him still and more muffled voices shot back and forth around him. Something slammed shut and he was jostled, sending a fresh shock of pain through his body. Then the familiar rumble of an engine gunning, and yet more waves of pain rolled through him, until his darkness finally settled and dragged him down into its comforting depths.

CHAPTER NINETEEN

It had been two weeks now of no messages, no Skype dates. His calls weren't going through, emails weren't being answered. Ty checked his contact list again, praying for that fucking bubble to turn green, and when it didn't, he threw his phone onto his desk hard enough for it to skitter off the edge and land on the floor.

He buried his fingers in his hair, bracing his elbows on his desk. Where the fuck was Cam? One scenario after another raced through his mind, each worse than the last. What if he was dead? Izzy would call, wouldn't she? She would reach out and tell him, surely.

No, Cam couldn't be dead. *Don't be an idiot.* Ty ran his hands over his face and turned back to his computer, where a story was waiting to be edited. The words blurred together on the white screen until everything was a gray blob.

What if Cam wasn't responding on purpose?

After the god-awful party with the strippers, their connections had been even fewer and farther between. Messages sent over the phone once every few days. One quick Skype chat that got cut short because Ty needed to be on air—Cam had looked like death warmed over.

It wasn't only that their schedules didn't match up; at least it didn't feel that way. Cam had been withdrawn during the last call, sunken into himself, giving one-word answers and not really interested in anything Ty had to say.

Letting him go back into the field had been a mistake, and Ty wished he had done more to convince Cam not to do it. Fuck the UN and their humanitarian crisis. What good would Cam be to anyone in the state he was in?

The radio silence wasn't only about Cam's PTSD—Ty didn't know why he thought this, but he felt it in his bones. Something was wrong.

He leaned over, grabbed his phone off the floor, and tapped the familiar Skype icon. Still no Cam. He scrolled through his phone until he found the other number he wanted.

It rang, and rang, and rang. He was about to hang up when it finally connected.

"Hello?" The greeting came out more as a groan, and Ty only then remembered what time it must have been in New York.

"Izzy? God, sorry. I forgot about the time difference."

Izzy groaned into the phone again. "Ty?" She took a sharp breath and let it out in a huff as if her brain were struggling to keep up. "What the hell? Aren't you in the Middle East?"

"Yeah, Abu Dhabi." Ty rested his face in his hand, his elbow on his desk. "Sorry for waking you up."

She groaned again.

"Listen, have you heard from Cam?"

"Huh?"

"Cam, your brother. Have you heard from him?" Ty resisted the urge to shout at her.

"Cam?"

"Yes, Cam." Ty bit back a retort.

"Ugh, I don't know." She sounded muffled. "Probably sedated. Do you know what time it is?"

"What? What do you mean, 'sedated'?" Ty shot out of his chair, sending it flying against the wall behind him.

"What are you talking about?" Izzy whined into the phone.

"Where is Cam?" He drew it out, saying each word with precision.

"Cam? He's at NewYork-Presbyterian."

"He's at a church?" That couldn't be right.

"Yeah, he's at a church, at this time of day." The grogginess cleared from Izzy's voice. "No, dumbass, he's at the hospital. Where else would he be?"

"Why the hell is he at the hospital? In New York?" Ty shouted, not caring how awake Izzy was, or if his voice carried through the walls of his office.

A beat passed in silence, and Ty fingers hurt with how hard he was gripping his phone.

"Wait, are you saying that you don't know?"

"Don't know what?" Ty growled.

"Oh my god." Something brushed against the phone's mic before Izzy came across stronger and clearer. "Ty, you really don't know? Cam was emergency evacuated a couple of weeks ago. He was in Geneva for a week before they got him back here. He's been in the hospital ever since."

Ty stumbled, missed his chair, and ended up on the floor. His heart stopped beating and the air was devoid of oxygen. All of a sudden, he was eight years old again, in the hospital room with his mother lying frighteningly still on the bed. He could still smell the astringent antibacterial cleaners, hear the beeping of the machines. Pain unfurled in the middle of Ty's chest, and his vision narrowed to a pinprick of light.

"Ty? Ty? Are you still there?"

Izzy's voice sounded distant and fuzzy, and it was only after a minute that he realized he had dropped his hand away from his ear. He blinked, training his eyes on the chair that sat a few feet away. He forced his diaphragm out and, after a couple of shaky breaths, finally got oxygen back to his brain. "Is he okay?"

"He's in pretty bad shape." Her voice wavered a bit, and it felt like a sledgehammer swinging against his heart. "But he'll live."

He'll live. It took a moment for the words to register, and then his brain to imbue meaning in them. *Cam's going to live; he's not going to die.* "Tell me. What happened?"

"Ty." She paused for a couple of beats. "You seriously didn't know about this?"

"No." Ty shifted on the floor so he could lean against his desk. He planted his feet flat and propped up one arm across his knees. Every breath was difficult, but he forced himself to suck in air and then spit it back out. "Haven't spoken with him in weeks now."

Izzy sighed. "God. I'm sorry. I should have called you the minute I found out. Cam's been in varying levels of drugged up since the incident; I should have realized you wouldn't be able to get a hold of him."

He hung his head, heart still beating erratically, tremors shaking his limbs. "Can you please tell me what happened?"

She exhaled into the phone. "I don't have a lot of details. Cam's not talking about it. You know how he is. All I know is what the UN told my parents."

"Which is?" Ty grit his teeth together, trying not to imagine the worst and, at the same time, not sure what the worst would be.

"He was in a car, with security, and they were driving back to the refugee camp from . . . I don't know where. And then they ran over a bomb."

"What?"

"A bomb. You know, on the road."

"An IED," Ty clarified, more for himself than for Izzy.

"Yeah, one of those bomb things on the road."

His heart seized, and he rubbed his free hand hard up and down the middle of his chest. It could have been worse, Ty told himself. Cam could be dead. IEDs killed people. "How badly is he injured?"

"A concussion, broken leg, a really bad gash across his back. That's the worst, I think."

That didn't sound too bad. He would live. That was the most important thing. "He's okay," Ty said, more as a reminder to himself than as a question for Izzy.

"He will be," Izzy said softly.

"I'm coming home." The words were out before Ty had even formulated the thought.

"What?"

"I'm coming home." As quickly as he had shut down at the news that Cam was in the hospital, declaring that he was going home jumpstarted Ty's internal processes. He was an adult and had resources and options; he could choose to go home to be with the man he loved. He might not have had any choices as an eight-year-old watching his mother die. But goddamn it, he wasn't eight years old anymore, and he wasn't about to watch Cam die.

Izzy was speaking, but he missed it as he pushed himself off the floor, grabbed the office chair, and pulled it back toward the desk. "Huh?"

"I said, don't you have to finish out your contract?"

"I'm not on contract."

"Oh, so . . ."

"I'm quitting." His mind was setting plans several steps ahead already, and his heart raced as if it were trying to make up for the earlier lack of beating. "They don't need me here. They can find a million other people to do this job. I'm needed at home."

"Really?"

Ty paused with his hand on the mouse, ready to look up flight schedules. Really? Throw his career away? Yes. Really. Absolutely. It was scary as fuck, but it was the right thing to do. He'd regret it if he didn't go back. He'd be left wondering for the rest of his life: what if? What could they have been?

Ty didn't believe in ghosts or spirits or any of that shit. But at the moment, he could have sworn he felt his mom in the office with him. And she said one word: go.

"I'll be on the next flight out."

"Ty . . ."

"It might take a couple of days to sort everything out and get back. But I'm on my way. I'll touch base with you when I'm State-side again."

"Yeah, okay."

He thought he heard sniffles over the line, but that wasn't important right now. He needed to get himself booked on the next available flight back to New York.

"Ty?"

"Yeah?"

"Be safe, okay?"

"Yeah." He took a moment to squeeze his eyes shut and take a deep breath. Images of a hospital bed flashed in his mind, but it was empty. His mom was dead and gone and whatever remained of her was inside Ty's heart, now sharing space with the man he loved. And that hospital bed didn't belong to Cam, either. Because Cam would recover, and they would salvage whatever it was they had, even if Ty had to fight until his last breath for it. He heard that one word again: go.

"I will."

Ty knocked on the door to Cam's apartment, his clothes damp with multiple rounds of sweat from his travels, his hand tight around the strap of his duffel bag. He'd spent the last couple of days packing up what little of a life he'd had in Abu Dhabi, stuffing it into two suitcases with room to spare, and running to the airport.

He had quit the day of his call with Izzy—it had not gone over well. But the only thing on his mind had been getting on that plane and back to New York.

The first thing he'd done when his plane landed was ring up Izzy, who had told him that Cam had been discharged that afternoon and they'd brought him back to his apartment. So here he was, heart beating so fast, he thought it would escape up his throat.

The door opened, and Ty almost pushed his way inside. The only thing stopping him was Cary, standing in the way with a look of surprise. Ty's glare was fueled by twenty-four hours of lack of sleep.

"Is Cam here?"

"What are you doing here?"

They spoke at the same time.

"Let me in," Ty growled.

Cary shot him an exacerbated look and stepped back. "He's resting."

"Hey, is that Ty?" Izzy's voice floated from beyond the doorway, accompanied by the sound of footsteps. "Hey, Ty." Izzy appeared from around the corner and peered past him. "Oh my god. Did you come straight from the airport?"

Ty shot a glance at the suitcases sitting behind him in the hall. "Yeah," he bit out. "I was hoping to catch Cam before it got too late tonight."

"Come on in." Izzy grabbed one of his suitcases and dragged it inside. "Have you eaten yet? We're about to order dinner. Cam's in bed and he's heavily sedated, so he's a little out of it right now."

Ty followed Izzy inside and stashed his duffel bag on top of his suitcases. "How is he?"

Izzy sighed, and Cary leaned silently against the kitchen counter, arms crossed.

"He's . . . I don't fucking know." Izzy ran a hand over her face. "Physically, he'll be okay, at least that's what the doctors say. But otherwise?" She shrugged with eyes wide, and threw her hands in the air.

"Has anyone spoken to Dr. Brown about this?"

Izzy shook her head. "She came by the hospital once, but Cam was asleep. She wouldn't say anything definitive until they've had a full session."

Ty crossed his arms, feet in a wide stance. "They were supposed to be doing regular Skype sessions while he was out there. She couldn't say anything based off those?"

One of Izzy's shoulders lifted, then dropped. "She wouldn't say anything."

"Can I go in and see him?"

"Why not? Those sedatives are so strong, I doubt a raging bull could wake him." Izzy led the way to Cam's room and Cary followed behind.

She eased the door open and stepped out of the way for Ty to slip through. Busker was lying on the bed next to Cam, and he lifted his head as Ty approached.

"Hey, Busker," Ty whispered, giving the mutt a pat before the dog settled himself beside Cam again. He walked around to where Cam lay, so silent and still. The only evidence of his being alive was the slow rise and fall of his chest.

Cam's left leg was wrapped in a cast, and the blankets had been arranged carefully around it. He wore a bandage on his head, and his face was a mosaic of gashes and bruises. The incident was supposedly two weeks ago, but he looked like he'd only been through the meat grinder yesterday.

Ty sat down softly on the empty space at the edge of the bed. Not even a stir from Cam. It was so much like another bed from so long ago, when he'd climbed up and watched his mother sleep a deep, drug-induced sleep. And like that time so long ago, tears prickled his eyes while he tried to blink them away.

Ty closed his fingers around the hand sitting on top of the covers. It lay limp, like his mother's had, but at least it was warm. He squeezed it gently.

"Hey," he whispered, the word coming out strangled and thick with fatigue and emotion. He wiped at the tear that escaped down his cheek. "It's me. Ty. I came back as soon as I found out what happened."

His throat closed up, and he took a second to force the muscles to relax. How many times had he sat next to his mom and held one-sided conversations with her while she slept? He had talked until his little eight-year-old voice was hoarse, and then he'd snuggled down and fallen asleep next to her. On the good days, he'd woken up to her running her fingers through his hair. Sometimes she'd even remembered bits and pieces of what he'd told her. Why was it so much more difficult with Cam?

"I—I quit my job. They're pretty pissed, but . . ." Ty shrugged and wiped at more of the tears running down his face. "Anyway, I'm back. I'm here. And you're going to get better. The doctors said so. We're going to do whatever it takes, okay? Whatever it takes to get you better. We're going to get you back on your feet. You're going to be okay, and we're going to be okay."

He had to believe it, because that truth was the single most important thing in his life. Ty suddenly felt so tired, his eyes drifting shut and his head hanging down to his chest. Every cell in his body wanted to stretch out next to Cam and hold him until he woke up.

But he stank and needed a shower. And his stomach grumbled because he hadn't had the appetite to eat anything on his way back to New York.

A grunt and a snore came from Busker, but still no response from Cam. Fuck it. He could shower and eat later. Right now, this was more important.

He nudged Busker until the mutt shifted to the foot of the bed, and Ty lay down on top of the blankets facing Cam. Cam's chest rose and fell, rose and fell. As he watched, his eyes drifted shut again. Cam was going to be okay. They were going to be okay.

CHAPTER TWENTY

He was running. No, not running. Limping. His left leg was wrapped in a cast from foot to thigh. So, he limped as fast as he could, even as his head throbbed and his back pulsed and pulled. He huffed with each step, sweat pouring over him, but still, he limped. He had to get away.

Behind him was the mob again, their feet pounding the ground. But this time they were accompanied by a loud rumble. He risked a glance behind him and nearly stumbled at the sight of a gigantic armored vehicle rolling along behind the mob. It was huge, looming in the background, far larger than any armored vehicle built on earth.

He tried to turn to keep running, but his right foot caught on his cast, and he tumbled to the ground. The mob caught up with him and, like every other time he dreamed this dream, they ran past without giving him a second thought. The armored vehicle drove past too, directly over Cam, its wheels passing on either side of him as he lay on the ground.

He couldn't catch any of them this time. None of his scrambling and shouting did any good to slow their progress toward whoever was in their sights. He pushed himself upright, hopping on one foot as he regained his balance. Then he limped along again, struggling to keep up as they descended upon their victim.

By the time he caught up, the mob was gone, leaving behind the evidence of their savagery. A cry bubbled up from Cam's chest, and he clamped his hand over his mouth at the sight. Patsy and Osman lay on the ground, brutalized. The two dead guards lay beside them, bullet holes in their heads. Ty lay there too, dressed in a sharp suit, covered in chocolate.

He backed away, one unsteady step at a time, and turned. He couldn't look at them anymore. His head was going to explode, his back was on fire. He ran with what little was left inside of him. He ran until . . .

Cam hurtled toward consciousness, breaking through before he was quite ready to surface. He gasped as his body exploded in pain—head, back, every joint. His mouth was full of cotton, suffocating him. Cobwebs stuffed his ears, disorienting him. When he blinked his eyes open, it was dark, and it took a couple more blinks before the varying shades of black formed into identifiable shapes.

Something wet and cold pressed against his neck, and the accompanying whine told him Busker was in bed with him. Cam groaned and tried without success to shirk away from Busker's nose.

As his heart rate gradually descended, he took a quick inventory of his body and the aches and pains he'd been tracking for the past week or so. None of them felt any better; if anything, his back was tighter from the stitches that kept the deep gash together, and his leg was itchy as hell under the cast. And he was so goddamn tired. But his bladder screamed at him, and he didn't have the humiliating luxury of a bedpan at home.

Cam lifted his arms, trying to get them far enough under his body to leverage himself up to sitting. He grimaced at how they protested even that simple movement. He tried an experimental push—nothing but the radiating pain across his back and his arms giving out before he even got an inch.

Busker barked at him, loud even as it filtered through the cobwebs in his ear. "Busker, shh."

Footsteps echoed beyond his door. Great. Cary and Izzy were still here. He had told them to go home and come back tomorrow. The door opened, letting in light from the living room.

"I'm fine. Really." Cam tried to preempt their complaints. "I need to pee, that's all, goddamn it."

"Here. Can you lift your head?"

That was the last voice Cam expected to hear. He jerked his head around to check if it was actually Ty so quickly that the movement set off a dull explosion of pain, and he froze with his eyes squeezed shut, waiting for it to ease. "Fuck."

"Whoa. Slowly. Are you okay?" Ty rushed to his side.

He forced himself to breathe through the pain, and once it finally died down, he bit out, "What are you doing here?"

Ty's hands on his shoulder and behind his neck stilled, and for a brief second Cam feared he might pull away. But he didn't, to Cam's relief. They were warm and familiar on Cam's skin.

"I'm here because you got your stupid ass blown up, that's why."

Ty's low, rumbling voice penetrated through the fog of darkness that had enveloped Cam for the past several weeks and found that vulnerable, precious part of him deep inside. He didn't respond. He didn't have enough words to describe how he felt about Ty being here: some nuanced concoction of joy, relief, comfort, hope.

"Come on. Let's get you to the toilet."

Cam gritted his teeth but couldn't stop the cry of pain that burst from his throat as Ty helped him up. His fingers dug into Ty's shoulder and forearm, unable to let go because he'd only fall back down on the bed. "Crutches." He jutted his chin sideways.

Ty kept one hand on him and reached for the pair that leaned against the wall. With great difficulty, Cam managed to swing his legs around and gently lower the one with the cast down to the floor. He was covered in sweat, trails of it running down the sides of his face.

Busker barked once, watching them struggle to stand up from the bed. By the time he was upright, Cam was so exhausted, he wanted to lie back down. He wasn't sure he could even operate the crutches. He took a tentative first step and would have fallen over if Ty hadn't been there, steadying him. With excruciating slowness, they made their way out of the bedroom and into the bathroom, and by the time he was situated in front of the toilet, he was shaking so hard he thought he might go into shock. Maybe he should invest in a goddamn bedpan.

"Do you want to sit?" Ty asked.

Cam shook his head. Sitting was torture on his back, pulling at the stitches in a way that made it feel like it would split open again. But standing while peeing in his state was going to be tricky. Fucking goddamn shit.

"Do you want me to stay?" Ty's tone was matter-of-fact, as if there was nothing amiss about an adult man not being able to pee on his own. Cam could have kissed him for that if he'd been able to move.

He gave a slight nod. "Can you . . ." Cam glared at the drawstring of his pajama pants. If he let go of his crutches at this point, he'd end up on the floor. Besides, his fingers had stiffened around the handles, and he doubted he could unwrap them even if he tried.

Ty stood behind him, pressing chest against back. After the initial flash of pain at the contact, it eased into a dull throb, and Cam leaned against him. Ty's hands were quick and sure, pulling his pants down far enough to access the equipment.

"Do you . . ." Ty spoke low beside his ear, his hands firm on Cam's hips.

Cam squeezed his eyes shut and fought the inevitable. He shook his head. "Can you?"

There was no hesitation, only efficient motions that had Cam's junk out and pointed in the right direction while Cam leaned his head on Ty's shoulder, eyes squeezed tightly shut, turned the other way. Ty's hands were warm against his skin—not arousing, not weird—simply a second pair of hands holding his penis in place so he could pee in the goddamn toilet and relieve himself.

"Go ahead."

Ty's chin was on top of Cam's shoulder, the side of his face pressed against Cam's neck, the solid mass of Ty's body behind him, holding him upright. It was comforting in a way that might not have made sense to other people, but it was what Cam needed at that moment. He bit his bottom lip and told his bladder to let go.

The relief caused another flood of sweat to pour from Cam's skin, and as he finished, what remained of his strength drained from his limbs. He didn't remember Ty cleaning him up and putting him away. There might have been muttered curses and shouts of pain as they maneuvered back to the bedroom. By the time Cam was horizontal again, the blissful darkness had taken him.

Cam sat by his window, leg propped up on a second chair. He stared out at the fire escape, focused on the pattern of rust decorating the railing. This was his third cigarette. It didn't feel like enough.

It had been two weeks of being back in this apartment and crawling out of bed when all he wanted was to bury deeper under the covers. They had forced him to do a Skype session with Dr. Brown—much good that had done; she only wanted to talk about things he didn't want to talk about.

Possibly the only constructive thing that had happened was Teresa calling with an update on Patsy and Osman. Osman had lost a leg but would survive. Patsy was in similar shape to Cam, and he wondered whether she would go back into the field after she recovered. The peacekeeper who had been in the front passenger seat had died, and Cam hated that he hadn't even learned the guy's name.

He took another drag on his smoke and considered lighting up a fourth one. Busker bumped against his good knee and sat beside him, head raised for a pat. Cam brushed his fingers through Busker's mane.

"Do you want to eat something?" Ty asked from across the room.

That was the other thing—Ty. He had been around constantly this entire time. Not leaving in the evening to go home, not leaving in the morning to go to work. He was around all the fucking time, coordinating with the cleaner, sending the laundry out, ordering food, and generally being helpful. It was so goddamn sweet. Cam gritted his teeth together. "No."

"You have to eat something." Ty's annoyance mirrored how Cam felt.

"I don't have to eat a fucking thing." Besides, if he ate now, there was a good chance he'd end up vomiting it back up. Something about the drugs they had him on and his renewed bout of PTSD left his body with an unpredictable relationship with food.

"Fine. Food's in the kitchen if you change your mind."

Ty padded softly away, and Cam's heart sank into the pit of his stomach. The last thing he wanted was to be an asshole to Ty. But every time he opened his mouth, the most asshole-y thing came out. He stuck the cigarette butt into the glass jar and grabbed his crutches. He could live without the fourth cigarette.

With one last pat for Busker, Cam tried to leverage himself into a standing position. His good leg had fallen asleep, and the attempt to stand on it sent shooting pain through the awakening nerves.

He got halfway up and dropped back into his chair, a layer of sweat developing on his skin. Busker whined while Ty stood at the doorway, arms crossed, watching.

He tried again, hopping a little and regretting the movement as it sent sharp stabs of pain radiating through his back, reigniting the throbbing in his head. He breathed through it and tried yet again, except this time his body gave out, and he started falling, nothing within arm's reach to break his fall.

Nothing except Ty, apparently, who was suddenly there, arms wrapped around him, holding him up. Cam attempted to fight it, but was unsuccessful as he leaned into Ty's warmth, letting him take his weight.

"I didn't ask for your help." The words escaped his clenched jaw even as he held on to Ty with a death grip.

"I'm not offering." Ty's response was equally strained.

Together, they hobbled over to the couch, and Cam eased down onto it with his eyes shut tight, teeth grinding together, and prickling breaking out across his skin. His darkness called for him, and Cam reached for it with both hands.

The next time he opened his eyes, there was a pillow under his head and a blanket covering his body. The sky outside his window had turned dark, and Ty was gently shaking him awake with a hand on his shoulder.

"Hey, time for your meds." He held out his hand to drop the pills into Cam's.

Cam pushed the blanket away and managed to sit up on his own with only marginal pain. Ty handed him a glass of water, then disappeared back into the kitchen. He returned with a plate of baked macaroni and cheese and a side of salad.

"You have to eat something or the drugs will burn a hole through your stomach lining." He set the plate on Cam's lap and held out the fork.

Cam traded the glass for the fork and stared at the mound of food. He hated Ty caring for him, being thoughtful and supportive, anticipating his needs before he even realized he had them. It was worse that Ty had done it without Cam once asking for his help. And there was nothing he could do but take and take, without giving anything back. He was supposed to be the problem solver, not the problem that needed solving.

Ty sat next to him on the couch, leaning forward with his elbows braced on his knees. His hair was tussled, like he'd run his fingers through it several times that day and had forgotten to straighten it out. A bit of scruff was growing on his chin and above his lip, but his cheeks were still baby smooth—that must have been several days' worth of growth.

"Thank you," he whispered, realizing he hadn't said those words the entire time Ty had been around. And he meant them, in spite of the asshole-y words driven by the uncontrollable urge that was even darker than his darkness.

Ty glanced over his shoulder. There were bags under his eyes that Cam had never seen before. The slope of his shoulders and the way he held his head screamed *tired*. Tired of taking care of him, of hanging around an invalid who couldn't get his shit together. And yet, those eyes hadn't lost their laser-precision ability to cut past Cam's defenses—thicker now than they had ever been—and see exactly how messed up Cam was.

He dropped his gaze back to the mac and cheese, as if that had ever prevented Ty from seeing parts of him he didn't want to acknowledge. And then that urge that had latched on to him after the incident came rushing to the fore again, pushing out words Cam wasn't sure were his.

"You don't have to stay, you know." Cam cringed at his own vehemence and the twinge of pain in his heart.

Confusion was written all over Ty's face.

"I mean, you don't have to stay and take care of me every day. Don't you have work or something?" Cam's heart hurt with every single word, but he couldn't stop them.

"And who else would take care of you?" Ty's question hit Cam hard, and he grimaced at the reminder of how helpless and alone he was. He started shaking.

"Izzy. Or Cary. Or my parents." Not that Izzy or Cary were good options. His mom would be there in a heartbeat, but then he'd wish he really had been killed by the fucking bomb.

"Yeah, right." Ty glared back at him.

Cam refused to meet his gaze. “I’m serious. You don’t have to stay.”

Ty rose to his feet and paced away as his fingers found their way into his hair again. “Honest to god, Cam, you’re driving me fucking insane.”

“Then leave!” Cam jumped at the force of his own words. This urge inside of him had taken control of his tongue, and he couldn’t seem to stop it.

“I’m not fucking going anywhere!” Ty spun around and threw his arms out. “So get the fuck used to it.”

Despite the outburst, Cam’s heart thrilled at Ty’s declaration. Not that he could admit it; he was too deep in the thralls of this thing to be able to respond genuinely. Instead, he stabbed at his food, and the aroma of cheese wafted up to him.

“I’m not worth the trouble.” He didn’t know were the words were coming from. “Don’t you have better things to do with your time?”

Ty dropped his arms, and they slapped against his thighs loudly. He came back to the couch, took the plate from Cam’s lap, and set it on the coffee table before inserting himself in between Cam’s legs. He put his hands on either side of Cam’s face, holding him in place and giving Cam no choice but to look the man he loved in the eye. As terrifying as that was.

“I told you. I’m not going anywhere. You can try to push me away as much as you want, but it’s not going to work.”

Cam frowned. In the rational, logical part of his brain, he knew Ty was telling the truth. But knowing something in his head wasn’t the same as knowing something in his heart, and his heart was in full defensive mode. “I’m not trying to pu—” He was cut off by Ty’s fingers on his lips.

“It’s okay. You can yell at me, shout at me. Be angry, be sad, whatever you want. I’m here. I want to be a part of it.” Ty dropped his hands and sat back on his heels. “Unless . . . Do you really want me to leave?”

Cam stared into Ty’s eyes and saw a kernel of doubt that was so unlike Ty. No, if he was truly honest with himself, he didn’t want Ty to leave, not when they’d found their way back to each other. He shook his head.

"Good. There's nowhere in the world I'd rather be than here."

Cam scrunched his nose because the alternative was to give in to the angry, violent tears threatening to spill over. He gritted his teeth, clenched his fists in the blanket covering his lap, and fought them back.

Ty brushed his thumb along Cam's jaw. "You need a shave and a haircut." His fingers ran through Cam's hair, combing it to one side. "Some kind of grooming. You're looking as shaggy as Busker."

The dog barked half-heartedly from where he lay on the floor.

Cam lost the battle against the tears, as that uncontrollable urge rose up inside him. He tilted toward Ty, ignoring how the motion pulled painfully at his back, and Ty shifted to meet him, positioning them until the pressure on his back eased. The tears came, savage and unadulterated, and as they rushed past Cam's eyelids, an accompanying sound of anguish escaped his throat.

He clung to Ty's T-shirt, thin and soft under his fingers; his forehead lay on Ty's shoulder. He cried. He yelled. All of the rage and resentment, the agony and terror. It all came out in a surge too strong to be held back. Through it all, Ty held him, a solid mass anchoring him to reality while his own world spun out of control.

When the tears finally slowed and his throat was hoarse with the yelling, Cam turned away from Ty as much as his back would allow. He still shook with the aftershocks of the ugly cry, his face a mess of tears and snot. Ty let him go and disappeared momentarily, only to come back with a box of tissues and a fresh glass of water. As Cam cleaned himself up, he was fully aware of Ty sitting on the couch next to him, thighs touching, his arm wrapped gently around Cam's back.

Cam's limbs felt heavy, as if they'd been pumped full of lead. His eyes hurt, and his head spun. He drained the glass of water before Ty pulled him back against him.

They settled on the couch, Cam tucked under Ty's arm, leaning against him, and into him. "Is this okay for your back?"

A couple of stray tears found their way down Cam's cheek, and he swiped at them while nodding. Ty pressed a kiss onto the top of his head, and a couple of more tears escaped.

He didn't deserve Ty's patience and understanding. He was damaged in his soul, complete with old scar tissue and fresh, new wounds. He was rough around the edges, and rough straight through to his core. He didn't deserve Ty's love.

More tears flowed, silent this time. He should let Ty go and find someone who wasn't a fucked-up mess. Because Ty deserved someone who didn't fluctuate between bursts of anger and bouts of depression. Ty deserved someone who was stable and who could give as much as he could take. Cam couldn't be that man; he didn't know how.

Unconsciousness took him, and still the tears fell.

CHAPTER TWENTY-ONE

Cam stirred the remains of his soup, his unreliable appetite not letting him finish it. His appetite was getting better, though, and he had been able to eat at least something for each meal the last few days. Or had it been a week already? The days blurred together, punctuated only by his weekly sessions with Dr. Brown. And even then, he couldn't quite remember when the last one had been, or when the next one was.

Ty was the only reason he made it to any of his appointments, or took his medication, or showered, or had clean clothes. Ty was everything, and with each passing day, Cam sensed the end coming. Ty said he wasn't going anywhere; Cam didn't believe him.

He snuck a glance at Ty, sitting perpendicular to Cam at the kitchen table, his own bowl of half-eaten soup forgotten while he tapped furiously on his phone, his lips pursed in a little pout of concentration. They hadn't talked about what came after this, when Ty went back to work, and when Cam would eventually have to go back as well. He didn't want to know.

He liked this twilight zone they were in, removed from reality. Here, he was safe and protected; his darkness didn't call as loudly, or try to consume him so entirely. Out there was the great unknown.

Ty must have felt his gaze, because he looked up before Cam could turn away. "Sorry." He put his phone down and folded his hands across the top of the table. "I was sorting out some things."

Cam debated whether he should let it slide and keep pretending the outside world didn't exist. But then the phone buzzed, the screen lit with a new email, and Ty shifted his gaze to read the notification.

"Go ahead, read it." The words nearly choked him, forcing him to face things he would rather ignore.

Busker chose that moment to amble up and put his head on Cam's lap. He busied himself with running his fingers through Busker's coarse fur and petting that soft spot right above Busker's eyes.

A couple of minutes later, Ty set it down again. "Sorry."

"What's it about?" Cam hated himself for asking.

"It's . . . work."

Cam tore his attention away from Busker; Ty's eyes were on him. "ANN?"

Ty cocked his head. "No, I quit. Don't you remember?"

"You did?" Cam racked his brain but came up with nothing. It made sense, though, what with Ty's suitcases still sitting in Cam's apartment, and his absolute lack of urgency to go back to Abu Dhabi.

"Yeah, I told you."

Cam nodded. "Why did you quit?" He didn't know what answer he preferred; they all seemed too overwhelming for him to process.

"It . . ." Ty shifted in his chair. "Wasn't what I thought it would be."

"Too many parties?" Cam meant it as a joke, despite how dryly it came out.

"Yeah, it was a little too much."

"Oh. But wasn't the work what you wanted?"

"It was, but . . ." Ty pinned him with a look. "I was wrong about what I wanted."

"Oh." Cam got the distinct feeling they weren't talking about journalism anymore.

"Yeah, so anyway, I need a new job. I ended up reaching out to those guys at Behind the Veil again. You remember that investigative journalism outfit I interviewed at?"

"I do." Cam went back to stroking the soft spot on Busker's head. "You were really excited about them."

A slight frown creased Ty's brow. "Really?"

"Yeah, weren't you? That was the impression I got when you told me about them. More excited than when you were talking about ANN, that's for sure."

"Huh." The edge of Ty's lips curled, and a little warmth blossomed in Cam's chest. His heart did that beat-skipping thing it'd been doing before he left for South Sudan—the first time he felt anything close to being the person he was before. He swallowed around the lump in his throat.

"Anyway, I figured it couldn't hurt to see if they still have a position open."

"And?" The short question came out as a croak.

"Well, the original position I interviewed for has been filled." Ty waved it off. "But there's another one: they need a host for their episodes."

That seemed like a good fit for Ty, but there was a touch of hesitancy in the way Ty spoke that made Cam pause. "And?"

"They said they wanted a visible minority as a host, to reflect the diversity of the society they're serving."

"So?"

Ty cocked his head and grimaced. "I get what they're trying to do, but it feels, I don't know."

"Forced? Disingenuous?" Cam had never seen Ty at a loss for words before.

"I'm being too sensitive, aren't I?" Ty peeked up at him, and Cam's heart skipped another beat at the uncertainty in that look. What had happened to Ty's easy confidence?

"I don't know. I don't have the best gauge on sensitivity."

Ty made an impatient sound. "I want to know if I'm being stupid for not wanting to play the race card."

Cam floundered. Not only had he never been in that position before, but he couldn't quite believe Ty wanted his opinion. What good was his opinion anyway? "Well, it's not like you're not qualified, right? I mean, I think you'd be a really good host. You're really passionate about what you're talking about, and you've got good presence on the screen."

A tinge of pink stained Ty's cheeks. "You've seen my clips?"

Cam dropped his gaze to Busker's head, still lolling in his lap. "I mean . . ."

"You have." The grin in Ty's voice was infectious, and Cam couldn't help but return it.

"Fine, yes, if you have to know. You're great on camera. You should go for this. You're qualified, and you deserve it." He meant every single word of it, even if it meant Ty leaving him. A world of success and fame waited for Ty; Cam didn't know anything about that world, didn't fit into it.

"They want me to do an on-camera audition." Ty's grin grew wider, if that was possible. "They've seen my clips and they like them. But this is a different style, so they want to test me out first."

"That's really great. Yeah, you should definitely do this." His chest constricted, and he forced himself to take a deep breath.

"So, um," Ty continued. "They want me to go in tomorrow. It'll probably be for half a day. I'm going to call Izzy or Cary and have one of them come over while I'm gone."

"No, don't be stupid." The words came out a little strangled. "I can manage by myself for the day."

Ty's eyes narrowed. "Are you sure?"

"Of course, I'm sure." Cam was barely convinced himself. "I've got to learn how to fend for myself eventually. I mean, you're not going to be here forever." He tried for a smile, but only got halfway, and then it turned into a frown.

"Cam." Ty raised an eyebrow at him. "I've told you before: I'm not going anywhere."

Cam pressed his lips together, and dropped his gaze. Ty kept saying that, and it would be true until it wasn't anymore. "You're obviously going back to work. I'm getting this damn cast off in a week. And life eventually goes back to normal. You can't be around here forever." He tried to keep his voice level, but it still wavered a bit at the end.

"That's all true." Ty seemed to choose his words carefully. "But that doesn't mean I'm going anywhere. Hey." Ty's fingers were warm where they landed softly on his shoulder, and Ty's other hand cupped his cheek, forcing him to look up. "What's going on?"

Ty leaned in close, his eyes darting back and forth as they examined Cam's own.

"What do you mean?" His heart raced under Ty's scrutiny. There was no way Ty could miss the nervousness and fear pouring out of every cell.

"Cam." Ty cocked his head. "Come on. I know you better than that. What's going on?"

"I don't know what you're talking about."

Ty sighed and drew his hands back. Cam almost reached out to stop him.

"Listen, I've been thinking about getting rid of my place," Ty said.

"Uh-huh?"

Ty pinned him with a look. "And moving in with you. I mean, if that's okay with you. We could get a bigger place. Maybe that way Busker won't keep walking into things. Something with a patio or backyard so you don't stink up the apartment with your smoking?"

Cam understood every word Ty had said, but strung together, they didn't make much sense. "You want to move in?"

Ty smiled. "Yeah, that's what I said."

"But why?"

"Well, I never go back to my apartment anymore. And I know you're getting better, but you're still going to have physical therapy for a while, and I can help with that."

Those were all good reasons, and yet none of them sounded very compelling to Cam. His disappointment must have shown, because Ty grasped his hand and squeezed.

"And because I love you, dumbass."

That was the reason Cam had been waiting for, though hearing it for the first time was so startling, he couldn't quite process the sounds. "What?"

"I love you."

Cam blinked and the words sunk in. "Oh."

Ty's eyebrows shot up. "'Oh'? That's it? I tell you I love you and that's all you have to say?"

"Um . . ." Something weird was happening. His heart felt big and growing, but fragile and delicate. "But, why?"

"Why?" Ty let out a dry chuckle. "You're going to make me spell it out for you?"

Cam stared because yes, he needed Ty to spell it out for him.

Ty leaned forward in his seat, expression intent. "Cameron Donnelly, you are the most difficult and frustrating person sometimes. One minute hot, the next minute cold. I never quite know which version of you I'm going to get."

A frown creased Cam's forehead—none of those were lovable qualities.

"But some things never change with you: your unwavering sense of responsibility, your determination to fight when everyone else tells you to give up. The way you open yourself up and invite me in—no one's done that for me before, no one's made me feel like I'm a part of something."

His heart was going to burst out of his chest. Ty must have been talking about someone who was a lot more put together than he was, someone who knew what the hell he was doing. It wasn't so much that he drew Ty in as one look from Ty had all his armor falling off and all the garbage inside spilling out—dirty and damaged, laid out in plain sight. And yet, Ty was still here, saying he loved him.

"I love you too." It was like speaking a foreign language, his tongue and lips moving around the unfamiliar sounds, knowing in his head what the words meant, but not fully understanding their meaning.

A grin was plastered on Ty's face, but he didn't say anything.

"I love you," Cam repeated. It was less weird this time, more like a statement of fact, like saying the sky was blue. He reached across the table, ignoring the slight pull on his back, and closed his fingers around Ty's hand where it lay on the table. "I love you."

He pulled Ty toward him and caught Ty around the back of his neck. The kiss was soft and gentle at first, then hungrier and more desperate as his body came alive for the first time in a long time. He broke off the kiss only because of the yawn that overtook him.

"Glad to know I'm so entertaining," Ty said, their foreheads still leaning against each other.

"Sorry." He clung to what he could reach of Ty, not wanting to let go in case it was all a bad nightmare and he'd wake up alone.

Ty chuckled. "Tired? Should we get you to bed?" He tried to push back his chair, but Cam pulled him to a stop. "Hey, I'm here. I'm not going anywhere, remember? Let's get you to bed."

"Come with me." God, he was such a child, begging Ty not to leave him.

"Sure," Ty said with his grin.

Cam reluctantly let him go and then did the awkward shift and push to move his chair away from the table. Busker wandered off to lie on the floor. He planted both hands firmly on the table and hoisted himself to standing, hopping on one foot until he caught his balance.

That move was getting easier with each day, but it still gave Cam a bit of a head rush. When his head stopped spinning, he took the crutches Ty held out for him and swiveled toward the bedroom.

He could mostly maneuver without Ty's help now, but the hand Ty kept on his back was comforting and safe. He dropped himself down onto the bed with a grimace, his back throbbing at the sudden jolt, then handed off the crutches to Ty.

"You okay?" Ty stashed his crutches and pulled at the covers with quick efficient tugs.

"Yeah." Cam shifted until he was snuggled down in a position that didn't aggravate his injuries. With his eyes, he followed Ty as he moved around the bed, admiring that simple confidence that had first drawn Cam to him. When Ty climbed up next to him, Cam reached for him, needing to reassure himself that Ty was actually here, in the flesh.

Ty chuckled as Cam pulled him in for a kiss, no finesse, no tact. Simply a press of lips together and bodies imperfectly aligned. Despite having been physically home for weeks, Cam finally felt at home in that moment. Ty made his heart soar, set his body alight, and was a balm for his damaged soul. He didn't know what good he'd done to deserve this, but he would hold on to Ty if it was the last thing he did.

Need curled in his gut, made more potent by the love they shared. He yearned for something to seal the pact they'd made with their words. He trailed a hand down Ty's chest and stomach, landing right between his waist and hip. "Please, Ty, I need you."

Ty's eyes narrowed and his lips parted in a silent gasp, but he held himself aloft. "I don't think you should be overexerting yourself like that."

Cam tried to tug him closer. "Please?"

Ty paused for a moment. "I've got a better idea."

It was Cam's turn to gasp when Ty reached for the drawstring of his sweats, Ty's breath warm where it blew across his stomach. Cam let his hands linger on whatever body part was within reach—Ty's hair, shoulders, back—and his cock quickly filled as Ty's long fingers wrapped around it.

"Is this okay?" Ty asked.

It was more than okay. It was everything. "Yes," Cam said shakily, the sight of Ty bent over his lap igniting a riot of emotions.

Cam wasn't fully hard yet when Ty's lips closed around his cock. Growing harder inside the wet heat of Ty's mouth felt so right, like Ty was the master of his desire and could tease it out of Cam at will.

But this was no ordinary blowjob. Ty locked eyes with Cam as his tongue worked back and forth. Fingers fondled Cam's heavy balls, squeezing right when Cam needed a little more. The physical pleasure was exquisite, but the emotional connection was his undoing. Ty's eyes never left his, and Cam didn't let himself blink.

Ty snuck a hand under Cam's T-shirt, sliding across his skin until they skimmed over a nipple and pinched. Cam wanted to arch up into the touch, to buck into Ty's mouth, but the cast on his leg and the stitches in his back forced him to lie prone and take whatever Ty gave him. Cam reached under his shirt and found Ty's hand, twining their fingers together over his heart.

He didn't last long, his body yearning for release and his heart bursting with all the love he never thought he'd ever experience. When his orgasm came, it was a slow rise from deep in his gut, spreading through every cell of his body until everything was filled with a glowing light. And through it all, he never lost sight of Ty.

Through barely open eyes, he watched Ty clean him up and tuck him back into his sweats. The kiss Ty gave him was sweet; Cam couldn't do any more even though he wanted to. Ty settled down, pressed against his side, and rubbed their cheeks together. The feeling of Ty's smooth skin against the hairs of his beard was warm and comforting.

He fought the unconsciousness, wanting to bask in the moment forever, but the pull was too strong. With the last of his strength, he wrapped his arms around Ty and murmured, "I love you."

CHAPTER TWENTY-TWO

A few rays of sunshine shone through the window, brightening the office with natural light. The plant Cam had thought was fake turned out to be real—he had rubbed a leaf in between his fingers to check during his last appointment. Colorful paintings he hadn't noticed in previous visits popped against the soft-gray walls.

"How have you been sleeping?" Dr. Brown took her seat opposite Cam.

Cam thought for a moment. "I still have nightmares, if that's what you mean. But I'm sleeping more than I used to."

"The same nightmares?"

"Similar," he said with a frown. "Now there's an armored vehicle in it."

Dr. Brown nodded, her fingers steepled. "That makes sense."

"So how do I get them to stop?"

She cocked her head. "You ask that every week."

"Because you never give me a satisfactory answer."

"And I'm going to give you the same answer as I have before." She dropped her hands to her lap, fingers playing with a pen. "You can't make the dreams stop, you can only control what you do when you have one."

Cam nodded, unsure if he should confess what was on his lips. "Ty helps a lot with that."

"After you wake up from a dream?"

"Yeah, it's nice to have him there. Like a solid thing to hold on to. He talks me through it usually." A grin tugged at his lips. "And when he's not there, Busker's a pretty good substitute."

"Your dog can talk to you?" Dr. Brown's smile was teasing.

Cam laughed. "You know what I mean."

"What was that about when Ty's not there? I thought you two moved in together."

"We did. But with his new job, he's working all hours. And sometimes they shoot on location somewhere, so he's taken a couple of overnight trips."

"And how has that been? Him being busy and not at home?"

Cam paused again. He didn't love it, but he didn't begrudge Ty one second of it. Not when Ty crawled into bed in the wee hours of the morning with an exhausted grin on his face. "I'm okay. He loves it, so I'm happy. We make it work."

Dr. Brown nodded and flipped back through her notes. "You mentioned last week that you were going to visit his mother's gravesite and that you were nervous about it. How did that go?"

Cam took a deep breath and sighed. "Better than I expected."

It had been her birthday, and Ty had asked Cam to go with him, so they'd driven out to New Jersey, stopping at a florist along the way. Ty had been silent during the entire drive, turning in on himself like Cam had never seen before. Suddenly, he was the chatty one, trying to lighten the mood, and it was strangely nice to be on the other side of that dynamic. "I felt like I was actually going to meet her. But it didn't end up as awkward as I thought it was going to be."

The gravesite was simple but well kept, and Ty had bought roses, saying that her perfume had always smelled like them. He had kneeled in front of the grave, with one hand on the tombstone, and Cam had immediately pictured a little eight-year-old Ty struggling to understand what it meant to be alone in the world. He vowed in that moment that he would do everything in his power—even if he was a fucked-up, damaged mess—to make sure Ty would never be alone again.

"And your work?" Dr. Brown continued, scanning her notes. "You went back last week?"

Cam blinked as he refocused on her question. "Yeah." He grimaced. "That hasn't gone as smoothly. Everyone's treating me with kid gloves."

"That's to be expected."

"Well, it's annoying as fuck."

She nodded. "You need to be upfront about what you need from them. You can't expect them to know. If you need more engagement or more space, whatever it is, make sure you communicate that to them."

That sounded nice, but Cam wasn't optimistic. Knowing what to do didn't make doing it any easier.

"And your darkness? How often is it making an appearance?"

Cam shrugged. "It's always there, sometimes more prominently than others. More often at work than at home."

"Do you still feel like escaping into it?" She scribbled something down as she spoke.

He cocked his head as he thought through it. "Sometimes, but not as often as before."

"What about the anger?"

That was the new urge he'd picked up after the bombing. After Dr. Brown had diagnosed it, suddenly all his blowing up at Ty had made more sense. "Again, comes and goes. Ty seems to end up taking the brunt of it."

"That's normal too," she said with a nod. "You're around him most often, and you're most comfortable with him, so your filter is going to be the thinnest with him. When you get angry around people you're less comfortable with, you'll naturally try to temper the anger. Have you guys talked about it?"

"Yeah, he gets it. It's still hard though. We get into shouting matches about once a week." Cam rubbed his fingers along his brow. He didn't need to mention how the makeup sex took the sting out of their fights.

"It's important to keep talking about it, especially after an argument. Once you've both calmed down, you should go back over what made you upset. See if you can identify the trigger and work through what a more appropriate response should be."

"Sure, okay." That didn't sound as fun as having makeup sex.

"Good. You're making good progress, Cam." She raised a questioning eyebrow. "How do you feel about where you're at?"

He took a moment to inventory himself: he still had the nightmares, though they were less frequent; it was difficult to concentrate at work sometimes; he was finally putting on weight; and the mental exercises were helping with his triggers. "Okay, I suppose. Yeah, I guess you're right."

She shook her head. "It doesn't matter what I think. It matters how you feel. We can go over some other exercises next week if you'd like. But unless you had something else you wanted to discuss, I think that's our time for this week."

"Thanks, doc." Cam grabbed his cane and used it to hoist himself out of the armchair. There was only the slightest twinge in his back now, and the cast on his leg had come off a few weeks ago.

"You're going to physical therapy?" Dr. Brown asked as Cam hobbled his way to the door on his cane.

"Yeah. It's a pain." Cam reached the doorjamb and steadied himself.

"Take it slow. Don't be so hard on yourself." She held the door open as he shuffled through.

"Will do. Thanks, doc. See you next week." Cam called for the elevator and then tapped his cane against the floor as he rode the tiny box down to the first floor. When the door opened, he let out the breath he'd held during the ride and found Ty standing there, looking as gorgeous as he had that first time Cam had seen him in Kenya.

"Hey, stranger." Ty's lips curled up in that sexy, smoldering grin. "I was about to come find you."

Cam stumbled forward and let himself fall against Ty, a smile spreading across his own lips at the feeling of Ty's arms coming around him. "Hey. I told you not to wait around for me."

"Yeah, but then who would get you these?" Ty held up a new package of cigarettes, and Cam groaned in appreciation. "See? You can never say I don't love you when I notice when you've sucked through your last cigarette."

"Thank you." He tried to snatch the package out of Ty's fingers, but Ty was too fast, hiding them behind his back where Cam couldn't reach while he leaned on his cane.

"Nope, what's the password?" Ty looked pleased with himself and cocky as hell.

Cam glared but the smile stayed on his lips. "I love you."

"I love you too."

The kiss they shared in front of the elevator stole Cam's breath away. When they broke apart, he'd almost forgotten about the cigarettes. As they planted lingering kisses on each other's mouth, Cam eased his hand along Ty's hip, reached forward and grabbed the package before Ty could wrench it away. With his prize in possession, Cam made a beeline for the door, not caring that Ty was hot on his heels. Because he knew that no matter where he ran, Ty would always catch him and bring him home.

Dear Reader,

Thank you for reading Hudson Lin's *Inside Darkness*!

We know your time is precious and you have many, many entertainment options, so it means a lot that you've chosen to spend your time reading. We really hope you enjoyed it.

We'd be honored if you'd consider posting a review—good or bad—on sites like **Amazon, Barnes & Noble, Kobo, Goodreads, Twitter, Facebook, Tumblr,** and your blog or website. We'd also be honored if you told your friends and family about this book. Word of mouth is a book's lifeblood!

For more information on upcoming releases, author interviews, blog tours, contests, giveaways, and more, please sign up for our weekly, spam-free newsletter and visit us around the web:

Newsletter: tinyurl.com/RiptideSignup
Twitter: twitter.com/RiptideBooks
Facebook: facebook.com/RiptidePublishing
Goodreads: tinyurl.com/RiptideOnGoodreads
Tumblr: riptidepublishing.tumblr.com

Thank you so much for Reading the Rainbow!

RiptidePublishing.com

ACKNOWLEDGMENTS

In a previous life, I worked in the field as an aid worker, and though I wasn't a lifer like Cam, my experience left a profound and lasting impact on me. International development and humanitarian aid is challenging and complex—sometimes the best of intentions cannot mitigate negative consequences. I hope I was able to provide a brief glimpse into what it can be like to work in the field.

As a Chinese Canadian, my life has been a study of intersecting cultures and figuring out how to be both Chinese and Canadian at the same time. As I hope Ty's story shows, it can be confusing growing up as an Asian in Western society, but I am a firm believer that embracing diversity leads to stronger and more resilient communities.

I want to give special thanks to my writing group for believing in this story when my own faith wavered, and especially Arden and TK for multiple rounds of beta reads. I want to thank Suzanne for our many long discussions about living in between two cultures. And, lastly, to all my friends working in development and humanitarian aid—you have a strength of character that I could never muster.

ALSO BY HUDSON LIN

Lessons for a Lifetime
Stepping Out in Faith
Three Months to Forever

Between the Tension series
Between the Push and Pull
Embracing the Tension

ABOUT THE AUTHOR

Hudson Lin was raised by conservative immigrant parents and grew up straddling two cultures with often times conflicting perspectives on life. Instead of conforming to either, she has sought to find a third way that brings together the positive elements of both.

Having spent much of her life on the outside looking in, Hudson likes to write about outsiders who fight to carve out their place in society, and overcome everyday challenges to find love and happily ever afters.

You can follow Hudson on Twitter and Facebook, subscribe to her newsletter for information on new releases, and visit her website for more of her writing.

Newsletter: eepurl.com/dbFqhT

Website: hudsonlin.com

Twitter: twitter.com/hudsonlinwrites

Facebook: facebook.com/hudsonlinwrites

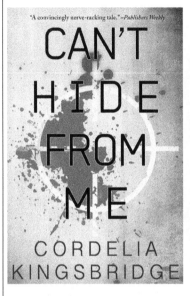

CPSIA information can be obtained
at www.ICGtesting.com
Printed in the USA
LVHW03s1921120718
583537LV00004B/681/P